THE AGILITY OF CLOUDS

VOLUME ONE OF THE HELLEBORINE CHRONICLES

A novel by C.J. Pitchford

Illustrations by Marjorie Schott,
Cover art by http://selfpubbookcovers.com/Shardel

Illustrated Trade Paperback Edition
ISBN-13: 978-0-9850882-3-1
ISBN-10: 0985088230

Also available:
iBook Edition
ePub Edition

Published by Chris Pitchford Publishing, LTD

Play the game "Airship Agility Free," available on iTunes App Store.

Dedication

I gratefully dedicate this book to my mom, Paula, for all that she's done, yet I wrote this for my daughter, Kate, to read someday, in hope for all that she will do.

Gratitude

I am deeply indebted to the editor of this work, Karen Conlin, via http://grammargeddon.com, for all her incredible work. (Yet, any mistakes still found in this volume are entirely mine, and mine alone. Sorry about that)...

I would like to express my profound gratitude to: Stacy Black, for reading the unedited dailies while I wrote this novel, providing encouragement and generally being the sweetest while putting up with my writing; Linda Huscher, for providing insights and critique and catching blunders I missed; Marjorie Schott, for providing the definitive visualization of Seramis like no other; Nesbi Maret, for her critiques and encouragement; I want to thank the Keeper of My Heart, Kristine Shafer, for providing Seramis' voice; and, Shannon Cross, for providing invaluable encouragement and inspiring the character of Seramis Helleborine herself.

And I would certainly like to thank the years of support from my dad, Joel, and step-mom, Ellen.

Epigram, with a note by the author

To see a world in a grain of sand
And a heaven in a wild flower,
Hold infinity in the palm of your hand,
And eternity in an hour.

A robin redbreast in a cage
Puts all heaven in a rage.

A dove-house fill'd with doves and pigeons
Shudders hell thro' all its regions.
A dog starv'd at his master's gate
Predicts the ruin of the state.

A horse misused upon the road
Calls to heaven for human blood.
Each outcry of the hunted hare
A fibre from the brain does tear.

A skylark wounded in the wing,
A cherubim does cease to sing.
The game-cock clipt and arm'd for fight
Does the rising sun affright.

Every wolf's and lion's howl
Raises from hell a human soul.

The wild deer, wand'ring here and there,
Keeps the human soul from care.
The lamb misus'd breeds public strife,
And yet forgives the butcher's knife.

The bat that flits at close of eve
Has left the brain that won't believe.
The owl that calls upon the night
Speaks the unbeliever's fright.

He who shall hurt the little wren
Shall never be belov'd by men.
He who the ox to wrath has mov'd
Shall never be by woman lov'd.

The wanton boy that kills the fly
Shall feel the spider's enmity.

He who torments the chafer's sprite
Weaves a bower in endless night.

The caterpillar on the leaf
Repeats to thee thy mother's grief.
Kill not the moth nor butterfly,
For the last judgement draweth nigh.

He who shall train the horse to war
Shall never pass the polar bar.
The beggar's dog and widow's cat,
Feed them and thou wilt grow fat.

The gnat that sings his summer's song
Poison gets from slander's tongue.
The poison of the snake and newt
Is the sweat of envy's foot.

The poison of the honey bee
Is the artist's jealousy.

The prince's robes and beggar's rags
Are toadstools on the miser's bags.
A truth that's told with bad intent
Beats all the lies you can invent.

It is right it should be so;
Man was made for joy and woe;
And when this we rightly know,
Thro' the world we safely go.

Joy and woe are woven fine,
A clothing for the soul divine.
Under every grief and pine
Runs a joy with silken twine.

The babe is more than swaddling bands;
Throughout all these human lands;
Tools were made and born were hands,
Every farmer understands.
Every tear from every eye
Becomes a babe in eternity;

This is caught by females bright,
And return'd to its own delight.

The bleat, the bark, bellow, and roar,
Are waves that beat on heaven's shore.

The babe that weeps the rod beneath
Writes revenge in realms of death.
The beggar's rags, fluttering in air,
Does to rags the heavens tear.

The soldier, arm'd with sword and gun,
Palsied strikes the summer's sun.
The poor man's farthing is worth more
Than all the gold on Afric's shore.

One mite wrung from the lab'rer's hands
Shall buy and sell the miser's lands;
Or, if protected from on high,
Does that whole nation sell and buy.

He who mocks the infant's faith
Shall be mock'd in age and death.
He who shall teach the child to doubt
The rotting grave shall ne'er get out.

He who respects the infant's faith
Triumphs over hell and death.
The child's toys and the old man's reasons
Are the fruits of the two seasons.

The questioner, who sits so sly,
Shall never know how to reply.
He who replies to words of doubt
Doth put the light of knowledge out.

The strongest poison ever known
Came from Caesar's laurel crown.
Nought can deform the human race
Like to the armour's iron brace.

When gold and gems adorn the plow,
To peaceful arts shall envy bow.
A riddle, or the cricket's cry,
Is to doubt a fit reply.

The emmet's inch and eagle's mile
Make lame philosophy to smile.

He who doubts from what he sees
Will ne'er believe, do what you please.

If the sun and moon should doubt,
They'd immediately go out.
To be in a passion you good may do,
But no good if a passion is in you.

The whore and gambler, by the state
Licensed, build that nation's fate.
The harlot's cry from street to street
Shall weave old England's winding-sheet.

The winner's shout, the loser's curse,
Dance before dead England's hearse.

Every night and every morn
Some to misery are born,
Every morn and every night
Some are born to sweet delight.

Some are born to sweet delight,
Some are born to endless night.

We are led to believe a lie
When we see not thro' the eye,
Which was born in a night to perish in a night,
When the soul slept in beams of light.

God appears, and God is light,
To those poor souls who dwell in night;
But does a human form display
To those who dwell in realms of day.

William Blake, "Auguries of Innocence,"
From *The Ballads (or Pickering) Manuscript* (1801-03)

In writing a novel where history is altered (in what I hoped to be ultimately an improvement), I was saddened at the thought of some of the things might never exist in the imaginary timeline. Especially where this verse is concerned; how could I add this as an epigram to a story where it might never exist? Thus, I added some lines (except for the famous first stanza) throughout the text, sometimes in an altered form, sometimes not. I leave it as an exercise for the reader as to note the appearances of the verse.

Table of Contents

Prologue: The Quick Exit 1

PART ONE: The Old World 11

Chapter One: The Entrance 13

Chapter Two: The Meeting 17

Chapter Three: The Study 27

Chapter Four: The Accusation 35

Chapter Five: The Confession 43

Chapter Six: The Interlude 51

Chapter Seven: The Mission 61

Chapter Eight: The Aftermath 69

PART TWO: The New World 75

Chapter Nine: The Journey 77

Chapter Ten: The Arrival 85

Chapter Eleven: The Conspiracy 91

Chapter Twelve: The Rebuilding 99

Chapter Thirteen: The Prediction 105

Chapter Fourteen: The Objective 113

Chapter Fifteen: The Transport 119

Chapter Sixteen: The Departure 125

Chapter Seventeen: The Consequences 135

Chapter Eighteen: The Loss 143

Chapter Nineteen: The Sacrifice 149

PART THREE: The End of the World 157

Chapter Twenty: The Recovery 159

Chapter Twenty-One: The Pact 167

Chapter Twenty-Two: The Aspiration 175

Chapter Twenty-Three: The Plan 183

Chapter Twenty-Four: The Rescue 191

Chapter Twenty-Five: The Enemy 199

Chapter Twenty-Six: The Battle 205

Chapter Twenty-Seven: The Confrontation 215

PART FOUR: The World, Split Into Two 225

Chapter The Last: The Parting 227

Prologue: The Quick Exit

In which a night at the Royal Palace of Lisbon turns sideways

"Her name is Helleborine. Seramis Helleborine." Upon hearing herself predicated in those words from a voice cold and cruel, Seramis Helleborine froze, smile in place.

The former Marchioness of Cambridgeshire's pale skin, made all the more so having been freshly powdered, set off her ruby lips and kohl-painted eyes. Although in her dress and deportment she matched the other nobility at the ball in every way, Seramis felt conspicuous and exposed. Her first mission as an agent of the Crown of England wasn't starting as smoothly as she had hoped.

It hadn't helped hearing her name spoken aloud, although the Portuguese lilt as spoken softened the effect somewhat.

The speaker was behind her and, if Seramis remembered correctly upon passing her, was none other than the Infanta Francisca Josefa of House Braganza, sister of King João. The words of the infanta had sounded drawn out and over-articulated to Seramis—as to be expected, as time passed more slowly for her than for most, and had done so ever since she had known of the difference. Seramis studied the reactions of those around her to see if they had heard her name as well.

But to the Count of Harcourt (Joseph de Lorraine, a distant cousin) and to the other courtier who had been in conversation with Seramis, the Count Pedro António de Noronha, the words had no apparent effect. Seramis could see no change in the eye movements of either noble or hear any change in inflection that would indicate they had heard the infanta call her out.

When Seramis spoke, she unconsciously did so just as slowly in practiced imitation of what she heard, intoning slowly and carefully, "My lords, your welcome is a most gracious introduction, as this is my first visit to Lisbon."

As she spoke in a manner that hid her true perception of time, Seramis spent that time wishing she could lose herself in the sumptuous decoration that graced the courtyard on this early summer's evening, and even imagined herself exploring the many grottos and circular alcoves that lined the garden walls that enclosed the space. The extravagant architecture might itself inspire such feelings, Seramis thought, although the thought of a princess seeking her out for unknown reasons may have also prompted this desire to hide.

"Dear cousin," Count Joseph said, smiling. "Please request of me anything that your heart desires—"

"—as this place isn't named the Palácio de Necessidades without reason," finished Count Pedro. Both men wore light coats trimmed with velvet and decorated with medallions and martial ribbons. All three—Seramis included—wore periwigs, although the false hair of the men curled down their shoulders, while Seramis's was styled with hair piled upwards as she would style her natural blonde hair. Even the servants wore wigs, although of much simpler design with ribbons tying 'ponytails' at the back. Seramis wished she could trade her heavy wig for one of the smaller perukes, but ignored the discomfort while the men continued speaking.

"Although built in an answer to a prayer to Our Lady of Needs—" began Count Pedro.

"—the construction of the palace was funded, of course, by commodity imports from Brazil," Count Joseph finished knowingly.

Their habit of finishing each other's sentences would have been amusing at any other time, thought Seramis. "How long have you been in King John's court?" she asked, using the anglicized version of the king of Portugal's name.

"At the end of the War of Spanish Succession, I believe—" Count Pedro started.

"His Serene Majesty was still a young man—" began Count Joseph.

"My brother, the king, is still a young man," prompted a voice behind Seramis. "Younger than your King George."

As she was the only person of pure English blood in sight, Seramis thought the phrase 'your King George' could only be addressed to her. Turning quickly, and flashing a charming smile that won her many an admirer, Seramis froze once again, this time in astonishment at the look of intense hatred directed at her.

Count Joseph interceded, attempting to resolve the situation. "Your Highness, might I humbly introduce my cousin Cambridgeshire, the daughter of the late Duke of Cambridge—"

"Seramis Helleborine," Infanta Francisca once again interrupted the count. "Daughter of the traitor executed and stripped of his titles by the first King George of England, no?"

Both Count Joseph and Count Pedro were silent. The revelry surrounding the exchange only heightened the awkward silence, the music a syncopated mixture of Mughal Ragas and Trinidad rhythms, performed as quavers, semiquavers, and crotchets, *tum ti ti tum tum, tum tum.*

Another noblewoman standing next to the Infanta Francisa Josefa whispered something into the princess's ear. The eyes of the infanta narrowed as she listened to her confidante, whom Seramis recognized as Duchess Ana Maria de Lorena.

Seramis wondered how the two most powerful women in Lisbon knew of her, and what they could want. She dreaded she was about to find out.

"What are you doing here?" the infanta asked her.

"*Sua Alteza Serenissima a Infanta,*" Seramis curtsied as she answered. "I was invited to the palace by Princess Sophie Dorothea, sister to King George—"

"No," Infanta Francisca interrupted as Duchess Ana Maria actually crossed her arms. "What are you doing in Lisbon?"

. . .

Earlier, after Baron Thomas West had returned from his meeting with Princess Sophie Dorothea, he asked Seramis a question. "Do you know why we are here in Portugal?" Impatiently tugging at the ruffles on his cuffs, he awaited an answer.

Seramis had just returned from a musical performance in honor of the same princess who had cut short her meeting just to hear her play. "I suppose, my lord—"

"No, you do not," the baron, also known as Lord De La Warr and living down to his reputation, snapped.

"Is that because I am a woman, milud?" Seramis asked, teasing out her reply in a West End accent, as if from Drury Lane or worse. "And I don' know 'bout such high matters?"

"Don't play games with me," De La Warr growled. "Princess Sophie Dorothea cut short our meeting, and I don't know why—"

"That I do know, my lord."

"Are you still toying with me? I'm warning you." De La Warr was squinting at the late afternoon sunlight that came in through the open windows of the palace antechamber where he met privately with his ward. "Even a paranoid would stagger at the array of enemies aimed at England."

"Princess Sophie Dorothea is not an enemy," Seramis replied knowingly. Emboldened by the reception the sister to the king of England had bestowed upon her, Seramis was annoyed by the baron's condescension.

"Our position here in Lisbon is tenuous, my dear." He is still lecturing me, thought Seramis, but she waited for him to continue. "I've arranged a meeting tomorrow to adjudicate a trade dispute, but our presence here is mere pretense."

"That I know as well," Seramis answered. "But you asked why we're here—what of the real reason for our presence, my lord? Before we left England, you mentioned plans of some sort—war plans?"

"Not exactly, but the plans do represent a new kind of armament," De La Warr said. "A new—very deadly—way to wage war."

"As if the old ways weren't deadly enough."

"If our enemies could sail over our heads using clouds for cover, there would be no force sufficient to stop them!" he whispered.

"What do you mean?"

"That's what *you* have to find out."

"Me?" Seramis's eyes widened.

"You will have to infiltrate the palace under cover of darkness and steal the plans—if they exist—for a man-o-war that sails through the skies!" De La Warr looked askance at her, and Seramis wondered whether he thought her capable of handling such an assignment.

"But why now, my lord? And why look for mere plans here?" Seramis waited, but no answer came. "Why not wait until Portugal—now our ally—starts to build your flying flotillas and steal the working plans at that time? Surely you have a spy at your disposal who could be given that sort of assignment." But as soon as she spoke, she knew her patron would never wait for a threat to actually materialize. With an 'array of enemies' to concern oneself with, it would be best to neutralize any threat before it could actually threaten.

"Why aren't you getting prepared?" De La Warr waved a glove in her direction and turned to depart. "You will need to improvise a disguise for the purpose of infiltrating the privy antechambers. Hide it under your gown or whatever you will, as we've been invited to a dance."

"You can't be serious!"

"It is the reason why I've brought you here, my dear." De La Warr grinned as if the answer should be obvious to her. "You'll never be suspected."

. . .

"Thank you," Seramis said to the handmaids who had been helping her dress. She needed to invent an excuse to be alone. "It is that time where my tides follow the moon's cycle, and I need some privacy to prepare." Ignoring their replies at how well versed they were at tending to ladies at that time, Seramis remained steadfast.

The maids looked at each other briefly before curtseying and turning to withdraw. Seramis Helleborine was left alone to stare at herself in the ornate gilt-framed mirror. A simple girl with gray eyes and blonde hair stared back at her with crossed arms, framed by the complicated ornamentation surrounding the solitary figure.

After a moment of introspection, Seramis turned to the garments laid out on the chairs. It was going to be a chore to dress herself, but first, she had to assemble the materials for her mission. The gown, like her attendance at the ball here in Lisbon, was mere cover for her true objective.

Lord De La Warr had provided the directions to locate her objective within the Palácio das Necessidades, and she had committed the route to memory. But first, she must make the careful arrangements for a transformation suitable to espionage.

Her formal gown, while suitable for the event she was about to attend, would be completely useless in secretly traversing dark hallways unobserved. Quickly yet delicately, she ripped the seams on either end of her skirts' pocket-slits; she would need them to be larger than the usual. From one of her chests, she removed two middling-size drawstring pouches and opened them fully, tearing the drawstrings from their casings. Then, flipping over the wire-framed panniers that would provide the fashionable shape to her gown, she partially sewed the pouches into their framework.

The new hidden compartments were lightly filled with containers of facepaint and light garments—a puppeteer's blouse and hose—in one, and a cap, dark gloves, and light leather moccasins in the other. Seramis sewed up the compartments once they had been filled. She planned on later destroying the panniers upon securing her alibi for the evening, but first, she needed to secure her disguise.

A sudden knock at the door elicited a sharp "*¡Um momento!*" from Seramis as she swept her chemise over her shoulders and threw an underskirt onto the upturned and obviously modified panniers, hiding them from view.

As the door opened and a handmaiden blithely entered, Seramis whispered a stern "*...Se agradar*," that stopped the young maid in her tracks. Covering as much of her underclothed body as she could, Seramis continued, mixing some Spanish into her instructions to close the door as if to appear unnerved. "*¡Fechar la puerta!*"

The servant hesitated at first, but eventually responded by closing the door. Unfortunately, she remained on this side of the door, turning to offer more unsolicited help.

Sighing, Seramis stopped the girl from proceeding with a look. Seramis signaled for the maid to turn around as if from modesty. Although she looked puzzled at the request, the maid did as she was instructed.

Keeping one eye on the girl, Seramis straightened her chemise, then fastened the panniers about her waist. Swiftly, she donned the underskirt without assistance (no mean task, to be sure), its fabric covering the wire frame and hiding the newly added compartments within.

In Portuguese, Seramis told the girl to go fetch her handmaids as she would need some help with her corset and the many fasteners of the gown. She continued talking as the girl left, telling her not to hurry and how she would prefer to don her hose in private, as she was accustomed to doing so in her English home.

Later, as the handmaids completed their fussing and primping, Seramis considered the overall effect in the mirror. Her face had been covered with powder, her hair with a wig, and her secret tools for spying with silk brocade.

. . .

"Need I ask again?" The Infanta Francisca Josefa grew even more irritated. "Why are you here in Lisbon?"

Seramis continued to smile, although her nerves were beginning to fray at the confrontational manner of her hostess. "I apologize, *Vossa Alteza*. I'm traveling under the visa granted to my patron, the Baron Thomas West—"

"Yes." The infanta looked at the duchess beside her, and then nodded in the direction to the right of Seramis. "The Lord De La Warr. I know."

Seramis followed the gaze of the infanta to see her patron in an affected, foppish pose, talking animatedly to other guests she didn't recognize. "Are you asking why the baron is here?" Seramis turned back to the infanta. "As his ward, I know nothing more of his plans than his schedule. Tomorrow, he is to meet—"

"I know his schedule, as well, blood-traitor," the infanta replied sharply. Without warming her tone, she addressed the counts. "Dom Pedro, Dom Joseph; please excuse us." Without a word, the nobles bowed deeply before retiring.

"I pray you, please forgive my familial sins, *Vossa Alteza*," Seramis curtseyed again before straightening.

"And what of your sins of omission?" the infanta asked, leaning in towards Seramis.

"I don't understand, *Vossa Alteza*," Seramis said, holding her hands away from her gown despite instinctively wishing to use them to cover her secrets—the disguise she guiltily kept hidden under her gown. Her discipline helped to her to appear neutral, while every fiber of her being screamed at her to run away.

"You still haven't told me why you're here," the infanta said. "I've heard rumors of an odd occurrence right here in my home."

"Odd? Are you referring to the music I performed this afternoon for the sister of my king?" Seramis wasn't aware of any animosity between the two princesses, and she was completely surprised by the infanta's condemnation of her father, and by association, of her. "I could, if *Vossa Alteza* wished it, play some more—of your choosing, of course. Or not at all, if you wish I would rather not perform..."

Seramis let her embarrassed repetitions fade as the duchess once again drew the infanta's attention by whispering in her ear.

The infanta continued her interrogation. "Your name appears in mathematical treatises, no?"

Blinking, Seramis was taken aback. "I..." She wondered what the question might have to do with anything, and hoped to draw out the reason for this questioning. *What else does the Infanta know of my past?* "I'm flattered that it had somehow come to your attention, *Vossa Alteza*. I didn't think that being mentioned in passing in forewords and assorted apocrypha would be worth your royal consideration—"

The infanta hissed her next words, reminding Seramis of nothing so much as a threatened adder. "Do not attempt to flatter or distract me. You may be tolerated where you come from—"

"Tolerated?" Lord De La Warr stepped forward, bowing deeply as he spoke. "Oh, *Sua Alteza Serenissima a Infanta*, she is ever that and more!" He took the infanta's proffered hand, brushing his lips across it briefly before rising. "Had I but known the Continent's enchantment with child prodigies, I would have brought my ward before your court years and years ago. You would have been amazed at the performances, thrilled at the recitatives and awed at the spectacle." He concluded with a flourish better suited to a popinjay than a colonial viceroy.

Seramis had noticed Lord De La Warr making his way over to where they had been speaking, and her reaction was mixed: a curious balance of relief and trepidation, as he was simultaneously the instigator of her present situation and likely the only person who could help her escape.

"You think you would distract House Braganza with your 'spectacle,' no?" The infanta nearly spat the word as she looked down her nose at him; he had yet to rise from his exaggerated bow.

"But if I could, *Vossa Alteza*," the baron continued, his tone growing even more unctuous, "I would make my entreaties the more palatable, my comportment the more tasteful, if only you would but instruct me."

"It will not be I," the infanta said, lifting her chin, "who will give you the instruction you crave, De La Warr." She turned away from him without the smallest gesture of recognition. "You think us fooled by your act, no? Leave us, I command you."

"*Sim*, as you will, *Vossa Alteza*," he replied, yet without withdrawing. Instead he took to one knee, just as the duchess gently tugged on the infanta's arm before kneeling as well. The signal wasn't strictly necessary, as the noise of the royal retinue announced its presence long before obeisance became necessary.

Seramis knelt, too, when she saw the king, and did so only in the moment before the infanta turned and curtseyed before her brother. The king was surrounded by servants leading monkeys and birds in a riotous procession of sight and sound. Servants led peacocks from Portuguese colonies in India, parrots from Africa, and toucans from the New World. Monkeys chattered incessantly while punctuating their remarks with high pitched shrieks. One parrot had apparently been trained to sing melodies by the recently departed composer Domenico Scarlatti, but couldn't do the tune justice when accompanied by other birds whistling *modinhas*.

In the midst of the chaos, as the king took his sister's hand and bid her rise, Lord De La Warr looked up, expecting to see the infanta call out his ward once again. But to the surprise of all present—even that of King João, who knew of his guest only by reputation—Seramis Helleborine had seized her opportunity during the moment of distraction, and had abruptly disappeared.

PART ONE: The Old World

A masquerade promises more than divertissement.

Chapter One: The Entrance

In which our heroine finds leisure to be a labor

Not long before, but in a different lifetime when thoughts of leaving England were only the most abstract of dreams, Seramis Helleborine lost herself in a daydream, her imagination soaring through the sky and unburdened by the present. She returned to earth when her carriage suddenly and unexpectedly shifted. Smoothing the silks of her gown, the Marchioness of Cambridgeshire thought sadly that escaping the limitations of her life and the expectations of her position would have to wait, such ideas probably being entertained no sooner than after tonight's masquerade and dance.

Whilst she rode, thoughts of escape and flight hovered about the mind of Lady Seramis like the clouds of dirt and dust sent up by the hooves of the horses. English dust—like any other, except that it seemed less likely to stay on the ground where it belonged—hung in the air just outside the carriage door before the wistful gaze of the marchioness. But the floating motes illuminated by the setting sun could not alter her route to the annual start-of-season party hosted by Baron Thomas West, her sponsor and protector, otherwise known as the infamous Lord De La Warr.

For all their noise and speed, the horse's hooves still sounded plodding and dull to Seramis Helleborine as she brooded upon the evening's upcoming events. Eventually, the hooves grew silent as the carriage stopped at the gates of the De La Warr estate.

Power in this new age of a United Kingdom, thought Lady Seramis, can apparently be measured by how long one makes one's guests wait, and what one forces them to do upon their arrival. Her thoughts turned from escape to resentment as she remembered that she would soon be immersed in the dreaded masquerade.

"What on earth could they be doing?" asked a lady-in-waiting sitting next to Seramis, the young Susan of Sussex, daughter of the earl, as she peered out of the carriage.

The three young attendants (only one of whom had spoken) had been sent by their families for tutelage and instruction at Helleborine Hall in Cambridgeshire, in the east of England, to spend the spring and summer of 1730 among others of their station. And as Elizabeth had stated, slaves were in fact hastily tying velvet bags upon the sweaty and dusty hooves of each of the horses

"I heard that the horses' hooves were to be muted—bagged if you like—for the ride up to the estate," said Elizabeth of Shrewsbury. "It's to prevent each guest's arrival from disrupting the pristine air."

"That's not all that needs to be bagged, if the pristine air is to be preserved," joked Mary of Northallerton, speaking at last, while the other girls held their noses and laughed.

Lady Seramis smiled in patient condescension, tempering her approval accordingly as their instructor and patroness. Their innocence lifted her spirits, and Seramis promised herself that she would try to enjoy the evening's entertainment for their sake.

The marchioness was scarcely a few years older than the others, yet her quick intelligence combined with a seemingly endless patience had made her the adopted sister to so many whose families aspired for them to be ladies-in-waiting to princesses and queens. Whilst the young girls learned their adopted mannerisms—by means of studying others and winning their approval amongst their ranks—they also formed a convenient shield wall between Seramis and society at large: part of an unquestioned and implicit routine that served her well in these requisite social encounters.

When the muted travel of the carriage came to a stop at the Neo-Palladian grand entrance of the De La Warr estate, Lady Seramis braced herself against the inevitable and unavoidable scrutiny she was about to face: a slight pause, to anybody who noticed. For most, including her ladies-in-waiting, experiencing an existential anxiety might make the moments of tedious delays and expectation seem merely a bit longer than they actually were. But to Seramis a moment's hesitation felt like a drawn-out lull. An awkward silence seemed to become a near-frozen eternity. For her entire life she had been experiencing time thus; for a lifetime she had been hiding this secret. She had learned painful lessons as a young girl, leading her to hide her unique perception of time, and despite growing more proficient at the deception as she grew older, it became ever more painful to maintain the pretense that she shared the same inner timekeeping as everyone else.

The truth of it was that being exposed as unique and fundamentally different from her peers both terrified and excited Lady Seramis. A single accidental slip betraying the extent of her abilities, and the secret she had hidden for a lifetime would be out. All she would have to do was reveal her secrets, and she could bring about the end of the world for herself as surely as if the planet itself ceased to be.

But the world did not end as the carriage doors swung open and the ladies-in-waiting first descended—stepping sideways through the carriage door as demanded by the panniers worn under their skirts. Their silk dresses flowing upon steps placed on the ground by liveried servants, the women were to be guided by gloved hands towards the entrance leading to the great hall. Men-at-arms with ceremonial halberds stood, stiff and menacing, on each side of the passage. The young ladies-in-waiting, followed by Seramis, made their way into the recently constructed palace. The entire scene one that conveyed to the latter the increasing prosperity and newly won power of England's colonial viceroy, the Lord De La Warr.

Before she slipped her mask into place, both externally as required for all of the attendees and internally for her own benefit, she broadly winked at one of the guards whose undisciplined and roving eyes had clearly been captured by her beauty. As if acting upon a whim, the young marchioness left behind her reserve, if only for a fleeting fraction of a moment. Dipping her nearest shoulder and cocking her head as might better befit Moll Hackabout of Drury Lane in London than Seramis Helleborine of Cambridgeshire, she flashed her teeth in a broad grin which was just as quickly hidden by a reserved smile as she returned to her earlier pace and continued past the confused soldier.

The guard, who saw only a flicker of movement so fast that it barely registered, beheld nothing so much out of the ordinary with the exception of the casual beauty of Lady Seramis Helleborine.

. . .

Unlike the gaze of the confused man-at-arms in the great hall who recognized beauty but knew not the name of the lady who possessed such qualities, the gaze of Patrick Tempus came to rest upon (and immediately identified) Lady Seramis as she entered the ballroom. Yet it cannot be said that he had ever countenanced beauty or charm, or even simple grace. The finer qualities were of no importance to him and as such they simply had no meaning or presence.

Even amongst the finery of the ball, the exquisite costumes, and the delicate and bizarre masks worn by the participants, Patrick Tempus had chosen to wear as his costume his priestly Jesuit disguise, a suit of severe and almost unrelenting black. Of course, this had the effect of making him stand out even more amongst the revelers. But perhaps more importantly, it also had the effect of keeping the rest of the party at bay, in that none would engage him or even exchange a glance with him.

"Is that her, Baron? Will you be introducing us?" Patrick Tempus asked of his patron, Lord De La Warr, who turned at the questions and noted a level of emotion in his assassin's voice he had never heard before.

Baron Thomas West carelessly balanced a crystal chalice of wine in one hand and held his mask in place with the other, smiling as he answered his assassin. "All in good time, Father."

Chapter Two: The Meeting

In which parties and plans cast their long shadows

The party was all chaos and tumultuous activity, greeting the new arrivals with a scene of an almost staggering incomprehensibility. Fabrics featuring oriental patterns mixed with others displaying the colors and dyes from the New World, begetting such gaudy spectacle as would defy rhyme and reason were it not for the traditional cuts and shapes of the clothes worn by the revelers. The cuffs and ruffles were a bit toned down from last season, as if to provide a nod to some sophistication or, at least, an attempt at balance.

The air was filled with melodies from pipes, reeds, and horns, accompanied by sweetly scratching viols and theorbos while punctuated by the pops of tambours and shaken cymbals, all directed by the continuous thudding of the stick that the master of musicians slammed into the ground at regular intervals in his almost fruitless effort to keep the instrumentalists in time. The fashionable dances of this season rehashed the same tunes from previous years while giving them new life with exotic rhythms and faster tempos, as if the staid tunes had been superficially infused with vigor without really being transformed into something new, or worse, *foreign*. Such was the unspoken hope of fashion.

Some of the young lords and ladies were milling about, either going to or coming from the sideboards where they had found unusual cakes and sweetmeats and an endless supply of various liquors and cordials. Others danced in groups, shouting their approval as the music started, or their displeasure when it only very briefly stopped. Into this mayhem strode Lady Seramis Helleborine. Her ladies-in-waiting flowed deftly amongst the guests and, by some unspoken yet shared strategy, intercepted those young lords who sought the attention of Lady Seramis.

After a brief discussion, where Elizabeth had spoken to an earnest and hopeful young noble while the others made their way towards the dancers, the group reconnected and Elizabeth whispered her report of what had transpired, fairly bouncing with eagerness. "My lady, my Lord Albion begs that you hear a quatrain he composed in your honor. I think it might please you, if..."

Of all the girls, Elizabeth was the most enthusiastic about romance, and only barely held her excitement in check.

"My dear Elizabeth," Seramis Helleborine replied, "if it might please you that I hear from this gentle lord, I would be remiss if I didn't. But please don't allow him the apprehension that my approval means that I might furthermore agree to dance or otherwise dally."

"My lady, it is already accomplished, and I thank you!" Elizabeth said quickly before returning to the anxious suitor. Mary and Susan deftly moved aside while talking to still more hopeful attendants. Soon, Elizabeth returned with Lord Albion, and curtseyed. "My lady, might I introduce the Duke of Gloucester, Lord Henry Albion..."

All too eagerly, Lord Albion interrupted, speaking while still bowing. "My Lady Cambridgeshire needs no introduction! For my part, I am utterly at your disposal..." His speech was somewhat distracted as he fidgeted, but he found at last a piece of folded paper hidden within his sleeve. The duke would have begun but for Lady Seramis's own interruption.

"My lord Gloucester, please permit me the honor of gratitude for your attendance," she said in an attempt to engage him in conversation. "Your poetic renown precedes you."

Lord Albion blinked, forgetting for a moment his lines, and stammered briefly before Elizabeth clicked her tongue, distracting him and extracting him from his stage fright. "The honor is all mine, my lady." Recovering, he continued. "As is my heartfelt gratitude for my lady's preference for the quatrain, and other—briefer—forms of song," he said this last as he nodded to Elizabeth, who had previously provided this intelligence.

"If my lord Gloucester will indulge a simple matter of taste—" Lady Seramis attempted again to engage him in discourse. To conclude this quickly was an unspoken hope of the marchioness.

"Indeed! My lady, if I may?" Lord Albion said, hastily continuing without inquiring further regarding matters of taste in what was intended to be an opening for a conversation by Lady Seramis.

As Lord Albion rushed to commence his reading, Seramis inhaled deeply, and hoped to sooner reach its conclusion by simply saying, "Please, Your Grace."

"*In your beauty, should—*" Albion began, pausing inappropriately in the middle of the first line of his quatrain, looking up at the marchioness as if she would disappear at the instant he started. Upon noting her continued presence, however, he returned to his poetry:

"*...the Sun and Moon ever doubt, shall their light immediately go out! Let he who doubts in what he sees drop without pause upon his knees—*"

"Your Grace," interrupted Lady Seramis in that instant, "I'm flattered by your appreciation! But I must apologize for not having the strength to bear your attentions. Your sentiments are so strong!" Smiling, she attempted to soften the interruption, but the tall duke seemed to visibly shrink.

"My lady, I beg your forgiveness!"

"Your Grace, please, make no mistake, I am well pleased but also not just a little embarrassed by such depths of feeling. By your leave, I will take some refreshment, and perhaps we can continue later?"

Smiling and bowing once again, Gloucester appeared to recover, saying as he straightened, "Until then, my lady, it will seem like an eternity!"

"For us both, Your Grace." Having already turned to leave, Seramis repeated, "for us both..."

. . .

As Lady Seramis and her ladies-in-waiting extricated themselves from the group of admirers, they stepped lightly in their colorful gowns amongst the waves of revelers. Gently moving amidst the darting dancers who flew like swallows, Seramis, Elizabeth, Susan, and Mary floated like graceful, beautiful swans—but were pursued in turn by an unlikely combination of cock and crow. The rooster in question was the lord of this hall, Baron Thomas West, the Lord De La Warr, vainly attempting to get Lady Seramis's attention, while the dour crow was the brooding Patrick Tempus, following close behind.

"My lady de Cambridgeshire?" shouted the baron, raising his chalice to further his cause for recognition. At the sound, the ladies-in-waiting pivoted so naturally and so effortlessly that their concerted maneuver to impose themselves between the gentleman callers and the marchioness had the effect of causing an onlooker to suspect they hadn't changed direction at all.

Of course, upon being intercepted by the ladies-in-waiting, Lord De La Warr and Patrick Tempus both stopped to bow deeply, while Lady Seramis only turned just enough to peer over her shoulder, with the aim of choosing whether to engage or escape.

"My lady! Please forgive my boldness," continued the baron as he straightened, a broad smile upon his ruddy and whiskered face. "Do you have but a moment?"

Seramis turned, her features radiating joy at recognition. "My dear baron," she began, and the effect her smile had upon him was immediate as his grin grew lopsided, relaxing his usual squint. Presenting her hand, she continued, "For you, if I could I would present time itself as a gift worthy of your grace." Other lords in attendance nearby recognized the voice of the marchioness and sought her out, but their attentions were held in abeyance by the ladies-in-waiting, who gracefully turned from Lord De La Warr and Patrick Tempus with brief curtseys.

Taking her hand, Lord De La Warr kissed her satin glove, his grinning expression matching his outlandish clothes. "My lady, you do this old man too great an honor! But if I can ask of you a further boon: will you call me Thomas, as once your father did?"

At the mention of her late father, Lady Seramis's insides twisted and her voice stopped in her throat, so painful the memory was still. Calling upon her reserves of strength and fortitude she curtseyed in response, her coiffed head turned slightly to one side in hope of concealing from him her reaction. "For all the efforts your governesses took to instruct me as a little girl, my dear Thomas, when you saved my family and my line from destruction upon the passing of my father"—a tear escaped from one eye—"I would call you Nuncle as I once did!"

Tears also burst from the pinched eyes of Lord De La Warr. "Why, you haven't called me that in years!" Pausing for a moment, he sharply inhaled before continuing. "It's so good to see you!"

The moment of emotion soon passed, however, and he appeared to remember his objective. "I know your studies and your duties keep you scarce around this court, and please forgive me for drawing you forth with the charms of an entire masque and ball, but if I could have but a moment of your attention..."

Lord De La Warr paused, having just noted that Patrick Tempus was still hunched in a bow, having remained in that position during the entire exchange. "Good heavens, Father. Please!" But Patrick Tempus remained still until Lady Seramis finished her curtsey.

De La Warr continued, "My lady, please allow me to introduce Father Patrick Tempus." Turning to Patrick and raising an eyebrow, he said, "Father Patrick, this is the Marchioness de Cambridgeshire—once my ward and my glory, though the honor was all mine—Lady Seramis Helleborine."

"My lady," Patrick said and bowed, again, "it is both an honor and a privilege to meet you." His words had an ironic undertone, as if this truly, in fact, was neither. His voice—betraying none of the excitement it had held when he had privately talked with Lord De La Warr—deepened as he continued. "Your accomplishments in science and alchemy at such a young age have been extraordinary."

He tries to pay me compliment, thought Lady Seramis, *but rather the effect is accusatory.*

"Almost legendary," Patrick said at last, as if he could contain himself no longer.

"Very gracious, Father." It had to be evident to all (not just to her), she was certain, that the venom in this priest's words contradicted his calling. "Likewise I admire your discipline, even among Jesuits, who are famous for their imposition of—"

"My dear!" said the baron. "Oh, forgive me. I thought you said 'inquisition' and I thought a debate was about to begin in earnest.

But that is almost why I wanted you to meet! As if you two were the opposite sides of a brilliant metal coin—"

Laughing, Lady Seramis interrupted. "Indeed! Father, I believe I see the red cloth of the monsignor's habit under your cloak. But where is the traditional hat?" *Am I the only one to see the incongruities in this disguise?* "You seem to be much more important just beneath the surface, if I'm not mistaken, than your attire would have me believe. I'm confused, I'm pained to say, and, dear Thomas, not feeling at all brilliant at present."

"Of course, my dear, of course," De La Warr answered, "aren't all men of the cloth, regardless of their station, just shepherds of our souls?" She wondered if the baron was truly deceived, or if, as part of his work in the service of the king, there was something else here—possibly something dangerous.

"'Tis a pity, my lady." Father Patrick's practiced smile faded. "Truly, 'tis a pity that you weren't born a man, to use your talents to their fullest."

As Lord De La Warr observed carefully, Lady Seramis tipped the fan she carried toward the crucifix Father Patrick wore, saying, "And apparently by your calling, 'tis not a pity, but instead a mercy, that neither were you."

In an instant, her unique perception permitted her to observe his subliminal reactions, unseen by any but her.

She had, she concluded, angered him.

Lady Seramis wondered whether to press her advantage, but felt that this might not be the best of circumstances to unmask this so-called Jesuit priest. She quickly changed her approach. "Tempus is an unusual name for an Irishman, is it not?"

Father Patrick looked surprised at the change in topic as well as tone. "My lady, you may indeed be correct. I can neither confirm nor deny your induction. I was an orphan, a foundling without any known relatives. To this day, there is no clue to my origin."

Lady Seramis could tell he was confused as to why he vouchsafed such secrets.

Including Lord De La Warr in the conversation, she nodded and said, "Knowing one's origins may not always be the gift some consider it to be, and if you'll have my story from someone else, I would be most grateful! Of course, I give leave to you, dear Thomas, to share what you will, as you know best both for the services you've done me and those rendered to the king." She wondered at her own pity for Father Tempus's orphaned upbringing. *Was that why she had cut short the conversation that Lord De La Warr had apparently gone to great pains to arrange?*

"My lady, your presence has repaid any debt many times over," said Lord De La Warr, again bowing. "It is I who shall forever be in your service."

Taking his cue, Father Patrick also bowed, "Until we meet again, my lady."

"Indeed," replied Lady Seramis, "some other time, Father."

. . .

Having retired to a private parlor in another part of the estate, Patrick Tempus waved away a servant and closed the doors himself, so that only he and Lord De La Warr remained.

Standing in the center of the candlelit room, the baron smiled in apparent victory. "Was she not everything I described?" he boomed. "And more, if I'm not mistaken. If your Jesuit training had been any more lacking, she would have—"

Patrick Tempus stopped walking towards him and interrupted coldly. "My lord, she has a formidable intellect, but I don't see what use you might have for a woman in any event." Turning away, he continued as he recalled the meeting. "Even one of her considerable skills."

"What do you mean?" Lord De La Warr could not conceal his incredulity. "Can't you see it? She's always three steps ahead of you, and never at a loss for an answer. It's like she has all the time in the world, while you're left struggling to keep up." To himself he muttered, "I never could piece together the disparate stories of her youth—"

"My lord, she is still young!" Patrick Tempus was dismissive, but turned toward the baron, not realizing the words were not meant for him. "What stories?"

"Ah," De La Warr paused to drain his chalice. He thought that it might be good to sound out what he had heard, despite his tendency to keep personal histories close to account, in case the information could prove useful at some future time. "That's just it. They don't make any sense. The old maids thought her funny in the head... She didn't talk until well after the other children, but when she did, she seemed to be a prodigy. She could repeat anything perfectly. I have no idea how she does it, or how she finds the time to do all the experiments she does—"

"How is it that you do not know?"

Lord De La Warr archly replied, "You forget your place—"

"Forgive me, my lord. I thought nothing happened in this country without your knowing about it."

"Of course I know everything about where she goes, who she meets, when she meets them, and what they have for dinner. But she appears to devour ideas, and takes on so many tasks. As if she has a twin... or twice as many days as have been allotted to the rest of us." Dejectedly, he continued, "I would have my spies find out, but her privacy is unassailable. She commands the loyalty of all her people." He waved his empty chalice at Patrick. "And you saw how even those girls—her guests, really—they protect her at any cost!"

Seeing at last the value his patron had placed on this marchioness, Patrick slouched in defeat. "My lord, you will never be able to control her."

Placing his hand on Patrick's shoulder, De La Warr rejoined. "No? I've previously procured the services of someone else as considerable, as useful, as mysterious... Don't you think I have a plan? As soon as there is an opening, as soon as she slips, I'll be there. To pick up the pieces, no doubt. And I'll have her."

Dejectedly, the false father asked, "Like you have me, milord?"

Laughing, De La Warr crossed the room to the sideboard to fill his chalice with brandy. "Don't be petulant, Patrick! You are too independent to be a mere prize to be won. I need your independence! If you're at all thought of as being in my thrall—which you know you are not—who would approach you?"

Patrick bristled. "My lord, this was a test? You put me in the same arena with that lady to see what would happen?"

"And you both passed brilliantly! If she had not been at least your intellectual equal, then she would be of no use to me. And if you had not gone from steadfast adoration," De La Warr teased, "to blazing hatred so genuinely, then I would have known you had your own designs, or were in league with someone else who had designs upon her!"

"Never, milord!"

"Of course not," De La Warr said, changing topic as he had truly confirmed his test of Patrick with this exchange. "Now, quickly, tell me the reason for your visit."

"The rumors you've heard are true, milord; the Continent is full of tales from France and Portugal of new weapons, new designs for war."

"Aren't they always, Patrick? What is so different this time?"

Forgetting their earlier disagreement in the excitement of reporting his discovery, Patrick continued, now gesticulating animatedly. "If I hadn't seen it with my own eyes in Lisbon, milord, it would be a fantasy dismissed right out of hand. But the plans describe a fleet of death that can float through the air, built in either the French or Spanish colonies in the New World!"

"Surely you jest, Patrick! What is it this time? A flock of birds tethered to a raft? Are you wasting my time?"

"Milord, if you held the diagrams in your hands, you would know it to be true! A man-o-war with fifty guns, whose round sails pull the craft through the skies!"

"To get my hands on those plans would formerly have meant that they passed through yours. But you will never again be admitted into Portugal to get those plans, sadly, unless the charges against you could be dropped... No matter. You said the New World? That is where the designs for the fleet came from?"

"I did say so, milord."

"Then, go immediately to the colonies—"

"You're sending me away?" Patrick was aghast.

"You must find the author of those plans, or anything connected with him or the so-called fleet. Destroy everything. Leave nothing." De La Warr's face was clouded by doubt. "I'll have to find a way to get the plans." A sudden memory, a vision from his past concerning the arrest and execution of a duke on charges of sedition, and Lord De La Warr recalled that he had never let anything thwart his ambition before.

"How, milord?" Patrick asked anxiously.

Lord De La Warr's features hardened until no hint of humor or leniency remained. "It's only a matter of time, Father."

Chapter Three: The Study

In which virtue proves no defense against casualty

After the encounter with Father Patrick Tempus, Lady Seramis was left with the burden of victory. Should she have risen above the insult coming from the so-called priest? Dancing with the other lords and ladies gave her time to reflect upon the exchange. While the other dancers felt the rush of the music and were forced to concentrate upon the succession of steps and movements, she found the music to be slow enough, and the steps simple enough, that she could let her mind wander.

Unfortunately, even after considering many possibilities, she could fathom nothing while she effortlessly anticipated the changes and completed the forms of the dances. *What was the connection between the tall, dark misanthrope and Lord De La Warr?* The latter publicly acted as the driver of the king's economic engine in the New World while privately negotiating the halls of diplomacy here in the Old. *But what of this new player, the supposed Jesuit priest with the unlikely moniker of Patrick Tempus?*

Tempus? Time? As she danced, she wondered if there was a lesson of no small import to be gained from the meeting. *Perhaps this meeting signalled that it was time for an official change in religious tolerance in the colonies?* Lady Seramis wondered whether her reaction was being judged. One could never be certain regarding the byzantine and often contradictory beliefs that support and uphold a state religion.

She had thought she would be seeing more of Lord Albion, but he was nowhere to be found. The evening's mysteries became more and more distracting until, at last, the masquerade concluded without resolution.

Saying their goodbyes, Lady Seramis and her ladies-in-waiting left the ballroom. Exiting the estate via the same great hall whence they had arrived, they stumbled upon what could only be described as a scene. A small girl with draggle-tailed hair burst through an open doorway from a side passage and ran straight for Lady Seramis. An exasperated governess soon followed in chase.

Calling out, the governess chided the little girl, "You'll be caught, with fever bright!" Just in front of Lady Seramis, the governess caught the little girl, snatching her up. "And soon returned to her own delight!" Squealing and struggling, the little girl was hoisted onto the shoulder of the governess, who curtseyed to the guests and returned to the side passage.

"Curious!" noted the lady-in-waiting, Mary. But it was much more than that to Lady Seramis. The little girl's cries were seemingly directed towards her, and the last she saw of the two of them was the back of the governess and the outstretched arm of the little girl, before they were swallowed by the shadowy passages.

The image in front of Lady Seramis instantly changed, replaced by the memory of a younger version of herself, in roughly the same condition as the child she had just seen. As the memory swept over her, the little girl in the vision cried out while being picked up by a governess.

Just beyond the little girl, her disheveled and bloody father, once the Duke of Cambridge, knelt in front of three soldiers. With neither pause nor mercy, one of the soldiers clubbed him hard across the face with the stock of his musket, knocking him senseless to the ground. The little girl, Lady Seramis in her youth, screamed in the apparition as another maid cried out, "Go! Get the child out of here!"

The marchioness, lost in this sad reverie, only returned to her senses in her carriage. Unaware of how she got there, and remembering none of the intervening travel, she had been completely absorbed in the memory of the single most tragic loss of her life.

The moment her father had been arrested on a charge of sedition by the first King George and summarily executed was burned within her brain, the memory of that day seared into her vision. But seeing the little girl had, for the first time since the dire event itself, triggered the full-blown immersion in Lady Seramis with an attention to detail that overwhelmed her senses.

. . .

The ladies-in-waiting were exhausted by the evening's events, and had all but assumed by Lady Seramis's silence that they would each retire for the evening. Despite her weariness, Seramis, for her own part, had no such intentions. She had recently been making excellent progress in her work, and felt that today—with the day having been spent in preparations for the evening's masquerade—was a day she could ill afford to lose.

Dismissing her maids as well as the ladies-in-waiting, she sought out her study instead of her bedchamber, stopping briefly in her dressing anterooms to remove her gown of silk and her petticoats. She replaced her clothes with a protective coat of canvas. Except its color—white—it was a copy of a full-length jacket used to protect oneself while smithing or working with chemicals, although covered with a multitude of pockets and loops for tools.

Her tired fingers deftly rearranged the blonde tresses piled high atop her head and quickly fashioned them into braids. Removing the powder and face-paint she wore revealed the high cheekbones that framed her smooth face. Her gray eyes momentarily studied themselves in her mirrors, but in no time at all Lady Seramis transformed herself from the public face of a young noblewoman of high birth into the woman of science and alchemy that was her inner self.

Arriving at her study, which also served as a laboratory and occupied an entire wing within the upper floor of Helleborine Hall, Lady Seramis proceeded immediately to her desk, half of which was covered with the parts of several apparatuses. They had been carefully taken apart and readied after her last experiments, the contents of which spread to adjoining tables to the left of where she sat. The other half of her desk was covered with ink pots, quills, and papers filled with her own writing and the notes from her reading, the sources of which filled the mechanism to the right of her desk, opposite the tables.

Standing seven feet tall in the shape of a vertically revolving wheel, the reading 'bookstand' could hold a dozen books open at a time, each within its own balanced and movable basket and propped open to a particular page of her own choosing. She could consult one tome, and then by freely rotating the giant wheel either up or down, could position another comfortably within reach. Whenever she wished, she could then return to the same page of the book she had left just by rotating the wheel back to its previous position. The idea for this giant crane-wheel of knowledge had come to a young Lady Seramis from a book describing a swing used to delight children (called a 'pleasure-wheel' in the Ottoman mountains). Upon studying a mill wheel in the western part of England when she was but twelve years old, she put the two ideas together.

As soon as she returned to her desk, her weariness dissipated as she threw herself into her work. She almost missed a knock requesting her attention. Lifting the goggles she wore, she called out, "Come in!"

The housekeeper—once the young maid that had long ago carried Seramis away from her father's arrest, now middle-aged—entered the study carrying a tray. "My lady, all have retired for the night, but I knew ye'd be working, so I hope ye don't mind that I made ye some refreshment..."

Lady Seramis smiled and removed the long, thick gloves she wore when experimenting. "Thank you." As the housekeeper lowered the tray to a small serving table, Seramis asked hesitantly, "Mrs. Persson—Nannerl—you knew my father, the duke, did you not?"

"Yes, my lady." The housekeeper's head remained bowed. "We rightly miss him, we do."

"I do, too. And sometimes I can't help but think and feel like the little girl I was, last I saw him. I'm still surprised at the time that's passed," Lady Seramis stepped towards the servant, and tenderly took her hand. "But I guess I'm no longer the little girl looking up at you."

The housekeeper clasped Lady Seramis's hand with both of her own and looked straight at her. "My lady, he was a good lord, but..." Starting to cry, she blurted out, "But you've grown into a great lady!" Mrs. Persson uttered a little gasp and reached up, fidgeting with her cap as she apologized. "Oh, look at me! I'm so sorry..."

Wordlessly, Lady Seramis sympathized while her housekeeper recovered. “We all wish we could have spared ye,” she continued through her sniffles. “But more’s the truth, there’s not a one of the house would not do any and all that we could for ye!”

“Thank you!” Lady Seramis replied, not entirely sure what to make of the statement. Brightening, she said, “And that is why I must continue to work! Work shall be our salvation and keep those old wolves at bay!”

“Will there be anything else, my lady?” the maid wiped tears from her eyes.

“No, I must return to my work, and it is late.”

“...And soon returned to her own delight!” the housekeeper said as she left. Pulling on her gloves back on, Lady Seramis called out a good night before Mrs. Persson’s words had registered. Disconcerted, she resumed her experiments.

. . .

First, that night’s study had started with a review of the *Hermetica* of Hermes Trismegistus; then, Seramis continued with the newly acquired works of another alchemist, Maria Prophetessima. So, it was only natural that after completing her review of the *Principia* of Sir Isaac Newton, she would proceed with her experiments now molded within the framework found in the works of the chemist Thomas Boyle.

“If truly the summation of my experience of time is infinite,” Seramis absently spoke aloud, “hence the operation of integration within time, that is, the original function of the passage of time can be recovered from its derivative...”

Of course, to the calculus of Lady Seramis’s reason, this made complete sense and was exactly what she had referred to as ‘the work that kept the wolves at bay.’ Although the formulas of Newton and Leibniz, following upon the work of Cavalieri, and before him, al-Haytham, helped her to understand and even quantify her secret abilities, it had become increasingly clear to her that only experimental alchemy would actually achieve her aim.

But towards what goal, she asked herself, do I aim? *Should I rid myself of my burden, so no longer shall I perceive time as a variable that differs from those around me? Would removing my unique abilities prevent the danger of discovery and condemnation that would be my undoing? Could I loosen these bonds that hold me to this plane, and find solace up amongst the clouds that move so gracefully across the skies?*

She paused to consider how her love of exploration and investigation had been aided by her abilities. *Should I not celebrate my differences? Am I not an individual with the inherent right of uniqueness within mankind?* Of course, she knew within that question lay the answer: For as long as she was not a vested individual—all the lands and wealth belonging to her title being held in trust until marriage—she risked jeopardizing herself, her name, and all that she knew or had ever known. This so-called enlightened age still held a terror for women, as she knew all too well the fine line between her reputation for intelligence and unfounded accusations of witchcraft that could bring all to ruin.

As Lady Seramis continued her exhausting pace late into the night, she grew careless. In her haste and excitement at isolating a gas that was lighter than air—a substance she knew to be unstable, requiring great pains to prevent its accidental release—an immense quantity of the volatile stuff accumulated about the ceiling instead of dissipating. When she sleepily released a bladder full of the gas (only the most impervious of materials could contain it, yet the element seemed to be a part of ordinary water), she noted that instead of coming to rest against the shellacked panels of the ceiling, the gas bag floated several inches away. It was as if the buoyancy of the bladder somehow reached equilibrium. Lady Seramis was puzzled by this, as it could only mean that the density of the air at the ceiling was the same as the density of the highly flammable gas...

Her worst fears regarding the experiment instantly roused her from her dreamy pondering. Instead of dousing the candles that now posed disproportionate danger, she raced for the windows to open them in an attempt to flush the gas from within. Tragically, opening the windows disrupted the gas at the ceiling, pushing enough of it towards the open flames to cause it to ignite. The resulting explosion propelled Lady Seramis out through the open window. Her scream of terror was torn from her by the rush of fiery air as she plunged into the hedges below.

Chapter Four: The Accusation

In which loss follows tragedy

Scratched and stunned but otherwise unharmed, Lady Seramis watched helplessly as another explosion, this one caused by the fire reaching the previously distilled gas, blew out the remaining windows of her upper-floor study, engulfing her beloved Helleborine Hall in flames. Picking herself out of the hedge into which she had safely fallen, she dragged herself to a servants' entrance in the garden level, slowly picking up speed as she recovered from the shock. There, she retrieved a skeleton key hidden behind a false brick and unlocked the door.

Awakened by the explosions, their hazy first thoughts focused by Lady Seramis's shouts, sleepy servants rushed about in a panic until wiser and more focused heads prevailed, directing the evacuation. The marchioness abandoned her reserve, running faster and faster until the rooms and corridors down which she raced were mere blurry streaks in her vision. She stopped at times to exhort individual footmen and coachmen to get buckets from the kitchen and the barn as well as water from both before speeding towards the front rooms of the hall.

Upon reaching the grand staircase to the upper story, Lady Seramis stumbled into a choking and coughing maidservant, who conveyed that no one else from the upper floor had escaped. Apparently, this poor girl had failed to reach the guests and assist them and was forced to retreat from the smoke and the heat. Ascending the staircase in a blur, Lady Seramis rushed into the smoke-filled central hallway upon the upper floor.

Dodging flaming timbers and charred ceiling panels falling from above, the mistress of this great house blindly charged down the hall by memory, drawn by the screams of the ladies-in-waiting. Squeezing tears from her stinging eyes, Lady Seramis just barely managed to push one of the girls ahead of her and grabbed the arms of the two others. Choking on the foul-tasting smoke, they sought to escape the ruin by using the servants' back stairway that none of the girls thought (or knew about) to use.

Elizabeth stumbled and slipped out of Seramis's grasp, and was in mortal danger of being crushed under the crumbling ceiling if not first burned by the encroaching flames. With sections of the floor now giving way, Seramis sprinted to Elizabeth's rescue, kicking off the still-standing wall and executing a leap across a chasm opening in the floor.

The other girls had disappeared to safety down the servants' stairway in a route now blocked, leaving the lady of the manor and the lady-in-waiting to face the flames and smoke whence they had just escaped. Overcome by acrid fumes, Elizabeth of Shrewsbury slumped to the floor, only to be bodily picked up by her hostess. Struggling with the weight, the marchioness was assisted by dedicated and brave servants so that all could flee down the grand staircase and finally into the darkness outside to safety.

. . .

The early morning light revealed a scene of ruin as the glowing embers of the topmost floor of Helleborine Hall smoked and sizzled in the aftermath of the fire. Lady Seramis, disheveled and covered in dirt and soot, walked from group to group, checking and noting that none were missing. However, when approaching the ladies-in-waiting who were huddled and whispering amongst themselves, she noted that they ceased their conversation and stared, saying nothing while she handed them each blankets. Moving to another group, she heard them resume their talking, more animated than before, but their behavior was soon forgotten in the rush to recover from the aftermath of the fire.

Into this sad company entered a rider on horseback. Baron Thomas West the Lord De La Warr, in plain soldier's gear, looked almost as different from how he had appeared in his opulent and gaudy costume of the night previous as did the Marchioness of Cambridgeshire in her soot-covered coat. With the men he led arriving behind him, he sought out Lady Seramis.

"By your leave, my lady, might my company be of assistance?" Lord De La Warr asked.

Puzzled, Lady Seramis answered, "My lord baron, I know not what providence to thank for your timely arrival, but you have my gratitude!"

"My duty to my lady is thanks enough!" Noting the remains of the upper story, De La Warr inquired further, "We had heard of possible trouble... Whatever could be the cause of this tragedy? Wasn't that your personal study?"

"It was my fault, my lord—"

Almost whispering, De La Warr hissed, "You admit this?"

"My experiments escaped my control, with disastrous consequences."

"Was anyone hurt?"

"Some of the servants were injured in suppressing the flames, and..."

Suddenly, the captain of the company arrived and signaled De La Warr. The baron leaned from his saddle to hear the whispered report. As Lady Seramis watched without comprehension, the soldier left to collect the rest of his company.

Lord De La Warr raised his voice to address all present. "It appears no one was seriously hurt in the tragedy, but I fear a disaster has fallen upon us all..."

In an attempt to draw his attention, Lady Seramis asked, "What mean you, my lord?"

"By happenstance, this calamity has uncovered terrible accusations that demand an immediate and just reaction." And as he finished, the company of soldiers swiftly surrounded the baron and the marchioness. The unprepared footmen and coachmen of her household, worn out from fighting the fire, were cut off by the circle of muskets and helpless to assist their lady.

"Is this how you mean to assist, milord?" Lifting her palms, Lady Seramis shrugged. "Couldn't accusations wait?"

"The Marchioness de Cambridgeshire has admitted to causing the destruction of this hall..."

"Do not lecture me on causes, Baron." Lady Seramis couldn't control her reaction, and pointed an accusatory finger at her patron. "I have saved that which concerned me most—lives were at stake!"

"Only God, our Lord and Savior, can truly save the lives of the lost who are condemned to fire, as surely all witches are condemned?"

Struggling to understand what seemed a non sequitur, she could only ask, "My lord, what are you saying?"

"We have a witness who described the marchioness flying through the air. Bring her forth!" Elizabeth of Shrewsbury was thrust into the circle of soldiers that ringed Lord De La Warr and Lady Seramis.

"My lord?" Elizabeth addressed him in a shaking voice. "How did the fire start, if not by evil sorcery?" Turning to Lady Seramis, she cried out, "How could you have saved my life if not by foul witchcraft? Was I not already dead, surely to perish in the flames?"

"I am beginning to regret having saved you." Seramis narrowed her eyes and turned to De La Warr. "I can explain myself to you, but this girl has no science to understand the alchemy I undertook..."

Shrieking in fright, Elizabeth cried, "You flew! I've never seen such swiftness in any natural thing!"

"Well, my lady?" Lord De La Warr sat straighter in his saddle, "Do you have an explanation? Was it science that carried you through the air?"

"You demand an explanation, Baron? Then I will have my say in the House of Lords!"

"No, Lady Seramis," replied De La Warr calmly. "Charges of witchcraft will not be heard in Parliament."

What color remained in Lady Seramis's face was drained in that moment. "You—you are arresting me?"

"By order of the King," said De La Warr, flourishing a scroll. "His Majesty has signed the warrant already." He showed the royal seal to her, but addressed the crowd assembled about them. "I have it justly here, as God and King swiftly command that no unnatural acts shall ever darken our fair land."

"What of this household, Baron?"

Ignoring her pleas, De La Warr loudly proclaimed, "I hereby arrest you in the name of His Majesty, George the Second." To the soldiers, he called out, "Let none impede the King's will!"

Leaning down to whisper to Lady Seramis, De La Warr looked sadly at her. "You know that I have constant plans upon contingencies upon moves and countermoves! Ride with me, and swiftly we may yet have justice!"

In defeat, Lady Seramis said, "I fear justice will not come swiftly, my lord."

. . .

Having commandeered Lady Seramis's carriage but ordering his own men to drive, Lord De La Warr rode with her to his estate. Warm early summer rain began to fall, mirroring the dampened spirits and stifling oppression within the carriage. Although still wearing his plain riding gear, the baron had resumed the habits of a courtier and attempted to engage Lady Seramis in conversation.

"My grief is boundless, my lady, your suffering—"

"Do not speak to me of my suffering, Baron," she interrupted, "when your words are endless droning in my ears."

"I beg of my lady, do not judge me too harshly—"

"I cannot judge you at all, Baron, unless I am mistaken and you are under arrest!"

"You are too exceptionally brilliant, my lady, to be mistaken," Lord De La Warr demurred, in the mannerism of courtly flattery, "but you are also too smart to have saved yourself—"

"I assume, Baron, that you are not merely adding insults to a day already filled with injury."

"My lady, I meant no insult! If you were not so industrious and rational, you might have clearly seen the king's designs upon your ancestral lands—"

Interrupting, she retorted, "Politics do not interest me, Baron, but do not mistake my indifference for ignorance. I knew well what our Hanoverian cousin desired—"

De La Warr continued as if she had remained silent. "...And if so, you might have otherwise made plans or sought to ensure your family's continuation, as I have done."

"Why, yes, Nuncle, do tell me how you have ensured my family's continuation by arresting me for witchcraft!"

"Don't you see? As opposed to someone else delivering you into custody, you will still have my household at your disposal! With me, you will still be family!"

"You will forgive me, my lord, for not sharing your enthusiasm for your plans, as you saw fit not to share the existence of your plans with me."

"My lady, I couldn't trust that such secrets would remain hidden! How could I divulge confidences with you that wouldn't also find their way to the king?"

"Then why are you sharing your warnings with me now?"

"Be patient, and I will give my entire confidence to you."

Not sure if she understood what the baron had said, Lady Seramis answered simply, "I have been patient for what seems a long lifetime, my lord."

. . .

Pouring rain having washed away all traces of yesterday's festivities, Lord De La Warr's Neo-Palladian estate appeared gloomy and foreboding. The menace of the soldiers that yesterday had been but the outward trappings of power was today an actual threat of violence, as ceremonial halberds had been replaced with bayonet-tipped muskets. After the carriage came to a halt, De La Warr disembarked and attempted to offer assistance to Lady Seramis, who refused.

"You may wish to rest," he said, "Please allow my servants to provide anything you desire."

"I have not eaten nor slept since yesterday, but all I desire is my freedom, my lord."

Adopting a paternal air, De La Warr said, "You may eat and rest within, my child, and await my summons." Whispering, he continued, "And place your faith in me for the rest!"

Chapter Five: The Confession

In which plots are both revealed and concealed

I have finally reasoned why I feel so calm, almost serene, after the recent catastrophe. While I am imprisoned here in Lord De La Warr's estate, I am also, in a sense, free.

After having been fed, washed and dressed, the former marchioness had been deposited in a cold and lifeless room to write her confession. Warmed by a weak fire, lit by a single high window and containing only the desk and a long bench, the cell reflected the starkness the prisoner, Seramis Helleborine, now found to be her changed circumstances.

The irony of the situation demands explanation, of course. All my life I have carried a secret burden. Now, however, it is definitely no longer a secret, and thus, perhaps need no longer be a burden as well.

I wonder if you will understand what I describe as my secret, my burden. To begin with, there are many images—metaphors as such—for understanding time, as it were:

Rivers. Falling sand. Moving clouds. A wheel.

Wheels. Consider time not as a single wheel shared by all; consider instead each and every one of us has a wheel of time of our own. This may seem inconsequential to you, as you are likely to assume that all of our wheels are the same size and turn at the same rate.

While all of the wheels cover the same distance as they roll through time, from what I have been able to determine, my wheel of time is simply so much larger than yours.

She stopped herself. Putting down her quill, Seramis read what she had written. Her words appeared so different being intended for others, although she had written very nearly the same ideas privately many times over. She hesitated, dipping the sharp quill repeatedly into the ink pot. When she wrote again, it was with a fury.

I may sound like I'm boasting, but consider the point of view of the wheel. We experience time from the edge of the wheel—never able to stop—forever going round and round. But your passage through time follows the rapid rise and fall of the point on the little wheel's edge. My burden is to experience the same passage of time as a point on a larger wheel, arcing so slowly in comparison. I watch and listen to the onrushing of time as a slow wash. I will never know if you understand what it means for me to hear dirge-like laments accompany a near-frozen tableau while you watch what you describe as a rush of melody and the dancing of swift feet.

Taking a deep breath, she wrote more as she found her voice.

Unfortunate does not begin to describe the series of events that have transpired from evening last until this moment. I have been instructed to write a confessional, and this is that and more; everything I do or write confesses my guilt and my shame. Yet I myself have felt neither sadness nor recrimination.

I do not deserve pity—least of all, my own. My carelessness, as a result of my fatigue, could have hurt or killed those who trusted me; and while they—and I—were spared that, I have failed all who depended upon me.

This, I confess.

But this will be deemed insufficient, as I have been charged with witchcraft.

An invisible accusation, that—

Seramis Helleborine nearly crumpled the paper in her grasp, but continued writing while leaving the thought incomplete.

How does one deny something that exists only in the mind of the accuser? If I could give a factual explanation of events, if I could demonstrate the physical and natural conditions of what transpired in the early morning hours at Helleborine Hall, would I be believed?

I do not think anyone interested in pursuing a charge of witchcraft will be persuaded; won't they instead fear that they were being deluded? Could a judge show reason and temperance without themselves being charged of aiding a witch or, at least, being susceptible to a witch's power? I know that anything I do or say, including these words, will be used as evidence against me, so I freely admit; I have no explanation nor defense for my actions, save one: what happened, happened.

One final thought as it applies here: while I am glad to lay down my burdens, I will not lay down my responsibilities so easily.

The former marchioness stopped writing. The fury she had felt had fled from her, leaving her drained; her writing hand trembled. She knew she was doomed. The feeling was overwhelming, so much so that it seemed to pass right through sorrow and into a darker place where inertia dragged her senses and her feelings into a pit and left them there, hidden from the light of day.

Sadness overtook her. Carelessly, she wadded her confession into a ball and threw it into the weak fire to slowly char and burn. As it turned to ash, she collapsed on the bench and wept.

. . .

A maidservant wakened Seramis and brought her to Lord De La Warr's meeting rooms. De La Warr had exchanged his riding clothes for a simple waistcoat and breeches, similar in style to the plain dressing gown Lady Seramis wore. He doffed a felt hat as she entered, and stood up from the chair near the fireplace. Except for the circumstances that led to this meeting, the two of them could have been country neighbors meeting to discuss local issues of the day.

"My dear, please join me. Will you have anything?" he said diplomatically.

"I would have my freedom, my lord."

Lord De La Warr paused, then asked again for Lady Seramis to join him. "I believe you shall, but first, let us discuss some serious matters at hand."

"My lord," Seramis sat stiffly on the proffered chair, "the matter of my imprisonment on false charges is serious, is it not?"

"Yes, it is; and I know you think me your jailer, but truly, I am not. I will do everything possible to help." He examined his hands for a moment, turning them over and flexing his long fingers. "I know that if you had an explanation to answer the charges against you, you would offer it, but we both know the real reason for this campaign against you."

"Are you repeating what you told me earlier about the king?" Seramis looked at him for the first time since entering the room.

"I would tell you more, if you wish to listen. Pledge yourself to my cause, and you will have a solution to this trial, I promise." He gestured to a tray of cheeses, of which the former marchioness took note but refused to touch.

"And your cause, Baron?" she said, still looking at the food.

"I serve the King, of course, as we all do," he replied matter-of-factly. "In fact I have served him and his father through all points of the compass in all corners of the kingdom, and I am asking you to do so as well."

Lady Seramis raised an eyebrow at this, wondering at the turn of events. As unexpected as it was, it made clear what the baron's intentions had been all along.

"Please, let me explain." Her patron shifted in his chair. "You know that the father of the king, the late George the First, styled himself the Duke of Cambridge when he assumed your father's title."

"I'm painfully aware of that part of my family history."

"But you may not be aware that his son, the current king, still fears the power that your family represents." Seeing the plate of food untouched, Lord De La Warr picked it up and offered it when he finished speaking.

Ignoring the platter still, Lady Seramis dismissed the baron's statement. "There is nothing left save the ashen ruins of Helleborine Hall and the ancestral lands. Baron, you know this. I could no more oppose the king in force than I could stop the wind blowing across the fens and over Gog and Magog!"

"In spirit and idea, you and your family represent a challenge to the king." He selected a piece of cheese and popped it into his mouth as he spoke. "And as much as I've tried to dissuade him from acting upon the royal warrant he signed, I was charged to bring about your downfall so that the crown may assume your lands and title."

Swallowing, he paused before consuming any more. "Naturally, I was given leave to accomplish this transfer as I will, so I have seen to your safety and to your restoration."

Picking up a slice from the plate at long last, the former marchioness held it up. "For what would I thank you, good milord?" She dropped the cheese back onto the plate, shaking her head. "You speak of my downfall as casually as a summer divertissement, but my household consists of real people, people who are as much a part of my home as yours."

"And that will continue, as Helleborine Hall and all within may now be in the king's name, but the retinue are part of my household and my staff—the continuation of the trust that I've held since your father's death." De La Warr's expression pleaded his case as did his next words. "I need your assistance now, and if we're successful I can help restore all that you—and your father—have lost! Please help me, and we can save you and yours and possibly all of England at the same time!"

Lady Seramis was exasperated. "How? What is it that you require?"

"I know you have no explanation for the charges against you, but the fact is you have abilities beyond comprehension." Seramis Helleborine no longer felt like the lady of noble birth she had been when she walked into the room. At the mention of her abilities, she felt smaller by the moment. "Is this not so?" The baron continued, leaning forward as the young woman seemed to shrink within her chair. "Have I to list every accomplishment, all of your talents, each of your many amazing attributes? Your achievements are superhuman, yet you are human. You thrive and flourish among us ordinary talents, yet you are extraordinary."

Tears welled in Seramis's eyes as she spoke; sobs choked her voice. "And what can I possibly say to such accusations? I confess that I no longer wish to be extraordinary."

Lord De La Warr looked pained and offered a lace kerchief. "I suppose if I could work to that end as well, I would. But at present I have a mysterious puzzle that only you, and only your talents, can piece together. Help me, my dear, and I will help you!"

Through the receding sobs she said, "Enough, Baron, what is it you require?"

“We will go to Lisbon, my dear,” he said consolingly, as if the solution to his dilemma and hers were one and the same. “There you will save this land from a potential threat and an enemy that only you can judge, only you can stop!”

“Lisbon? What is in Lisbon, my lord?” The former marchioness had acquiesced, and her voice reflected not curiosity but resignation as her hands dropped to her lap.

Conversationally, the baron continued while he distractedly scanned the bookcases along the wall. “Well, the king’s sister—Princess Sophie Dorothea—is there, visiting... But, of course she is not the enemy I fear... Yet I need not remind you that you should, naturally, be wary of her.” Resuming his impassioned plea, he continued, “I will go on pretext of meeting with her and negotiating a trade dispute, with you as my trustee. But, your true goal is the acquisition of plans for war that, if left unchecked, could be the downfall of us all!”

. . .

From a small hidden antechamber just outside the meeting room, Patrick Tempus withdrew from eavesdropping at the mention of Princess Sophie Dorothea. He now had enough information so that he could continue collecting his intelligence on the Helleborine girl through a secret informant of his own.

Fearful at this new addition to Lord De La Warr’s retinue of spies, Patrick worried that his own position was now undermined. In response, he planned to activate his own network of associates and adherents without De La Warr’s permission or even his knowledge. With a feverish certainty, Patrick Tempus felt he would soon be a lord—and De La Warr would answer to him.

Going to the New World and appearing to follow the baron’s instructions would mean that he would have to use the services of another—a spy known only to him—who would act in his stead.

His thoughts swirling in his head, he planned to leave for his accomplice a set of instructions, which he drafted thus:

You, like a brother to me, but even more so; my compatriot who cannot be named, must anticipate our betters from where I but recently departed, especially the girl from my dreams that I have described to you.

Remember well the lessons I taught you. Never forget my foresight that there is not one world but many worlds. These many worlds will soon collide and only by our loyalty will we see the dawn of a new age where we will be ascendant. Be true to the cause. Be faithful to me.

For now, follow the fools who think themselves above us. Stay hidden and observe. If your targets separate, follow the girl. Get close—but not too much so. Never reveal yourself or make any mention of me, as only ultimate pain will result from such indiscretion and disloyalty.

You will find what you need in the agreed-upon location: gold for bribery, silver for travel, and copper for seed. Grow your fortune from such seed to meet any expenses as will arise. At long last, should you find yourself where I am destined to travel you will find my further instructions.

As he finished, Patrick Tempus was sick with jealousy. And as he prepared for his own departure, he remembered an appropriate quote from a play by the Bard, and let it settle into his mind awhile.

Any bar, any cross, any impediment will be
medicinable to me: I am sick in displeasure to him,
and whatsoever comes athwart his affection ranges
evenly with mine...

Chapter Six: The Interlude

In which an old life is left behind

The morning sky was overcast, but it failed to mute the constant din of activity in the port of Lisbon as Lord De La Warr and the former marchioness disembarked. The two walked unsteadily after weeks at sea, followed by a train of slaves carrying their goods from the Princess Jane, the barque that had brought them hence.

"Have you ever been to Portugal, my dear?" De La Warr asked as he scanned the multitudes traversing the dusty Rua de Cinturo. Portuguese cavalry cleared the traffic so that his personal guard could form a cordon of protection as they made their way up the hill to the Palácio de Necessidades.

"No, my lord, I've never journeyed outside of England before." Seramis Helleborine answered evenly, despite her rising excitement at the novelty and the bedlam of languages swirling about her. From Seramis's perspective, her first visit to the Continent was marked only by a view of the backs of tall musketeers.

She leaned upon De La Warr's arm for support while her balance adjusted to a steady firmament and a static horizon. Despite this, she didn't fully trust the baron since he had revealed himself as the principal behind her recent arrest. "I've also never participated in diplomacy before, my lord."

"Ah, but you have—you have... And you will have to use all the diplomatic tools in your disposal!" He laughed, but his eyes were cruel. "Today, your mission is to meet with the dowager duchess of East Anglia, a neighbor of yours in fact. It just so happens that she travels with the king's sister, the Princess Sophie Dorothea. Of course, I will meet with the princess."

"Will I be meeting with her as well at some point?"

"Not if I have anything to say about it." The smile disappeared from his face as he continued walking without elaboration.

. . .

Seramis Helleborine smiled sweetly, a pleasant enough mask arranged by her pretty features as she removed the point of the needle from her finger. She had intentionally stabbed herself while stitching to prevent herself from falling asleep.

The Dowager Duchess of East Anglia, the Lady Albion (also grandmother to the current duke of Gloucester), seemed stuck on the same pointless personal anecdote of her son's brave defense of the first King George in the near-rebellion of 1715.

Seramis hadn't drawn blood. It simply wouldn't be seemly for the former marchioness of Cambridgeshire to bleed upon her needlepoint while being entertained by her hostess.

"My dear," the dowager duchess added after another story, "you've hardly spoken a word since you've arrived!"

While that observation was indeed true, Seramis could hardly reveal the reasons for her silence. "Have I, Your Grace? I've been so entertained by your company, I scarcely noticed!"

This was, of course, a lie. But diplomacy had its place, not the least of which was this place: a parlor room of Lady Albion's guest quarters within the Palácio de Necessidades of Lisbon, where now sat two great ladies, one young, the other old, like two resplendent dolls, surrounded by the colorful spread and trains of their gowns, powdered, bejeweled, and bewigged.

"Well, my dear, since the king—God save our George the Second—retained the title of Duke of Cambridge upon his ascension to the throne..." The Lady Albion spoke as she worked a needle upon her project, without the added stimulus of puncturing her own fingers. "Your family's station has suffered somewhat, has it not?"

"Your Grace's concern is of great comfort to me," Seramis said truthfully, as she truly wished to cultivate the support she heard. "But I had hardly noticed, as in these matters I have less skill and even less knowledge surely than even the maids of my country estate."

This last was a lie and a necessity as her arrest had yet to be made public knowledge. Of course, if Lord De La Warr was true to his word, the whole incident would be made to have never happened at all.

Unexpectedly, a servant arrived and announced another guest, who was preceded by slaves bearing a great rectangular harpsichord into the parlor, gently placing it near the sun-filled windows. Seramis rose, handing her needlepoint to another servant. The silks and satins of her dress settled upon their panniers as she helped her older companion to rise, which the Lady Albion finally accomplished with some difficulty. The two ladies curtsied to the doorway, now temporarily emptied of footmen and departing slaves.

Entering with a flourish of her gown, the Princess Sophie Dorothea spread her arms bidding her attendants rise. The beloved sister of King George II of England, now the Margravia of Brandenburg, had apparently left the company of Lord De La Warr as soon as it had been possible.

The three women exchanged pleasantries. Another chair was retrieved, and they sat discussing the news of their travels and their circumstances. Diplomatically, no further mention was made of the former marchioness's titles nor her late father's unfortunate siding with James the Pretender and his sympathizers against the father of the newest guest.

"Your Highness, England will shine upon your return." Lady Albion spoke tactfully at first to the princess. "But your sweet mother's banishment to Hanover all those years ago, and then later her separation from you and your brother, were such a dark stain upon our country."

The princess replied gently, as Lady Albion's obsequiousness mitigated her tactless reminders. "You have our thanks, which extend also to our gracious guest," she said as she turned to Seramis.

"It was while in Prussia that I learned of my fondness for music," the princess continued. "Do you know that my husband acquires the finest instruments, but cannot or will not procure the services of a court composer? Our musicians, then, languish for want of someone to mold them, to instruct them. In fact, I brought some new music—still unheard—as no one in my service has the skill to play it."

In contrast to Lady Albion's round features, Princess Sophie Dorothea's face was, at best, pinched, and she rarely smiled due to problems with her teeth. While she spoke, she attempted to smile and wordlessly persuade Seramis to perform, by hint, rather than directly, as it was improper for noble ladies beyond a certain age to play musical instruments. The reputation of Seramis's musical proficiency had, in fact, preceded her arrival in Lisbon.

Seramis wouldn't have taken such casual hinting from anyone else, but this came from the sister of the king, after all. It seemed that this trip might provide the opportunity to cultivate support among members of the court, if she could play the music as the princess apparently desired.

Seramis sat upon the bench at the keyboard, adjusting the stops for the three decks of keys in front of her. Her delicate hands brushed the dark, polished keys, not yet uneven through too many performances and still responsive to the touch. A servant placed some sheet music in front of her, which she could see had been copied by a steady but unsure hand. It was as if the music had been reproduced on the page without the copyist truly understanding the harmony or the counterpoint.

"I had a copy made of some music sent to my husband by a composer from Leipzig, whose works I have long admired," the princess explained. "I have not been able to hear the composer's works performed as they should be—just as I was regretfully not able to attend the famed concerts you gave as a girl, my dear."

"Thank you, Your Highness," Seramis said, not quite believing that the parlor performances at her introduction to society had been noted, let alone remembered. "With Your Highness's permission, I'll start out of order. Say, with the *Andante*? So that I might get used to the instrument?"

"By all means, we await your pleasure."

As she had always found as she played, Seramis could review and imagine the entire score in the time it took the audience to listen to just the opening chord. It appeared to onlookers that she could play the music perfectly at sight despite its difficulty, at a tempo that her audience found stately and moving. To Seramis, the music fell under her fingers very naturally, despite a few errors in the copying—which she automatically corrected.

Each note of the melody was an isolated and lonely sonic jewel, played within her experience of time as slowly as she could stand, and hanging upon her ear like a lament. Seramis would confess she hated the arias she played in this manner, if she would admit to the truth of it. But to her audience—hearing it unaffected by Seramis's own perception of time's passage—it was a brilliant and emotive melody, filled with graceful ornamentation and a precise rhythmic touch.

Seramis followed the *Andante* by playing the opening movement from the same collection; it was playful, with melodies that soared. The two noble ladies were enraptured, and in fact the entire palace within earshot of the parlor was still, held in thrall to the beautiful music that came from within.

But it was the closing movement, labeled *Allegro assai*, where Seramis found a complexity to challenge her soul. The music had, in fact, been written as a concerto. The title page showed it was the second of six concerti for various instruments—in this instance, a *clarino* (a little trumpet), along with several other melodic instruments and a supporting *ripieno* with only the bass marked for a *basso continuo*—the copyist neglectfully leaving out the harmonic notation normally played by multiple instruments.

Seramis played all the parts—including the implied harmony of the *continuo*—on Princess Sophie Dorothea's harpsichord, naturally anticipating the melody changing from one hand to the other while counter-melodies punctuated the rhythm and simultaneously brought out the harmony. She played sequences of daring invention, the dazzling purport of which the small audience could hardly comprehend, content as they were to merely follow in rapt amazement as the music flew past their ears.

For her part, she slowly and steadily brought out each phrase as a neatly balanced and orderly structure. When it was over, while her audience clapped enthusiastically, she noted that the copyist had even reproduced the signature on the last page: *Joh. S. Bach*. She wondered if she would ever play its like again.

. . .

After the performance, the dowager duchess retired for the remainder of the afternoon, explaining that the musical performance had nearly sapped her of her remaining vitality. This left Seramis alone with Princess Sophie Dorothea. Although Seramis had been warned about her by Lord De La Warr, the princess soon put her mind at ease.

"My dear, that was a heavenly performance! You truly have a talent equal to the composer's genius. Sadly, the rest of the collection has never even been opened, and shall probably never be heard!" The princess's eyes fairly sparkled at the memory of the musical experience. "For such music, I am at your service, but I do have one small favor to ask of you," she said while she settled into her chair. "Pray tell me, how can you play such amazingly complicated works with seeming ease and grace?"

"In all honesty, Your Highness," Seramis answered directly, nearly forgetting diplomacy in the afterglow of performing such music, "I do not know where to begin such a tale." She hesitated, knowing that her performance would require some explanation, but would an explanation help or hinder her cause?

"I am a rational person, my dear," the princess said. "But there are miracles in this world beyond my understanding. Your musical performance surely qualifies as such!"

"I fear that sharing the truth will not bring you understanding, Your Highness. I would confess it all to you, except for an apprehension that such misunderstandings would arise that could never be repaired!" The words came out of the young woman in a rush. The confession she had earlier written and abandoned while held as a virtual prisoner returned to her mind unbidden.

What harm could there be in sharing my story at this point? Am I not already condemned? Seramis was torn. She had wanted earlier to confess all she knew, but felt that Lord De La Warr shouldn't be the person to hold her secrets...

Hadn't the baron warned me about the princess?

Looking concerned, but moving closer, the princess said, "You have piqued my curiosity, my dear; please tell me what troubles you!"

Her instincts had told her to withhold her secrets, but Seramis now felt differently. The maternal concern fairly radiating from the princess inspired in her feelings she had never felt before.

"I apologize for the explanation to follow," Seramis began. "I have no practice in sharing my story, and I can only hope to elucidate what has been a vexing problem despite what appears to be a simple difference of perception."

She began at the beginning, of course: how she had, since her first memory, perceived time to move like a slow, almost imperceptibly flowing glacier, and not the swift-running river so often described. The shadows upon a sundial may freeze; the songs of birds sound slow and serene in their passing; one spoken word heard by her would be equal in length to twenty imagined in response.

"How is it your voice sounds just as any other young woman's, my dear?" Princess Sophie Dorothea asked. "Do you truly think or hear any differently than anyone else?"

"Your Highness, I have mimicked those around me since my first word," Seramis said, suddenly self-conscious. "It would be as awkward for me to speak any faster than I do, as I imagine it would be for you to speak any slower."

"Remarkable—almost unbelievable... And yet perfectly suited to how you play! Your style and the ornamentation are perfect matches to the graces I hear the from the best musicians," the princess exclaimed. "And as I've attempted to perform the slower of the movements you played, I might possibly have successfully plucked one note to the ten or more that you performed."

"But I've never wanted this!" Seramis whispered, forcing the words out. "Your Highness, please believe me! Every moment that I haven't spent hiding my differences I've spent researching to find an end to this curse! I would try anything for release from this burden."

"Why? You have such a gift! I admit that I'm a bit nonplussed thinking that my voice drones in your ears, and I only wish for some tea so that I might speak all the quicker! You see, I've felt like you have—"

"Really? We share the same malady? I've never known anyone else—"

"No," the princess smiled as Seramis appeared momentarily crestfallen. "Actually, my dear, I've just felt time speed up and seem to slip away in a rush, as well as experienced the occasion where time almost stopped!" She paused. "Or so I've thought, and I think most people experience time fluidly that way. Why would you think this singular gift to be a curse, an affliction, when you can accomplish such marvelous good with it? Why on earth would you hide your ability?"

"I wasn't told not to reveal it," Seramis answered in a whisper. "But in fact I believe it is still a secret, Your Highness. That is, your brother, the king, has signed a warrant for my arrest as I've been accused of witchcraft—"

The princess's demeanor changed at that moment. "I'm... so sorry, my dear. And you were indeed right not to share that news with just anyone." The face of the princess blanched behind her rouged and powdered cheeks. "I should have guessed that if anyone suspected your abilities, knowing my family's designs upon your titles and lands, that this could indeed be the case—"

"Please help me, Your Highness!" Seramis moved to the edge of her chair, and would have fallen to her knees but for a sense of reserve. "Forgive me this plea, but I beg you! I'm desperate..."

Princess Sophie Dorothea's eyes widened at the request. "I dare not oppose my brother! I may have some small say in family matters, but... I'm so truly sorry that I am unable to assist you." Her features softened as she laid a gentle hand upon the young woman's shoulder that in turn seemed to crumble under the touch, as if its burden had become twice as heavy.

"Sharing your difficulties should lighten them, my dear," said the princess. "I'm truly privileged to have heard the startling truth behind your talents. It's such a shame that you've had to hide your remarkable abilities. More troubling is that your gifts have caused you such pain when they could clearly bring joy to others. But it occurs to me to ask, why are you here in Lisbon if you're under arrest in England?"

"I am to play some part in a plot by Lord De La Warr. Something about the acquisition of some war plans or the like, Your Highness. He has promised me that I may yet redeem myself."

"Lord De La Warr," Princess Sophie Dorothea said, a pained smile disappearing from her face, "Yes, that would make sense, and I now also understand his displeasure at the brevity of his meeting—he may have been trying to keep us apart." She looked gravely at Seramis. "It seems that you must play your role as skillfully as you played that music, but there may be consequences."

Stopping and brightening suddenly, the princess laid her other hand on Seramis's other shoulder to look directly into her gray eyes. The young girl's gaze was held transfixed by the older woman.

"Use whatever strength you possess, as well as all your talents, leave none for reserve, but throw everything you have into the game," the princess said. "I know that skill and genius such as yours will be successful!"

Shedding any royal reserve, Princess Sophie Dorothea hugged the tearful former marchioness, Seramis Helleborine.

Chapter Seven: The Mission

In which our heroine becomes a thief

As she fled past the numerous guests attending the royal ball at the Palácio de Necessidades, Seramis wished she could truly disappear. At the rate she was making enemies, she might soon need to. While everyone was focused on the king of Portugal, and King João himself was focused on his sister, the disapproving infanta, Seramis had swiftly and silently slipped away.

But she had come to Portugal to restore her life and her position, not escape. Lord De La Warr had persuaded her that serving him as a spy would protect England and redeem her in the eyes of the king. King George had seen her as a threat, as his father had been threatened by hers years ago.

Now, it appeared to Seramis that the most powerful women in Lisbon saw her in that selfsame threatening light, so she fled.

In her flight she moved more swiftly than any other, although she took great pains to do so unobserved. Although encumbered by the intricately embroidered gown she wore, she threaded her way amongst the guests at the royal ball as their attention was elsewhere. To Seramis, the dancers moved so slowly, and the spaces that appeared between, around, and behind them opened so clearly, it was as if she floated free amidst the captive and frozen souls of the dead.

Moving so quickly took her breath away. She paused for a moment once she had crossed the grand courtyard of the Palácio de Necessidades. Although she couldn't see the king, she thought she could still hear the monkeys and birds that accompanied him. She wondered for a moment if she had more in common with the animals, due to the apparent differences between her and the rest of humanity.

Seramis knew she would be enchained, imprisoned, or worse, should the infanta act upon the suspicions she voiced. The king of England had already seized her family's lands and the remains of Helleborine Hall, leaving her with naught to lose save for her freedom and her life. Simply because she was different. Not for any particular act she had performed, as she had never done anything criminal, or even distasteful.

Tonight, she would change that. Tonight, Seramis would cross the line.

. . .

Slipping into the shadows between a religious grotto and the outer wall of the palace, Seramis needed to discard her finery and put on the garments she'd chosen for her mission. The noise and distraction of the party continued, so Seramis waited for a moment before making another move.

Just as she considered herself free, and as she looked for a place to hide her gown, she was startled by the sudden appearance of a monkey. On the top of the shrine in the grotto, a macaque stopped its flight, a thin leash drooping from its collar. Chattering in either excitement or anger, it looked down at the shadows below where Seramis hid herself.

"Go away," Seramis whispered as loudly as she dared.

Speaking loudly in French, two servants called out to the monkey. Seramis froze, wishing for the animal to lose interest in her—if she could be seen at all. The animal bolted in the direction from which she had just come, and the servants followed in pursuit.

Seramis knew she should wait. While time appeared to pass much more slowly for her than for most, allowing her to move swiftly when she chose, that phenomenon made waiting an almost unbearable chore. Most of her life had been spent in pursuits that avoided her having to wait, but tonight she knew she must be patient.

At several various points during her self-imposed silence, Seramis could hear revelers wander over to the other side of the grotto. Scraps of conversation would float over the statuary and hint at politics, a subject Seramis had avoided due to her family history. But the general sense of a new common union, the birth of an identity of Europe, fascinated her and helped pass the time. A "League of Augsburg" was mentioned frequently, and Seramis lost herself in thought concerning the implications. A world at peace would be such a different place.

But before there would be peace, she would have to break into a secret section of the palace to steal plans of war, and to do so, she must secretly transform herself and be born anew.

. . .

As the sounds of the party died, and the distant lights were extinguished one by one, Seramis waited what seemed a lifetime for the opportunity to start her mission. The strains of the last dance faded away, once again the syncopated mixture of East and West: *dum di di dum dum, dum dum...* Sounding to her trained ear as crotchets, quavers, and semiquavers, the music made her feet tap quietly along as she embodied the rhythm.

Seramis silently removed her polished, lacquered shoes and powdered wig. Unfastening the pulls and buttons, she shed the expensive gown without hesitation, although with some difficulty in the process as she only occasionally had to dress or undress without assistance. The gown simply wasn't designed for divestiture by one woman, alone.

Seramis had disrobed to her simple chemise and turned out the panniers where she had hidden her costume. But first, she stuffed her hair into a dark cap and then removed her powder with cold cream. Simple hygiene was not the goal tonight, as she then applied liberal amounts of a black face paint to the exposed areas of her head and neck.

Her garments were simple, tight-fitting hose and a blouse. She bound her breasts with cloth bandages wrapped about her chest, not in an attempt to hide her gender—as that was not the goal, either—but to give her more freedom in movement than nature would normally allow.

It is far from perfect, but it's the best I can do. Puppeteers wore such clothing to hide themselves during shows, and if I wish to remain hidden, I best adopt what suits this deception best. She cast aside her chemise and donned her soft-soled slippers and gloves, hiding her entire frame, except for her large and expressive eyes that shone in her pitch-black face.

She waited to bury her garments until the silence of the darkest hour of the night seemed to smother any sound. Walking away from the grotto, Seramis felt as though she inhabited the shadows themselves and could pass unseen amongst the palace guard, the only other people still out and about at this hour.

. . .

Later, as Seramis silently crept along the walls of the Palácio de Necessidades in Lisbon, concealed by the dark shadows of the night, she realized what she had been missing all of her life. It wasn't her new clothing: the tight-fitting puppeteer's hose and blouse she wore, nor the gloves, small cap, and soft leather-soled and laced slippers, every piece colored black. Nor was it the stealthy and fleeting dashes from hiding place to hiding place and the avoidance of the guards. It was also definitely not the excitement and thrills—for this was the first time the former Marchioness had ever done anything remotely like cat burglary.

What had truly filled a void was, simply, maternal care: a connection newly forged, as the import of her meeting with Princess Sophie Dorothea intruded upon her thoughts even now. Pausing in her roundabout entry into the parts of the palace where normally guests would be forbidden, she reflected on the turn her life had taken. It seemed to her that she had quickly mastered some of the finer points of sneak thievery and the mental and physical challenges that accompanied such activity. But it fulfilled no longing, satisfied no need like her confessional with the princess earlier.

Seramis had been forced to pause in her illicit activity by the appearance of sentries who only now turned away out of sight, so she left aside her feelings for later, and continued her silent journey towards the couriers' entrance to the palace. There, she would have to slip past a single guard, ascend a staircase and, within the second vestibule on the left, penetrate a secret entrance to a privy stateroom wherein she would steal the plans from a locked bureau. Maybe it is better, thought Seramis, to think about relationships and feelings, rather than think too much, or even at all, upon the tasks ahead; that serves only to bring forth a bewildering cascade of questions to which I have no answers. *How can I possibly accomplish this? Why did I ever agree to such a scheme?*

. . .

As she sidled up to the couriers' entrance, Seramis was almost within reach of the guard whom she hoped to distract and slip past. But before she could initiate her plan, the hulking brute turned towards her, sniffing the air. *How could I have forgotten?* thought Seramis as the guard scanned blindly but inexorably about for her, frozen in place but announced just as surely as if she were wearing bells: the scent of her *eau de toilette*—mild as it was, and completely undetectable to her as she was so used to the fragrance—stood out to the guard as does the scent of violet in a manger.

It took but a moment for the guard to espy Seramis. He instantly reached out a meaty right hand that would have entirely encircled her delicate neck. At the last instant, she pulled back the exact three inches necessary to evade his grasp. At that point, he raised the stock of his musket in his left hand to club her, intending to smash it cruelly against her head.

Of course, she wasn't there when the weapon thrust downward. By the time it crashed into the hard ground, Seramis had spun around to kneel behind the guard and brought her enclasped hands to the back of his knee. Her move instantly brought him down exactly where she wanted him to fall: face first upon the barrel of the planted gun. If the gun had had a bayonet, the point would have speared him through his eye socket. Instead, the firmly fixed musket merely knocked the guard out cold after he smashed into it, sending him toppling silently to the ground, the whole sequence lasting barely more than a few seconds.

Shaking with the after-effects of the first violent encounter of her young life, Seramis slipped into the shadows of the couriers' entrance and doubled over, retching silently and feeling her bowels twist. Fortunately, she had not eaten at the party earlier, but she was now quite shaken and broke out in a cold sweat. She returned to bind and gag the guard, and found out that dragging the insensate bulk back into the shadows was the most difficult task she had yet faced during her brazen intrusion into the Palácio de Necessidades.

. . .

After gaining the stateroom, Seramis proceeded to open the bureau with a skeleton key she had slipped from within her waistband and a hairpin from under her cap. Scooping the contents into her arms, she then deposited the folded letters and rolled scrolls into the moonlight pouring in from an open window. She started with the scrolls, and soon found the object of her quest, described in Latin, complete with engineering drafts and schematics. It all seemed commonplace until the final result: caravels—complete with crenelated forecastles—designed to float upon the air. But instead of 'round sails' as they had been described to her by Lord De La Warr, she recognized bags of air holding the ship aloft. Seramis at once saw the daring in the proposal and also its certain failing. Yet, by her own recent and painful experience in distilling the flammable and buoyant gas she recognized an audacious, albeit reckless and potentially disastrous, possibility.

Replacing the schematics in the plans with single pages from other scrolls (she held on to the schematics of the aerial man-o-war for Lord De La Warr's benefit), she returned the contents to the bureau as she had found them. She then exited as she entered, pausing to check the condition of the guard that she had defeated earlier, only to find him still unconscious. Weariness tempered her elation as she stealthily returned to the apartments secured by the baron, just as the first birds began their pre-dawn chorus announcing the new day.

Chapter Eight: The Aftermath

In which betrayal leads to welcome support

For some inexplicable reason, thought Seramis, *Lord De La Warr prefers to annoy me by keeping me waiting, when we should be quite hastily leaving this country.*

Sitting in a sunny drawing room off of the main courtyard, Seramis was certain she had spied De La Warr's servants assembling her belongings separately from his own, but that at least meant preparations were underway for their departure. Upon the completion of her quest, she had arrived this morning and entrusted the stolen plans to the care of the baron's manservant before changing her costume for an embroidered gown. Noting she had exchanged the physical comfort of the clothes made for exertion for the mental comfort of traditional garments, Seramis nevertheless soon regretted wearing the pinching corset and layers of petticoats as she passed the time reading a prayer book that once belonged to her late mother, having kept it as a memorial token her entire life, but never having read it before now.

"This is a most distressing turn up, and a severe disappointment," boomed Lord De La Warr as he entered the sunlit parlor from an inner hallway. Lady Seramis inexplicably imagined exactly the same words coming from her father at just that moment, and was stunned into silence. She simply stared, speechless, at the newly arrived baron.

Returning her gaze with a stern and disapproving scowl, Baron Thomas West, the Lord De La Warr, stood in similar silence.

"You were seen," he finally declared. "And worse, you left the witness alive to tell his tale. If the Infanta gets to him, she'll make him say whatever she wants to hear."

The casual approbation of murder implied in the disapproval of mercy shocked Seramis still further into silence. The suggestion of torture also unnerved her. She no longer was sure she had been merciful when the thought of what King John's sister could do.

"Do you know what would happen to us both if you had been recognized?" De La Warr asked rhetorically, before sighing, "At least the guard was as bad at lying as he was at protecting the palace, claiming that he was overpowered by several large men in a tale meant to redeem himself. Of course, that untruth was disproved by the single set of footprints that didn't match his own, so he changed his story to the claim that a single stocky dwarf or the like had surprised him. The Infanta couldn't accuse you directly but remarked upon your disappearance. Damn your impetuousness..."

The steel had left his eyes as his voice trailed away. He sighed again. "What am I to do with you?"

The question popped the bubble of uncertainty that had surrounded Seramis. "Why, of course, you are to hold to your word and release me immediately upon our return to Portsmouth, Baron!" Her voice sounded thin and weak in her ears, especially as De La Warr didn't immediately affirm her repetition of his original proposal.

"How now, my lord?" she continued when he did not answer. "I could not and would not murder for the plans you sought. There was no need, as you said yourself that none would suspect me of being your operative!" Her hands shook as she recalled the violence she had perpetrated. "Would you, Baron? Would you have murdered for those mere scrolls?"

Speaking softly still, his eyes flashing, he circled her as a lion circles its prey. "My dear, you have no idea to what lengths I have willingly gone, nor of the depths I would plumb with neither hesitation nor question in the service of my King."

"Oh, but I do have an idea, my lord," she replied. "As I have seen first hand how you have entrapped an innocent and set her against your enemy in your cause!"

"But you are not so innocent, now, are you?" Lord De La Warr's voice lowered to a vicious growl. "Did you think that you could just go back to your books? Were you so naive to think that you could return to the life you just left?"

In truth, Seramis rather wished she would not, not after she had opened herself up to Princess Sophie Dorothea. But she had no idea how she could continue—exactly—except that with her new motivation and self-assurance, she would somehow find a way.

"No, in light of the Infanta's suspicions you are useless to me here." De La Warr announced. "I will send you to my lands in the Virginia Colony in the New World, where—You dare?" He shouted the last at the sudden intrusion of his personal manservant.

Eyes downcast, the manservant whispered, "The princess sends for the Helleborine girl, my lord, as a royal command."

Shrugging, Lord De La Warr turned from Seramis, submitting to the summons with seeming nonchalance. "Of course."

Accompanied by tall Hessian mercenaries, made even taller with their conical helms, the courier from the princess invited Seramis to withdraw from the parlor to return to the palace.

. . .

Her energy already drained from a harrowing, exhausting night, Seramis felt what little strength she had left being sapped from her during the ride to the palace in a horse-drawn coupe. It was all too much: from the fire to the arrest, the weeks-long journey to last night's thieving, and finally the threat of a thousand-league expulsion to this, a possible last-second reprieve.

It had taken a toll on Seramis. Unable to keep her eyes open, and also unable to stop the flow of tears, she was in quite a state when she arrived at the palace. The princess's maidservants took pity on her, and proceeded to wash and clean her. Seramis numbly left herself to their ministrations, as she was led to the chamber where she was re-dressed, after which for all appearances—save a hint of shadow under her eyes—she was ready to meet with the princess.

Although Seramis recognized the architecture from her visit yesterday and invasion this morning, she hadn't been in this part of the palace before. Yet, she recognized the sound of the instrument being played in the parlor she entered. A lively and pleasant tune came from it, though the sound overall was a bit muted.

"Your Highness," Seramis curtseyed when the princess had finished playing and the maids left them alone.

"My dear! I've always loved playing that prelude as fast as possible, despite everyone else almost universally hating that interpretation! I hope you liked it, of course—"

"I am humbled, Your Highness," answered Seramis, and her eyes filled with tears once again. "I don't know how I can ever repay you, as you've saved me from a fate that I can't begin to imagine!"

Princess Sophie Dorothea's thinly drawn facc screwed even tighter, as she was close to tears herself. "Before you begin to thank me, please know that I can't stop what will happen—whether the consequences are imposed by the infanta or the baron." She paused, as if considering what to say next. "No more than I could have prevented what has happened since last night, as much as I had wished to. If only you hadn't crossed the line... That is, I imagine no one else has any proof, of course, that it was you... I mean, you're the only person capable of what transpired last night..."

"What do you mean, Your Highness? I had no choice in what I did!"

"My dear, you always have a choice, do you not? Did you not choose not to kill the guard that only you could have bested single-handedly?"

"Your Highness, I was completely unaware of the existence of another option!" Seramis felt her world collapse around her, her vision tunneling and blocking nearly everything from sight. "You know that I was threatened with death if I was judged to be a witch! What would you have had me do?"

Princess Sophie Dorothea straightened. "I would have had you do your best, and invading a sovereign land as the minion of De La Warr and stealing secrets—although I doubt that your theft is known to any here but me—are far beneath your talents!" Seramis looked for disapproval in the princess's face, as she had seen in De La Warr's, but saw only sorrow. "Unfortunately, I can't directly and openly oppose even the mere baron while he is in the service—and likely under the direct order—of my brother, the king."

"Your Highness, he means to send me to the colonies!" Tears filled her eyes as Seramis spoke. "He broke his word, and now adds to the punishment and continues my indentured servitude!"

"Then, my dear, this gift shall mean all the more to you as you start your new life, which is what I hope you will do given this turn of events." Through her own obvious discomfort and sorrow, Princess Sophie Dorothea smiled. "Your future is yours by your will, and your choices determine who you are." She attempted to brighten her features and words, but Seramis saw the results as ineffective.

"Gift, Your Highness?" Seramis asked as the word broke through her sorrow.

"This instrument is my favorite," Princess Sophie Dorothea explained, as she ran her hand down the rectangular length of the harpsichord. "But, as I mentioned, the margrave keeps us awash in the finest of instruments in Brandenburg. And I shall be in London soon, and have my pick of any that I find there.

"Are you familiar with the courses within this instrument?" she continued, seemingly changing the subject. "The higher notes have such shorter strings, and naturally, they are closest to the plectra as they connect to the keys within the keyboard, and don't come all the way to this end of the instrument, do they?"

Seramis drew closer to the harpsichord, curious as to the sudden emphasis on musical instruction, but supposing that there was something else to be gained by all this.

"I want you to have this," Princess Sophie Dorothea said, brushing her fingertips along the masterfully carved wood of the case. Then, as Seramis looked on, the princess lifted the lid slightly (the muffled sound the instrument made earlier was the result of playing with the lid closed) and pressed what appeared to be a simple truss, moving it slightly and thereby pushing the back of the instrument's casing out about an inch away from the rest of the ornamental woodwork. Closing the lid, Princess Sophie Dorothea reached underneath the casing and pulled at the back of the instrument. Her movements revealed a hidden padded drawer at least a foot deep and three feet wide where it was flush with the casing, narrowing to about a foot—leaving room for the longer bass strings within the instrument—more than three feet into the interior of the instrument's case. And from side to side, top to bottom, the hidden compartment appeared to be filled with jewels, mostly polished and cut loose gemstones but some set in jewelry, as well as coins of precious metals like gold and silver.

"This is my gift to you, dear Seramis. I may not be able to stop Lord De La Warr from ordering your transport, but you can be free of all that has happened, and all that is trapping you here. Your choices will make your destiny!" Straining at a smile, Princess Sophie Dorothea added, "...With a little help from your friends, of course!"

Wishing she could fathom the reason for the princess's generosity, Seramis was nonetheless very grateful. Overwhelmed by the turn of events, she could do nothing but weep with joy.

PART TWO: The New World

Seramis in Lisbon using hitherto undreamt of abilities.

Chapter Nine: The Journey

In which travel produces unlikely results

Securing passage to the New World wasn't as difficult as Seramis Helleborine, now no longer the Marchioness of Cambridgeshire, had thought it ought to have been. Although she was persona non grata in her native England, her traveling papers described her as a freewoman sponsored by Lord De La Warr and a subject of the king, able to travel unmolested through any of the British colonies or lands belonging to the chartered companies.

Unattached as she was to house or family, and with her newly received fortune from the Princess Sophie Dorothea, she need be neither a servant nor indentured, but was free to determine her destiny independently. Of course, De La Warr was unaware of her just-granted riches, and had paid for passage upon a triple-masted sailing vessel bound for the Virginia colony via the Canary Islands. Although it was late in the season, the sailing ship steered towards Africa in the south before heading west from Morocco, in part to stop at the port of Santa Cruz in the islands before heading west, allowing it to avoid the westerlies that blew hard above the 'thirties' and would hinder even a deftly tacking vessel trying to sail against the wind.

Once again, Seramis developed her sea legs more quickly than her shipmates, save those who had years of experience. It was not due to any natural affinity for the sea, for the deck's rolling surface required the same balance from Seramis as it did from others. But her ability to see things as they occurred much more slowly than others allowed her to more quickly adapt and adjust. And for all appearances she could walk as gracefully about the pitching deck as she did upon land.

The weather was clear, with steady winds, so they made excellent time to their first port.

Once in port, some of the passengers more affected by travel returned above decks, including one gallant who appeared gray and wan, despite being dressed in the heights of fashion. Observing that he leaned upon his cane more often than he carried it, Seramis noted that he was slowly making his way towards her, standing as she was near the aft quarterdeck in the shade of the unfurled sails, out of range of the smells from the piers where returning fishermen deposited their catches. Whether to hide the smells coming from the docks or to try to hide his distress, the gallant covered his face with a kerchief while he bowed and presented himself to Seramis. "*Bonjour, mademoiselle, je parlez Monsieur Innes, et je suis à votre écoute—*"

"I thank the good gentleman for his attention," Seramis interrupted as she curtseyed. "And should I require you to 'listen' to me, I shall be the first to request you do so."

"A thousand apologies, my lady, your bearing and your fashion suggested your having come to the Canary Islands via Lisbon—our last stop—from Paris or Bordeaux, possibly Toulouse?" Innes said.

"Good sir," Seramis deflected his inquiry, "you're casting your net as wide as the fishermen who have already hauled in their catch, but I fear they have left none for you."

Spreading his arms in supplication and smiling weakly, Innes bowed again. "And I would only add my wish for you to avoid the fever and chills that I have most unfortunately caught in my travels, as you are the very picture of health—where I am in very, very poor spirits. I merely wish to make your acquaintance and, with your blessings, bask in the glowing radiance of your vigor."

Seramis watched Innes ingratiate himself with a good humor, but noted that he didn't display any physical signs of embarrassment that a courtier might; there was no placing his hands over his heart or briefly touching his face that she had seen time and time again played out in slow motion, seemingly without the courtier's awareness. The embarrassment might mask an ulterior motive, or reflect that the courtier really thought himself above such prostrations and affectations.

Not allowing her curiosity to be piqued by this unusual behavior, nor to be charmed by the good looks of the newcomer, Seramis merely wished him a good day and made to leave.

However, he called out, "Ah, my lady, I have offended, and I would make amends, but I know not thy name—"

"Good sir, if you disembark here, then you need not concern yourself with me, my name least of all, as I continue in my travels," Seramis replied without breaking stride, her concentration on maintaining an outward appearance of normalcy unimpeded by speech. "And if you continue on as well, then we have many, many days of sailing ahead where our paths might intersect. God grant you good health soon, if not presently!"

. . .

While the ship lay in port, and after returning to her small stateroom, Seramis wrote several letters and gave one to each of the ship's boys to take to the diplomatic post on the island. She knew that her letters would be intercepted upon arrival in England, so she dared not write directly to Princess Sophie Dorothea. Rather, she wrote neighbors and friends of the family as if nothing had changed in her station or position, saying that she was merely traveling on the advice of a trusted peer and asking that they write and keep her informed of news from 'home'—or so she wanted De La Warr to think.

Seramis had no home at present, save for wherever she found herself, and the solitary unstructured life of a traveler was very different from the socially demanding structured life of a noble. She hated De La Warr for it, but he was right: she couldn't simply return to Cambridgeshire as if nothing had happened—not after what she had done.

She didn't feel any different than she had before the fire which marked the transition from her old self to the new, but of course there was a part of her that naturally missed her old life. Although she no longer had a title, and no one aboard knew of her past station and fall from her position, she acted in the same courtly manner; her countenance and bearing spoke volumes about her.

The rest of the ship's passengers and its company simply assumed her to be a member of the peerage and acted accordingly, with the exception of a few like Innes, who seemed to operate outside the norm of aristocratic social conventions.

This line of thought led Seramis to write on this topic in her journal, using this time of solitude to reflect upon the many changes in her life. She hadn't had time previously to reflect upon her invasion of the Palácio de Necessidades in Lisbon, or so she told herself. But upon such reflection, how easy it had been to break the law and then act in a way completely unlike anything she had ever exhibited.

Just as she had told Princess Sophie Dorothea, it was true that she had acted under duress. Apparently she apparently needed no coaching nor enticement for her to act in a completely unethical manner. It had come naturally to her, as she had believed at the time she was acting in the right—even to the point where she felt that sparing the life of the guard was proof of the righteousness of her actions.

However, as she reflected upon the events of that night, she realized she had broken laws and conventions and stolen secret plans. Further, she had done so just as easily as she had previously instructed ladies-in-waiting in the finer points of conversation, or learned to play a sonata unaccompanied.

Seramis realized that she had without question acted 'virtuously' as a model peer and member of the nobility in her life in Helleborine Hall, in as easy and effortless a manner as she had taken on new 'vices.' Was she as virtuous as she believed? How could she know if not by her actions?

She realized that the princess was indeed correct; at all times she had her ability to decide, and this decision was the crucial difference in her moral bearing. Only by facing the conflict within herself and making the correct choice when it presented itself could she contribute to the moral weave that created the fabric of society. This became all the more important to Seramis, as she realized she would be facing some critical decisions upon her arrival in Virginia. She now had to actively plan every stage of the upcoming venture, considering especially the differences between the expectations of her position in her former life, where tradition and inertia confined and constricted her choices, to her new freedom and the meaning of its exercise.

She considered the moral implications of solitude—of a life lived apart from society—and how it provided the least morally hazardous route. She very quickly dismissed it, as she now knew the feeling of burdens shared and feelings reciprocated in friendship. She even wondered if she would find someone with whom to share her life as her parents had shared theirs—all too briefly—and as had their parents before them. But tradition need not be her only guide, where a suitor appropriate to her former station would first be judged by the circumstances of his birth before the suitability of his companionship. She would construct a new Helleborine Hall, better and more egalatarian than the first, but would she find a companion who wanted to share it?

. . .

Innes returned to the deck a day out from the Canary Islands a changed person. Gone was the seasickness as well as the fancy clothes. He was dressed suitable to the mid-summer warmth in a shirt, light vest, and breeches but without knee-length socks or hose. He stood out from the tanned and dark-skinned sailors in complexion, but not in spirit. While the watch commander led the deck crew in song as they worked, thus keeping hands from idleness, Innes drew and wrote in a small notebook.

It was this scene that Seramis witnessed as she arrived upon deck to take some sun and afternoon air, and was utterly swept away by the charm of it, even in the slow, languorous tempo that shaped all of her perceptions. Innes eventually noted her attentions and smiled to her, causing her to blush and turn away. *How is this happening? Am I really like a little girl invited to her first dance, that I should react so?*

Giving his notebook and pencil to a ship's boy nearby, Innes pulled himself up the rigging of the mainmast, hand over hand, to where a sailor worked on a beam. Seramis pretended not to watch, but noted his progress. *Does he truly think to impress me with shipboard acrobatics?*

Innes took in his hands one of the ratlines, or loose ropes that was tied far above near the crow's nest, which a sailor could tie about himself and furthermore lash to a yardarm for security in case of bad weather and for safety against being thrown overboard by a sudden squall. He pulled it taut several times in a test of its strength and its knot's secureness. But the weather was clear, and the sailor working nearby nodded and answered Innes's question with a reply that was carried away by the wind, so that Seramis could hear neither Innes's query nor the sailor's reply to the effect that he had no need himself of the ratline.

At the apparent affirmation, Innes launched himself into the sky, holding on to the rope, swinging out from the beam in an arc over Seramis's head and the heads of others who stopped to marvel at this impromptu show. Especially at the slow speed in which Seramis perceived it, Innes floated gracefully through the air, seemingly staring right at her—for her part turning in time with his swing—and returned to the spar opposite where he started. Reaching out with a free hand to steady himself in the rigging to the accompaniment of shouts and claps from the distracted sailors, he then tossed the ratline back to the sailor he had queried, who caught it and tied it fast to the spar.

Returning to the deck via the rigging, Innes began to walk towards Seramis, who honestly was as surprised by the maneuver as she was at the mere fact that he made an attempt to impress her. Striding confidently, he missed that a belaying pin had come loose and rolled under his feet—whether by a sailor's mistake or by design, none could rightly ascertain. His victory walk turned into a stumble and then a fall as he stepped directly upon the pin which rolled immediately away, taking his left foot with it, the rest of his body following thereafter.

Seramis quickly ran to where he lay and helped him to his feet, grateful she was not alone in her laughter, thankful he was not too hurt in either body or pride to join her in such. His swagger and braggadocio, however, had apparently been broken too badly to be repaired and were left where he had fallen; neither was missed as they chatted together for the remainder of the afternoon.

Chapter Ten: The Arrival

In which welcome is marked by farewell

"These past three weeks have been the most meaningful in my entire life," Innes said to Seramis, referring to the time spent in each other's company as they crossed the Atlantic. Life had become routine after so much travel, except for the novelty of the conversations between the two, who had avoided boredom just as the vessel had avoided the doldrums.

As they sat upon the balustrades leading up to the forecastle, they took in the moonlit evening. The sailors of the night watch had just settled in to their routine, but the two young people continued to talk as if only they existed in the entire world. "I never tire of listening to you, and I hope you never run out of things to say," Innes flattered, but in truth, Seramis noted that he was indeed an avid listener.

"Oh, thank you so much. I know that you'll soon tire of my nattering. But, you'll forgive me if I continue with the story of my friend, Susan, and her mysterious would-be suitor?"

Seramis spoke with great animation in both voice and gesture, as having found a casual and willing listener her thoughts and words flowed almost unceasingly. "There once was a gentleman caller who arrived at precisely the same time every morning," she began, "and would offer his card to a maid or servant who would then relay the same to Susan—Susan of Sussex, daughter of the earl, that is—while she would fret and dither over what to do next. 'What is the matter?' we would always ask, each time, until it built to the point where we would stand and wait in anticipation of the gentleman's punctual arrival and request, which of course Susan would refuse.

"Despite her refusals, the visits continued and continued and on and on until Susan simply had no other recourse but to eventually receive the caller. She would give us no reason as to why she refused all those times, and when she finally acceded to his request, she was equally as silent. None of us could muster the nerve of intercepting the gentleman and asking him his business, nor would we put up a servant to a task we wouldn't undertake on our own—although we all, Susan included, would tirelessly ask whoever received him after every visit about what he might want with Susan. Of course, we simply had to know what could have compelled the gentleman to persist in the face of such numerous refusals and why Susan so steadfastly refused. On the day of the meeting, the rest of us hid just outside the parlor, and spied, of course, upon the fateful meeting.

"We were simply amazed to see the gentleman drop to his knee and declare his intentions to ask Susan's parents for permission to be a suitor! Susan could only respond, 'What?' To which the gentleman offered a folded lace and linen kerchief, saying 'then I must return this to you,' but Susan insisted, 'That isn't mine, sir! Further, why would you ask my permission when my parents had already promised me to you after you finished in the Army?'

"We were stunned! But even more so, when he replied, 'I was never in the Army! Aren't you Susan of Sussex, daughter of Stafford and Amelia?'

"'Now I remember you!' Susan exclaimed, 'Stafford is my father's—Samuel's—brother! And you—there was talk of interest in my cousin, also named Susan! But my other cousin, her brother William, told me that a man had been promised me by my parents upon his return from serving the king!'

"'It was William,' the ersatz suitor exclaimed, 'who told me that Susan—my Susan—was here. But he didn't know that when we were children, we exchanged personal objects and that I promised to return one day after having secured a fortune for us—sorry, I mean, for myself and my Susan.'

"Well, some of us—I think Mary in particular—wanted to know just how great was the fortune before Susan—our Susan—should have rejected the ill-informed suitor."

Innes laughed, and asked, "Would it have made a difference?"

"To Susan, no. But to Mary? Possibly! He was a nice enough, if trusting, fellow. We entered the parlor on the pretext of inviting him to a tea, which went surprisingly well, after all the weeks of denied requests and the delay of an unrequited romance."

"After I win my fortune," Innes mentioned, "I may have a romance some day, although I would prefer it not be unrequited!"

"Sir, please temper your comments!" Seramis chided, although not harshly. "Although I'm too old for a chaperone, I'm not interested in conversations that dwell too much upon that particular subject."

"Of course, and please forgive me! But what would you do, in Susan's place, if you were expecting to be married off by your parents?"

"Innes, you've been very patient with your questions, seeking not to ask me to divulge personal and painful truths, but I will say that my parents didn't have much time to make those sorts of arrangements before I was left an orphan in this world."

"I'm so sorry," he said, sliding from the balustrade to the stairs that ascended to the upper deck. "And again, I beg your forgiveness for the personal intrusion."

"Since I cannot ever be in that position, what of you, Innes?" she asked as she looked down upon him. "Would you tirelessly and patiently be as persistent as Susan's mistaken suitor?"

Innes looked up directly into her eyes with a look of such earnest and heartfelt longing, that for the first time in her life, she felt time rushing past too quickly, in that her breathing was quicker, her pulse faster than she had ever known. Innes's words sounded almost rushed to her ears. "I know of one—just one—for whom I am profoundly unworthy to wait, even if I should wait a thousand days and be forced to endure every moment of every one of those days in baseless expectation and hopeless longing."

Even as her heart melted at his declaration, and even as a sweet rush of longing flooded the edges of her vision, a small part of her noticed what can only be described as a 'tell.' Without looking away from his eyes, she could see the pulse of his heartbeat as his lifeblood traveled through a vein on his upturned neck. Sharp shadows thrown by light from the deck lamps revealed that, despite the rush of words, Innes's heart raced not. While Seramis could feel her own heart beating at half again its normal pace, Innes appeared as cool as ice.

She fluttered her fan as if to recover from her passion, but it was actually meant to measure Innes's reaction, as if marking time with a metronome. "You didn't actually answer the question, Innes! But in all fairness, I shouldn't have stopped you from talking about romance only to ask you how you might act if you were a suitor."

Seramis, without actually changing her attention, noted how his eyes started blinking more and his breathing and heart rate also increased slightly when he said, "You are correct, Seramis. I wasn't describing how I would act, but how I felt."

She felt confused, wanting to believe what she perceived as contradictory messages, but thought that her inexperience in these matters could simply be at fault. Maybe a man could speak of passions he felt while not actually feeling them? She truly had never spent this much time alone in the company of a man who wasn't a servant—in fact, the only other man she had spent any time alone with was Lord De La Warr. She would need more information before continuing: more research, perhaps?

"You are about to seek your fortune, Innes, as you've said many times."

"A modest life that guarantees naught but hard work and simple rewards," he repeated, as he had discussed this with her previously.

"And so do I!" Seramis rejoined, "and until I do, I won't know if I'm profoundly worthy, or as persistent as needs be for the one that destiny sets in my path!" She made ready to leave. "Good night, friend Innes, you have given me much to think about!"

. . .

Seramis, Innes, and the other passengers and their belongings had been transferred to a smaller vessel upon arrival at the James River, after being sent off by the captain with a knowing wink seen by Seramis and Innes alone. Apparently, the time they spent together had been noted by the crew (as well as observed some of the more curious passengers). Soon it would be time for them to part, yet neither seemed anxious—anticipating the event with neither desire nor dread.

The single-masted sloop put ashore at Jamestown, where Seramis sent a runner to present her letter of introduction to the lieutenant governor. However, no sooner had she stepped upon the soil of her new home continent, about to marvel at the genteel mix of all stations and races, than a slave ship began to disgorge its cargo. She and Innes stared at the suffering, shambling figures, some with features downcast and crushed in spirit and others with proud, if not outright challenging and angry, expressions.

It seemed to Seramis that the inner light of the world had just gone out, and that everywhere she looked a pale and sickly patina had suddenly dimmed the shine that had been present. Looking at Innes, she realized that she had been surrounded by slaves all her life, and had taken no notice of the people they truly were, and had not given a thought at the conditions that they were subjected to, and the part in all this that she played.

She had no words for how sad she felt, and for a moment wished she could simply be back among the fens and hills of her former home. Yet, she also felt a renewed sense of purpose; retreating to her past would serve no one. The best way to work out her feelings would be to face them and make what changes and improvements she could.

Her voice sounded clipped to her ears as she rallied and said good-bye to her traveling companion. "Good luck and Godspeed, Squire Innes!" She had picked up the social graces of her new home quickly, although she was trying to put the best face upon her feelings of sadness.

"Until we meet again, Miss Seramis!" Innes replied just as a coach and wagon arrived to take her and her cargo to the governor's mansion up the road in Williamsburg.

Chapter Eleven: The Conspiracy

In which new plans are formed and reunions made

The coach ride to the governor's mansion was an eye-opening introduction to the colonies. Compared to Seramis's former home in England, the Virginia colony was hotter, meaner, and practically empty. Still, it was enough like home that she felt that in order to thrive here she would simply have to be cooler and tougher and would need to fill the spaces with her science and invention. She remembered riding in a coach back in England, dreaming of flight and freedom—but here, at the very edge of her world, she reconsidered that idea as hopelessly romantic and possibly, even quite immature.

Lieutenant Governor William Gooch feted Seramis Helleborine's arrival with a feast that evening. Seramis radiated sophistication in her gowns and powder amongst the simpler, and in some cases homespun, fabrics. No sooner had she begun to answer a question about European politics than she would be interrupted with a question about fashion or food.

On occasion, certain details would prove interesting, as when Lieutenant Governor Gooch inquired about Lord De La Warr. "Did you know, Miss Helleborine, that De La Warr's great-grandfather was a company governor of Virginia colony? The third Baron Thomas West—De La Warr is his namesake, I believe?"

"I didn't, Governor," Seramis answered. She thought that it might prove difficult to be as open as she wanted to be but remain circumspect about her patron. "But that might explain the unusual capitalization—Englishmen today would never spell his name in that manner. Why, the King himself spoke only French in his early years, despite growing up in Hanover. The baron himself mixes his French in ways most peculiar."

"Do you know the baron well?" he asked.

"Well, he was my 'Nuncle' as I grew up!" Seramis said to laughter all around, "But, of course, his business kept him busy."

"And is his business satisfactory these days, I hope?" Lieutenant Governor Gooch finally asked, truly curious and possibly truly fearful that he might be replaced if De La Warr's business was somehow deficient.

"I should think so, but I only know of my own small part which I hope to conclude soon. I've been entrusted with the portfolio of a number of engineering patents that should improve the efficiency of foundries and mining." Of course, Seramis was in fact describing the results of her own research. "I should like to examine the most rare elements of the local mineral wealth in exchange."

"Oh, my! How progressive!" One of the goodwives exclaimed, "I marvel at the baron sending a woman to do this work!"

"It's far from marvelous, I assure you." Seramis smiled and could see the resentment in the woman's expression. "And really, these are only the most mundane of propositions that no one else could be spared to do, given the amount of important work that must needs be done!" She spoke as if sharing a conspiracy; drawing them thus into her ersatz confidence, she could feel the tension dissipate.

"Will your work take you to the interior?" Gooch asked. "I could grant you a sizable parcel of land in Shenandoah and throw in some slave stock as a bonus. Science and industry will transform this land as the savages never could!"

"Thank you, no, Governor," Seramis replied, hiding her disgust at the suggestion. "But if we could discuss the transfer of some rather inconsequential land near the Fall Line, in Henrico Shire, I would be grateful..." Amidst the growing laughter, Seramis asked innocently, "What? Was it something I said?"

"For one so progressive," the governor explained, "you need to be educated on the local customs!" Seramis did, in fact, know what she was about to be lectured on, as he continued. "We haven't called them 'shires' in an age—although I suppose that technically that still is the name—but we call them 'counties' now."

"I'm grateful to you all for your instruction," Seramis said, smiling at having disarmed any possible resistance to a woman owning property. That might in itself be too progressive of an idea.

But having won them over, Seramis looked forward to getting on with her work, and to getting out of Williamsburg and away from these people as soon as she could.

. . .

Shortly after Seramis departed Jamestown, Innes checked for his new instructions at the local taverns, finally finding a letter for him from 'PT' that was only a few days old and contained instructions to meet at a lodging home down the peninsula road, which he immediately took in seeking out his master.

"Father Time, it has been far too long," Innes said in greeting to Patrick Tempus, grasping his forearm with both hands when he had caught up with him. They were alone in a drawing room where Patrick had been waiting for word from his spies who had traveled south and west beyond the English settlements into native, Spanish, and French territories.

Before Patrick returned the greeting, he stared into Innes's eyes as if seeking out a mote or some imperfection. Innes blankly stared back, as open and defenseless to his master as a chopped cutlet was to a chef.

Patrick was eventually satisfied, and suitably established in his dominance, that he embraced Innes, saying in false humility, "My brother in spirit, why do you persist in calling me that?" Smiling, he chided Innes, although he truly didn't object to the adoration, and was undauntingly determined to have Innes completely in his thrall.

"It was my dreams, my Father, that convinced me," Innes said in a rush, the fervor of his belief pouring out all at once. "How else could you be all things in all ways to me, except that you and time itself are one and the same!" Innes had, in being mesmerized by Patrick, created a very elaborate mythology, where in everything not concerning the false priest he tended to be practical and casual, if not even incurious and superficial.

"I do confess that each day that I've waited for your arrival," Patrick said as he sat, and gestured for Innes to the same, "has been an age in itself, but the nights have moved in every conceivable direction! Well, I'll tell you more of that later. What news have you? If you're here, it must mean that Lord De La Warr or Lady Cambridgeshire is here, as well. Is that right?"

"Aye, but she's simply Seramis Helleborine, as she travels."

"What about maids, escorts, guards? Anything?"

"No, and it was pretty interesting," Innes said, smirking.

Coolly, Patrick asked, "How interesting?"

"Oh, no. Not like tha'!" Innes protested, speaking with a thick brogue, having dropped his affected speech. "It took me th' full 'clumsy acrobat' stunt to wile her eyes! After that, o' course, she took to followin' me like a lost puppy!" Innes then changed his voice to the mild accent he used when speaking with Seramis. "Yet, for all her inexperience, she kept her integrity and her maidenhood—"

"How heavy did you press, Innes? What does she think of you now?"

"I played the most virtuous of roles, Father. I had a feeling about her—despite being a sophisticated lady, she seems to have led a rather protected life, so I stayed in my humblest of characters," he smiled as he talked. Tilting his head, he reflected out loud, "I suppose it could be possible, but is she for you? Do you seek out a mortal as your mate?"

"You know I have no interest in anything like that." Patrick dismissed him with a wave, continuing as he paced about the room, "What are delights to some are called perversions by others, and to me all are nothing. Forget you not the quote:

'th' expense of spirit in a waste of shame
Is lust in action, and till action, lust
Is perjur'd, murd'rous, bloody, full of blame,
Savage, extreme, rude, cruel, not to trust,
Enjoy'd no sooner but despisèd straight,
Past reason hunted, and no sooner had,
Past reason hated as a swallowed bait
On purpose laid to make the taker mad!'

"What does emotion, let alone love, mean to me?" Patrick stopped as he spoke directly to Innes. "Only my will is constant, and my only ambition is to further my will!"

"But what's her story?" Innes asked, still seated in deference to his master. "Besides the stories of her aristocratic life amongst the wealthy and the powerful—of that I've heard enough!"

"Like you, kin-that-should-have-been, she has been a frequent figure in my dreams! In my dreams, her avatar appears before my spirit as it wanders the astral planes, yet she never moves of her own volition, as if she were cast about by winds of time. Somehow she has the potential to be unbounded by time itself but is still but a prisoner... I think she may be the key to our destined escape from this temporal realm." Patrick knew the effect this mode of speech had on Innes. In fact, he played up the figurative and metaphorical aspect of his dreams so as to string his dupe along all the more.

"It is enough for me that you escape this realm each night, Father! Your appearances in my dreams have provided me with the guidance to make your ambitions a reality!" Innes said, nearly falling to his knees from his seat and all but clasping his hands before his breast. "But I saw nothing out of the ordinary in this Helleborine girl except her intelligence. She was as idealistic, imperialistic, and enthusiastic as any young aristocratic lass I've charmed."

"That's because she's the opposite of you in all those things," Patrick flattered. "But what would you have now? Would you continue your hunt for her inner truth? Like some well-fed lion displaying a casual interest in a tasty morsel?"

"Aye, Father, if you still have an interest, I will follow, and I will find her secrets!"

"Good, I will leave instructions for my spies to forward their information to you so that I might continue my quest."

As if seeing a private vision, Patrick's eyes widened as he spoke further. "It is time for me to take up the cause of Time and bring about the end of the separation of Past and Future!" His voice became a tense whisper as he continued, "The fiction of the present must needs revealed. If it take me to the end of the world, I will destroy the false barrier! I will destroy the non-existent 'now' that separates what has been from what will be!"

Patrick's eyes lit up with a fire of intensity he had been stoking for some time by this point, and Innes—who clearly didn't understand a word of it—was basking in that fire's glow as Patrick's oration grew in loudness and fervor. "I'm on the edge of the foretold that will take me out of our known world, and into that which is beyond Time, beyond Place. Now that you are here, Innes, I must go forth! I cannot falter! I cannot delay!"

Innes fell to his knees. "Oh, yes, Father! You must! You cannot!" he repeated, no longer caring that he knew not what it meant, but still believing in it completely. "I will await your sign!"

"Yes! You will know the sign when it comes. AND SO WILL SHE! You both will come. You will know when to follow, and when to reveal all!"

. . .

After writing to the deans of several colleges of Cambridge in an attempt to rebuild her library after the loss of her laboratory and study, Seramis took out her plans for New Helleborine Hall. Reviewing them, she added to the list of materials she planned to purchase as well as to the manifest of artisans and laborers whose services she wished to procure. Fortunately, all of the transactions could be drawn from the letters of credit provided by Lord De La Warr—which saved her the awkwardness of trying to pay for smithing tools and farm implements with precious jewels and bullion.

The letters were instruments in the standard form of currency in the Virginia colony: tobacco. Seramis had already noted that the plant was everywhere, and everything fairly reeked of it. She was careful not to add stimulants to her already unique perception of time, although she really shied from them because of what affects she might exhibit rather than what effects she might feel. Maybe, provided that the ubiquitous familiarity of the weed didn't turn her distaste into contempt, Seramis would try it. But for now, she was glad enough for a chance to visit the market and escape the stale air of the mansion.

Lieutenant Governor Gooch just happened to have a parcel of land in the southeast pocket of his immense holdings—his was a 'Goochland' of sorts, in tribute to his ambition and business acumen—at a bend in the James River where it tumbled and fell amongst the woods of the Fall Line, splitting into several tributaries before joining up again upon the coastal plain. Above and below the line were suitable for tobacco, but Seramis had a completely different estate in mind.

At the market, she advertised for laborers and artisans, carpenters and camp cooks, animal wranglers and gardeners, smiths and surveyors, milliners and maids (she sought three, but hoped they weren't named Susan and Mary and certainly not Elizabeth). Also, she bought her first mule. She actually bought several, as well as horses, dogs, and other animals, too, but passed on the carriage that the lieutenant governor thought would add the "right amount of class to their neck of the woods" although she did procure two high-wheel wagons that she was told would fare better away from the streets of Williamsburg and Jamestown.

On her return, Seramis met the man recommended to be her future majordomo and charges d'affaire, Colonel Cyrus McClure, and his wife, Sarah. 'Colonel' was an honorific title and not an actual military rank, although Cyrus certainly seemed every inch the part, from his steely-eyed squint and his sturdy frame right down to the dusty boots he wore.

Sarah and Seramis got along from the start despite Sarah's reserved nature, thanks to Seramis's polite enquiries about managing life and family and her asking Sarah for practical advice. Seramis gave Colonel McClure and the surveyors each copies of the plans for Helleborine Hall, leaving the former to assemble the mule train in three days' time, but exhorting the latter two to start for the interior immediately, to see if they could acquire the lay of the land from the neighbors, including the Tutelo natives to the south. Seramis herself planned to travel by boat on the James River to the Brooke farm and then continue the short journey overland from there.

Before she retired to the lieutenant governor's mansion (and she was in no hurry to do so), she stopped at a collier's guild to learn about the mining of coal in the region. She was used to it being easily accessible in her native England such that one could shovel it up from the surface, or even just chip away at "sea coal" exposed on the shores there, yet here in Virginia colony she feared whether she would have access to it or not.

Fortunately she learned coal was found a-plenty and even halfway between Jamestown and 'Goochland' that considerable iron ore and lead was mined and processed. Of course, there then followed the rumors that Lieutenant Governor Gooch's lands were rich in gold.

Sharing with the colliers the amalgam techniques she'd researched, she was able to acquire the rights to the raw materials she would need for equipment that couldn't be purchased and would have to be made. In addition, during the idle chatter at the close of her conversation, she learned of a curious substance that was called 'pitchblende' by the miners. This rock released an inert gas that suffocated and extinguished flame, a gas that was too light to settle dangerously in the shafts of the mines as it quickly dissipated. If this mineral was just a nuisance to the men, Seramis asked, could she procure some? With their promises and assurances ringing out after her, Seramis made her way back to her rooms for the night, puzzling over what she'd learned and planning for what she would soon be doing.

Chapter Twelve: The Rebuilding

In which the New World reveals opportunities

Autumn and the harvest were in full swing as Seramis and her crew continued to build New Helleborine Hall. As the nights grew colder, living in tents was soon going to become a problem, so the work continued at an energetic pace. First to be raised was the barn in the cleared space inland from the river, followed by the colonel's house and kitchens.

Seramis would hear neither Cyrus's nor Sarah's pleas for her to take up temporary lodgings in the new house. She insisted that the couple settle into their new residence, while she and the maids lodged in a walk-in tent as the autumn weather was still fine. Although the laborers could have found accommodations with Seramis's new neighbors, they stayed in their own tents and quickly became a tight-knit community, complete with Saturday night bonfires (to which the neighbors were invited) as well as something new to Seramis: Sunday sermons and classes.

For the most part, none of the workers had ever lived more than five miles from a church, where attendance was mandatory. But this prescribed day of rest for most became a day of instruction led by the colonel, whose taciturn and gruff demeanor softened once weekly on that one day, as he initially offered improvised readings and discussions from Seramis's mother's prayer book that she loaned to him. Soon that expanded to lectures in philosophy and history from him, joined by Seramis who could recite stories and facts from memory—or extemporize on the spot—much to the delight and wonder of her workers.

On one chilly Sunday, when the group had assembled in the barn after a quickly improvised cleaning and the animals had been moved out to the newly fenced and partially cleared pasture, the discussion had turned to the fall of Rome and the rise of

Christianity. Of the assembled group, only one of the maids and Mrs. McClure had had any formal schooling (the private tutoring Seramis had received as a child notwithstanding), although that had only taken them to the age of 10. With the addition of the colonel and the engineer who had taught themselves to read and write and had studied their individual areas of expertise, that was the sum of the educational experiences of the group.

Colonel McClure never spoke down to them, despite the immense gap in knowledge from their lack of schooling, and instead patiently answered and repeated the ideas and narratives with an uncharacteristic enthusiasm for the subject of the moment, whatever it might be, carrying them all through to the moral, lesson, or conclusion of the day. As the maids would of a moment go out to tend to the animals, and others go to help them or to help prepare the evening meal, breaks were a frequent occurrence, with recaps and summaries to bring everyone together again.

After one such break, a newcomer joined the assembly, which sometimes happened as travelers and neighbors were welcomed frequently. To Seramis's surprise, it was Innes, who waved at her but sat closer to the entrance with others to listen to how Rome became the center of a diverse community that previously had no such center.

"I think that if someone were to say that Christianity itself were the cause of the decline of Rome," the colonel lectured, "that would be overstating the case. Have you heard the saying 'All roads lead to Rome'? So, as Christianity grew, it must needs follow those roads, and necessarily converge upon the capital of the Empire. But if some other philosophy had taken hold there, would we convene here today as Mithraists? Zoroastrians?" Everyone laughed at the idea, but still thought about how everything that seemed predestined and was inarguably historical still hinged upon actual choices by actual people.

One of the carpenters asked, "Are you saying that history could have been different?" And in questions of this kind, all looked at the colonel except Innes, who looked at Seramis—and the look upon his face was clearly defensive, as if he thought the question was a challenge.

"That's an excellent question, Fletcher, and I'm very glad that you asked that." The colonel always prefaced his responses with a direct statement of acknowledgement to the questioner. "Your question about history—to me—also asks 'What is history?' which, we all know, is the kind of question I love!"

Again, they all laughed, and Seramis picked up on that. "I think you are right—history could have been different, if different events had occurred. If Caesar had not crossed the Rubicon, would the Roman Empire ever have followed from the Roman Republic?"

McClure continued easily, "And I was just pointing out how Christianity was one of several religions practiced in ancient Rome, and how possibly any one of them could have swept the others aside. But there is another question: whether there is such a thing as," he leaned forward and emphasized, "a history."

While the colonel paused for effect, Seramis saw that Innes had turned his attention to her; she winked at him but couldn't tell if he had noticed, as she had probably done it too quickly for him to see.

Continuing with his topic, Cyrus said, "Yes, we discuss 'History' with a capital H, and we can all see when a book has been published on, say, the history of England, but does that mean that history itself can't be changed? I say that history changes all the time!" The others gasped while the colonel and Seramis smiled. "No, I'm not saying that travelers go back in time and change everything we know, but that what we know changes all the time!"

The crowd hushed as McClure continued. "Just because a history is written doesn't mean that someone else might later dig just a little deeper and uncover another side of the story, and thus rewrite history!" Some started to clap, while others whispered. Both the colonel and Seramis had enough experience with this group to know this to be a cue to wait, that another question would rise from the precepts of what she had just established. But rather than force it out, they waited for it.

Eventually, it came: "But how do we know what we know?" Innes started. "Oh, I'm sorry. That just sounds ridiculous."

"It's perfectly all right," the colonel rejoined, "I'm used to sounding ridiculous so I don't think anyone here minds," and they all laughed. "But go on; no matter how they sound, questions are rarely, if ever, actually worthy of ridicule!"

"Well," Innes began, hesitating as he was unused to this kind of discussion, "How do we know what we know, when what we know keeps changing?"

"I don't care if anyone thinks that sounds ridiculous," Seramis said, "it is nevertheless a very good question, if you really think about it." Innes grinned at the compliment, but the others in the audience had heard similar expressions before from Seramis. While a few were still too shy to ask for themselves (Mrs. McClure, for one, although she sometimes prompted her husband to ask for her, which no one minded), many had felt the same feeling of recognition, a feeling of validation of sorts, in their community through the Sunday sermons.

"What do we do? At some point do we just say we know enough?" the colonel rhetorically asked, working his way to a near-theatrical flourish. "Do we say we can't know it all, so we won't try anymore? Or worse, do we give up? We could just stop—in fact, more than stop, we'll refuse any and all knowledge that comes our way, and roll back what we've learned!"

The colonel paused, then straightened his back, planting his feet firmly. "Or, on the other side of things, do we demand only the newest and most recent ideas? Do we cast aside all knowledge that had been hard won previously? Do we willfully forget and ignore all that came before, only to focus on the present? We could resist making any decision, coming to any conclusion, always saying we must wait for more and better facts." Raising his arm, he appeared as a preacher would: preaching, in this case, for learning.

"No, it's best not to do either of those things, as I'm sure you've experienced." Conversationally, he continued, "Perhaps you knew of a good remedy for an ache, but discovered a different one that worked better in some circumstances, so you adapted what you knew to the situation at hand." Smiling, Colonel Cyrus chided gently, "You still need to take care of that ache, however!"

Signaling the end of the sermon, he relaxed into his closing, "And we still need to go on. We still need to learn, but we can never be one hundred percent sure what we're learning is correct. And we'll never fix anything if we never try to establish some confidence in what we know. So that is where we are, balanced between hubris and indecision, simply trying our best."

. . .

At the communal dinner that night, Seramis invited Innes to sit near her and they quickly caught up with each other's experiences since they had arrived in the New World. He shared with her that he was working with a gold mining operation on Lieutenant Governor Gooch's land nearby.

"I understand that it's your amalgam that is increasing the yield of the gold in the mining," Innes said. "And I admit that at first I had a difficult time reconciling how such brilliance could come from the person who spied and played tricks on her friends in the stories you told me. Then I came here and I see all that you've accomplished! Is there nothing you can't do?"

"I can never tolerate flattery," Seramis replied in mock seriousness. In only a moment, however, she was laughing and thanking him. "But you just arrived, so I'll make an exception!" They shared their plans with each other as they ate, as she spoke of her intention to build a mill next to the falling river, and he talked about having just completed the main task he had been given.

"With the combination of my work and my share of the profits from the gold we extracted, I'm already done!" he said.

"Oh, congratulations, Innes!" Seramis replied enthusiastically. "What are you going to do now?"

He appeared troubled, and it was genuine. "Something about what was said by—you said his name was 'Colonel Cyrus'?—is sticking with me, on that very topic. I thought I was certain in what I knew, and now, I'm not so sure anymore." Innes paused for a moment and studied his boots. "Everything I know is from an authority, with the great certainty that comes from knowing that there is one infallible guiding light."

For some reason, this reminded Seramis of the Jesuit priest she had been introduced to by Lord De La Warr, but she only said, "Well, those seeking guidance may often desire a spiritual answer, and I suppose you might at least refine your questions if you joined the clergy, and perhaps even if you don't find the answers for which you search, you may help others with their questions? Although I met a priest a while back whose manner suggested that mercy and temperance were not given qualities among that class."

"Truth knows no mercy, indeed!" he said.

They could continue their discussion no further, as at that moment, a band of native warriors had silently crept upon the dining company through the late evening darkness, and—to the screams of the maids and shouts of the men—suddenly burst into the torchlight like an apparition of painted and fearful demons.

Chapter Thirteen: The Prediction

In which bonds of fate are forged for some

"Everybody HOLD!" The colonel commanded as he stood between the natives and Seramis, clearly realizing that their aggressive entrance was not an attack. She knew that they could have launched their arrows before announcing themselves, but they hadn't. The colonel's surmise was correct, and all were still, even the natives, until more of their number appeared from the shadows carrying wounded. Lowering their hatchets and spears, relaxing their drawn bows, and returning their arrows to their quivers, they adopted a more neutral stance.

"Notchy!" Innes exclaimed, recognizing the Natchez Indians and using a common nickname given them by the colonists. "What is a war party doing here?"

The colonel took charge while the maids and Mrs. McClure went for medicine and bandages; a few men guided those carrying wounded to the barn. McClure spoke at some length to the one Natchez that apparently had some English, and then returned to the table where Seramis sat and observed.

"First," he cleared his throat, keeping his tone low and even, "I want you to know that I had arranged that a man would leave and act as a runner if ever hostilities broke out. He has some forest skill and he's probably observing us from the ridge to the north. If anything happens, he'll head east to the Brooke farm to sound the alarm."

"I'm grateful that you had plans for this, and while I never suspected the particulars, I never doubted your ability," Seramis replied.

"Well, I want you to know that while I can protect you, I can't say the same about your estates, unless you want to wall yourself behind a fort!"

"Of course, I know well the risks," she concurred. "Even if we lose everything here, we'll find a way to rebuild, that's my promise to you!"

Cyrus nodded. "Very well. Now, I've been speaking to Octochay, who learned some English from his war chief, one of the wounded currently in your barn. They forded the river just above the falls, coming to shore on your land where they've left their horses and made camp. He says that they were attacked in their new homes far to the south—"

"They're a long way from home now," Innes interrupted.

"Indeed," the colonel said, appraising Innes momentarily. "After their defeat by the Muskogee, this group tried to resettle after escaping the Creek. They couldn't stop in Tutelo lands for fear that they'd be captured and sold as slaves—"

"So, they continued on to where they weren't considered useful even as property," Seramis whispered, her distaste at the notion of slavery once again coming to the fore. "I may not be able to defend the structures here, but I will defend our foundations! I will not abide slavery, as you know!"

"Well, if the tables had been turned, of course..." The colonel let the remainder of his sentence fade, as he supported Seramis's ideals despite their unpopularity. "What shall I say to Octochay? I recommend we give them leave to camp near the river, as we can guarantee their good behavior while their leader recovers—if he recovers."

"Of course, let them know, and keep tabs on our people, as their nervousness may test our fragile truce." Seramis had been surreptitiously observing her workers, seeing that they helped when asked, but sometimes less than enthusiastically.

"I'll have a few of the men rotate on a watch, and close camp while everyone tries to get some sleep."

"And now, I'll try to be useful as well," she said. "Innes? What about you? You're welcome to stay, and there should be an empty cot somewhere if our scout is not yet returned."

"I'd pledge myself to your safety, Miss Seramis, but I see that is already in very capable hands." He nodded to the colonel, who was about to leave but paused a moment to appraise him again, then nodded and left. "So, please allow me to help in whatever way I can!"

"This way, then. Let's see what has befallen the war chief of the Notchy."

. . .

The scene in the barn was one of both horror and hope. Fortunately for the war chief and for the household of Helleborine Hall and its guests, the prospects were hopeful. Yet, that same future was not shared by two other wounded warriors Seramis and Innes saw as they entered. Both faltered, stunned by what they saw and felt. She missed her step and would have fallen, had not he lightly caught her arm, steadying her for a moment before continuing.

While the war chief's wound was initially thought to be the more dangerous, as he had been shot in the neck, it turned out to be clean, with the shot having gone through only muscle and exiting rather than remaining within. But, for one of the warriors, having been shot in the leg meant fractured bones as well as a musket-ball still lodged within the festering wound. Sadly, the leg had turned the wrong color, and having been cleaned, the wound now appeared much more serious.

The emergency had transformed the reserved and shy Mrs. McClure, focused now as she was on making the Natchez's hazardous journey over several hundred miles through enemy territory end as well as it could. She took charge of the makeshift hospital immediately, tirelessly cleaning wounds and exchanging bloody bandages for fresh ones, which the maids did their best to keep in constant supply.

Mrs. McClure had learned terrible lessons in the Massacre of 1722 that she applied this night, including makeshift surgery that Seramis could neither assist nor even watch. Applying hastily readied butcher's implements, Sarah tried to save the life of the warrior, sacrificing his useless and destroyed leg in the attempt.

The war chief, Hanaawa, watched in concern and horror as he drifted in and out of wakefulness, roused by the cries of the wounded man while Mrs. McClure applied her 'remedy.' Seramis brought water for the war chief to drink, when he said what Seramis thought was a word of thanks to the Son for the draught. Seramis asked, "Are you a Christian? Is there something we can do?"

"No," Hanaawa replied hoarsely, "it is the Great Sun, the light, the God of all living in the person of the leader of my people. But that light will soon go out, I'm afraid."

"What happened?" Seramis inquired gently.

"Another has set himself up as a god, and is attacking family after family of my people. His skin may be pale, but his eyes burn," he said cryptically before fading out into merciful rest.

. . .

Seramis had returned to her tent, and barely just closed her eyes to sleep, it seemed, when she felt a gentle tug at her shoulders.

"Wake up, miss! Please wake up!" It was one of the maids, whispering in a panic. It seemed like only a moment ago it had been dark, but now the sun shone clear although seeming cold and heavy as the first chills of autumn arrived at New Helleborine Hall. Seramis woke and blinked at the girl before her mouth could work properly, and the words fell from her lips in a rush. "Whatisit? WhereisInnes? Whereisthecolonel?" Waving off the answers and the confused look on the maid's face, Seramis struggled against a sleep-deprived morning fog within her brain that belied the clear sky just seen through the open flap on her tent.

"It's one of the natives, miss. He's in a bad way, and the colonel asked to send for you." Seramis slipped on breeches and boots, piled her hair atop her head, and appeared in tomboyish contradiction to her usual appearance as she stepped out of the tent—and stumbled right into Innes's arms.

"I hoped if I waited here," he said, smiling, "that eventually you'd come forth, but this is altogether sudden!"

"I'm sorry," Seramis said, gently extracting herself from his embrace. "But one of the Natchez is doing poorly, and I must see to him."

Innes's smile vanished as swiftly as a snuffed candle flame. "May I attend? I don't know what I can do to help, but I'd be a cad for not offering!"

"As you wish!" Seramis replied, instantly regretting her terseness, but started to walk, nevertheless. He quickly fell in step as she continued, "I appreciate the support your presence has provided since your timely arrival, of course."

Arriving at the barn, built with wood that had barely been cured and (as the maids had noted) not even having seen the expected arrival of the next generation of farm animals before being used as an unexpected hospital, Seramis stopped just inside to talk with McClure.

"Miss," he said while nodding to Seramis in terse greeting. The "Sir" he offered to Innes was clipped, and he spared him not so much as a second glance, making it clear to Seramis that he had yet to accept Innes at face value. "I've sent for you, but not my wife, as I don't think anything can be done to save the young man and Hanaawa has repeatedly asked for you."

"Thank you, Colonel. Any other news?" Seramis steeled herself for the answer.

"No, miss. The Natchez and our own people are quiet. I've replaced and since tripled the contingency we discussed yesterday," he said, referring to the scout who had been sent out to observe and in case of any troubles, get help and inform the neighbors at Brooke's Farm if needed.

Seramis relaxed and appreciated the caution, as the Tutelo might have been trailing the Natchez, or worse: the burning-eyed self-proclaimed deity who had wrought all this might well be on the other side of the James River, although that was unlikely. "I've seen this before," the colonel concluded, "and it won't last long."

"What, Colonel?" Seramis asked.

"This," he replied, and indicated the young warrior, whose breathing was quick, short, and clearly insufficient. Seramis fairly reeled at the convulsions, which may have appeared as tremors to the colonel and others but to her perception comprised wave after wave of violent wrackings as the dying warrior's heart and lungs no longer pulsed with rhythmic vitality, but stammered and stuttered spasmodically in life's last vain efforts.

Seramis was lost in the sight of this condition; neither her science nor her religion seemed to be of any use here. Both the colonel and Innes gently assisted her, McClure leading the way to where Hanaawa still lay recovering, with Innes supporting her and following.

As they arrived, Hanaawa spoke first. "Does this land belong to you?" he asked.

Recovering thanks to the men's support, Seramis answered, "I belong to this land now, I think, and I wish I could better welcome you to New Helleborine Hall. Of course, you are free to stay until you have recovered."

Something in Hanaawa changed at that moment, "*I am a steward of my people, but my Mother is its head. We belong to her, but I do not know if she's dead.*" He spoke directly to her in a voice raspy and terrible yet strong, and the words seemed to have an effect upon her the moment they were spoken aloud. "*A spirit is about to take flight, but its direction is not clear. I beg for your help, from a maiden who is also a seer.*"

"Miss? What's he saying? I can't understand—" the colonel began. He could see the rapport quickly building between her and the war chief, but couldn't understand the source of that comity.

"Seramis, are you all right?" Innes interrupted, but she put up a hand that silenced them both.

"Of course! I believe he's asking for my help in the passing of his kin," Seramis said in a rush.

Joining in the meter and the tempo established by Hanaawa, she replied intuitively, "*The robin, red of breast, sits in a cage; putting all of heaven into a rage*," she said in sympathetic reply, as if the words emanated from another source beyond her comprehension. Their incantations provided a verbal focus to the energies and feelings they experienced. Despite just waking, Seramis felt clear and alert, and sensed that Hanaawa felt it, too, despite his injury.

"I can barely understand you, Seramis, you're speaking so quickly, I think," Innes pleaded.

Speaking slowly, she tried to calm his agitation. "Please, help Hanaawa to join his tribesman. We must help him best we can," she said as they all joined the wounded warrior who lay dying.

Hanaawa spoke to her in the same rapid sing-song he used earlier. "*We are all begun in the birth of our Sun, to return to dust is no loss, but an eternity to be won.*"

She joined in improvised verse, continuing, "*We join in this struggle, one we're destined to lose. But to win in this battle, knowledge and friendship do I choose!*" It seemed as if the dying man's struggles grew weaker. To Seramis the rest of the barn, even the colonel and Innes, faded away. The souls left were naught but hers, Hanaawa's, and a spirit about to be freed from its shell.

Although it was a clear and early morning, to Seramis and Hanaawa the world became dark and indistinct while they knelt on either side of the spirit of Hanaawa's nephew struggling to return to the source whence it came.

Seramis felt exposed and empty in the presence of death. She saw in this death that of her father before her. At the thought, her throat caught, and she let out an anguished cry. Innes would have gone to her and pulled her from the Natchez, but Colonel McClure stopped him with a single gesture.

"I'm all right," she said to the half-recognized shadowy forms that were the others still in the corporeal realm.

Hanaawa spread his arms and tilted his head back, in supplication and in steady strength despite his wounds, shouting hoarsely, "*Back to the origin, the Sun! Back to the original Mother! I give you a completed life! The wheel turns! Turn upon another!*" His was the penultimate push, the energy of his voice and the rhythmic force of his words channeling the forces felt by all present.

Seramis's clear voice rang out, and as it did, the light returned to her vision, just as the spirit departed the body in front of her that gave its last breath. "*From birth do we believe in lies, as we forget what is unseen by our eyes!*"

Tears streamed down her cheeks as she instinctively completed the ritual, "*Return to the truth from which you came, that part we all share, where we are all the same.*"

The giving of their energy, which Hanaawa and Seramis poured from themselves into the ritual of the passing of his now-deceased nephew, returned the gift in the form of prophecy.

Hanaawa lowered his arms and spoke directly to Seramis words that seemed to come from a distant, far-off source: "*She who respects another's faith triumphs over the time-starved wraith.*"

Chapter Fourteen: The Objective

In which an expedition is planned

"Let me see if I understand this." Innes's voice quavered, and he gripped the tent flap to steady his equally shaky stance. "You've just eased the passing of a Natchez war chief's nephew in a ceremony I can't begin to comprehend; the English colonists are allies of these same native warriors while fearing them all the while; there is currently a violent zealot cutting a swath of destruction that even the native warriors can't stop; and you, of course, are planning to seek out this zealot? Do I have that right?"

Seramis looked up from her packing to see him haranguing her from the tent opening, and answered neutrally, "Yes. That's about right."

"All right, then." Innes was sounding desperate; his voice rose a bit in pitch. "What are you going to do when you find him?"

"Why, I'll do the same as when confronted with any situation: observe. Analyze. Understand." Tilting her head with curiosity, she frowned a bit. "Really, Innes, I'm curious as to where you're going with all this."

"As am I," he exclaimed, "as am I!" His face was twisted in frustration. "I'm very concerned, for one, and I fear for your safety! If you're going to go poking at mysteries, what pops up may be more than you're equipped to deal with!"

"Innes, I'm grateful for your concern," she softened her tone slightly. "But you were there when Hanaawa led me through that ritual; you saw what I just went through!" Distracted by the memory, she looked away from him, staring at an unseen middle distance. "There is a more terrible threat here than can possibly be understood from the seclusion of one's study!"

"Oh, I was there all right! And I certainly don't understand what happened." His eyes went wide. "Seramis, please listen to me. I don't think I'll ever understand what happened to you in that Notchy ritual! If you could've seen yourself—"

"Innes, I am listening." She cut him off but didn't stop her packing. "And as you can see, I'm also preparing to leave. I've made up my mind on this, and you'll have to come up with something more pressing than a possible danger to my person in order to dissuade me." Lifting her chin, Seramis paused. "There are more important things that I must consider. I'm aware of the risks, but I'm prepared to face them. I won't try to convince you that I'm right in this, as I would rather use what little time I have to try to ensure the success of this expedition and the safety of this household." Seramis dropped the clothes she had been packing and stepped closer to him. "But I will ask you to trust me, and I will ask for your support, as it means so much to me!"

"I—I don't know what to say!" he confessed, looking at her closely, and for a moment, all his artifice melted away. "You, also, mean so much to me..."

"I think we should discuss that further," Seramis said gently. "When I return—"

"Oh no!"

"What?" The vehemence of his response took her aback.

"If you think I'm going to just muck about for gold, or sit here, or what have you, while you go forth into danger and adventure, allow me to offer a correction," he nearly shouted.

"What do you have in mind, Squire Innes?" Seramis said, smiling.

"I must collect my things from the mine site upriver, but I will return to be by your side!" He all but laid hand over heart as he spoke. Once more, she studied him, trying to see the heat in his frame that his words implied, but failed in her search.

"Well then," she said as she returned to her packing, "you must meet me at Newport, where I'm acquiring a ship."

"A what?" Shaking his head, Innes didn't pause despite his bewildered expression. "Consider me already there."

As he smiled, Innes's eyes made promises to Seramis, who gazed on him and drank them in while still wondering about the coolness of his composure. She could feel her heart racing, her chest heaving with each breath, while he seemed perfectly composed.

"I'll be waiting for you!" she replied.

He bowed, turned on his heel and left while Seramis returned once more to her packing, but with a pace and energy that had not been there previously.

. . .

"Thank you, Colonel. I've considered your recommendation, but I need you here," Seramis said, having just told him of her plans and her wish for him to stay and run the household while she investigated the mystery of the Natchez.

"Miss, will you allow me to expand on my point, and explain why you need me to come with you?"

"Certainly, Colonel. Your advice is always welcome!" Smiling, Seramis continued, "And be assured that I plan on countering your points with reasons of my own. Are you and Mrs. McClure available? Please meet me at the main entrance of the Hall."

Arriving at the front entryway of the still-incomplete New Helleborine Hall, Seramis asked the carpenters there to take a break as she and the McClures ventured inside. The sounds of hammering and sawing slowed and eventually stopped as the workers left for lunch, some talking about the arrival of the Natchez, others about the work that was ongoing, but all nodding or acknowledging the three as they left.

Seramis faced them squarely. "I want to hear your case, Colonel, as I value your advice. And Mrs. McClure, I would welcome anything you have to contribute as well, regarding my intention to solve the mystery of why the Natchez were attacked, and what led them here."

"Of course, miss," Mrs. McClure said. "I would support my husband, first," she said, looking at him devotedly. "And I would do all that I could in service to you, miss."

"As you demonstrated last night, with service above and beyond my imagining," Seramis said. "And I'm not alone in being grateful, I'm sure."

The colonel cleared his throat. When he spoke, it was with an authority born of leadership. "Miss, there's going to be conflict, and you'll need someone to take charge in the midst of the chaos that is an attack. Taking charge—being organized—it's the most important thing that can be done in that situation. The attacker's advantage of surprise assumes a disorganized response."

"Colonel, your leadership last night was evident, which is why I need you here. If I discover the threat to New Helleborine Hall, I may need the resources from here to effectively counter it. And that is the reason we're actually in the incomplete Hall."

Seramis moved to the harpsichord given to her by Princess Sophia Dorothea, covered by canvas and stored in the relative safety of the center of the great room with crates of her belongings while work was underway. Removing the canvas, she lifted the lid, and moved the internal brace which was actually a lever, allowing her to reveal to the surprised couple the hidden compartment. "I hope I'm not burdening you with the location of this, my hidden treasure!"

As the contents of the compartment were revealed, the light from the lanterns fell upon the glistening jewels and coins and splashed about the room in rapturous reflection. Both the colonel and the missus stared with their mouths agape.

It was Mrs. McClure who looked up and spoke first. "I don't mean to question, but I've never imagined such a treasure without the accompaniment of a host of armed guards."

"Naturally," the colonel agreed. "A score of men would be too few, if word of this gets out."

Seramis nodded, but waved off their concern with an open hand. "As far as I'm concerned, this is just an instrument gifted to me by the king's sister, as everyone knows. As such, it's treated like royalty, so I've never given any thought to any special protection."

"Nor should you, miss, as I can now see the logic of it," the colonel said. "That's as perfect a hiding place, secret in its conspicuousness, as I can imagine. But what happens if you play it?"

"It sounds perfectly normal, but that's a good point." Seramis closed the compartment and lid before replacing the canvas cover.

"My reason in showing you this is that the letters of credit from Lord De La Warr may come due at any moment. Until we've built the mill and generated some income for ourselves, I want to ensure I do not become indebted to Lord De La Warr, or fall subject to foreclosure by my creditors. Until I return, I wish to make this resource available to you."

"Until you both return," Mrs. McClure corrected, in an unusual display of loquacity. "I don't mean to be out-of-place, miss, but I've headed households under duress, whereas neither of you has. I've spoken my piece on this subject, and I hope you'll hear my counsel."

"It's sad but true," the colonel added, shaking his head. "During the Massacre of 1722, while I was out fighting, my wife acted the equivalent of a fort's captain. Something which I hope we never see the likes of again. But if we do, I know that my good wife will handle herself and ensure the security of this homestead."

Seramis appraised them both. "Well, it appears that I'm literally and rhetorically outnumbered and logically outmaneuvered!" Smiling, she quickly conceded the point and moved on to the matter at hand. "Colonel, I don't mean to stress that time is of the essence—"

"You needn't worry on that account," Mrs. McClure interrupted. "He's packed and ready. Has been since yesternight."

Laughing, Seramis surrendered. "I see that the transition of power here is merely a matter of formality! Then, let's set the quest in motion, and find out for ourselves what future lies in store for us and for the Natchez!"

Chapter Fifteen: The Transport

In which a suitable vessel is found

When Innes arrived in Newport to find Seramis haranguing a quartermaster of the port over supplies, he was stunned at what he saw. It was a fine ship, indeed—much smaller than the vessel which had brought them to this side of the ocean, but trim and fast-looking—with nearly two dozen men swarming over the decks and rigging while being watched over by the colonel and another man. This fellow, obviously the captain of the vessel, was dressed in Barbary finery topped off with a long black feather trailing behind a gilt-edged tricorn.

Innes could hear the quartermaster complaining as he walked towards the ship. "That much canvas will cover a fleet in sails, I cannot think why ye'd have so much!"

"Do you see any cargo, good sir?" Seramis retorted. "This is no trading mission, but an expedition under the English flag and the orders of Lord De La Warr!" With a volume to her voice that seemed improbable for her slight frame, she continued. "Get me the goods, as we will have our stores needed for this voyage. Well? We're waiting on you to depart in the King's name!" She set her hands on her hips, glowering.

Seramis's young features were stony, and her voice rang in the quartermaster's ears, leaving him no quarter, no room in which to wheedle and bargain. Admitting defeat in a manner not seen by many a ship's captain (it impressed the colonel and the others on board who stopped to watch), the quartermaster simply acknowledged her with the one word "Aye" and left.

Innes walked past the quickly retreating man. He strode directly up to Seramis, who was still standing with arms akimbo and her features stolid, until the quartermaster was out of sight. Innes bowed, and stayed that way, until Seramis let out a low whistle of relief, and ran to him, hugging him enthusiastically as he straightened. "Oh! Innes, I'm so glad you're here." In apparent shock at the familiarity, he hugged her back, but gingerly so.

As she pulled from their embrace, he smiled broadly, saying, "Not as glad as I to be in your forceful presence once again! You, miss, are an adventure in and of yourself."

Regaining her composure, but still genuinely glad to see him, she curtsied. "Speaking of which, we best get you settled in and up to speed." She called up to the main deck where the colonel and the other gentleman stood. "Permission for myself and my guest to come aboard, Captain?"

With an accent from knowing many languages, and often speaking a mixture of several, the captain shouted back, "Permission granted, Commodore!"

Avoiding the paired gangplanks leading to the main deck, Seramis instead pulled Innes after herself and ran to a long, single plank that led steeply upwards from the pier to the quarterdeck amidships, where it stopped at the top of the railing. Letting go of him, then hiking up her skirt and petticoats to reveal riding boots underneath, Seramis took off at a sprint up the bouncing plank to its upper end, where she jumped onto the deck.

Handing his roll and bags to a crewman, Innes pointed to the main deck to instruct him where to take his things. Looking up at the captain, the crewman received a nod, and started to tote the belongings on board. In the interim, Innes nerved himself. It was easily fifteen feet down to the water from the top of plank, which was only about a foot wide. But Seramis had demonstrated the only way to ascend: match the vibrations of the pliant plank with one's pace and bound upwards at a run, hoping one's step will peak just as the plank does.

Steeling himself, Innes swallowed and bounced, breathing in time with each hop. Once. Twice. And on the third, he started. Crewmen on the ship stopped to watch, along with Seramis, the colonel, and the captain. It began well, as Innes mimicked the actions she had so ably demonstrated, and he managed to take his first several steps before the natural fundamental frequency of the pliable and resilient plank began to reinforce the bouncing of his sprint.

Although the plank was at its most unstable when Innes was in the center, Innes actually missed a step just before the end, when his foot came down and the board wasn't there. Unfortunately, that caused him to pitch forward before his other foot could find purchase. He immediately pushed off with the foot that connected, intending to dive for the deck, but the bending of the plank proved treacherous and Innes landed belly first upon the railing, with his upper half neatly folded towards the deck, and his lower extremities on the other side, dangling over the water.

Innes's own body proved resilient enough as he bounced upwards from where he landed, and somersaulted as a result of his forward motion, to then land flat on his back and staring up at the furled sail of the mizzen. The landing had knocked the wind from him. Seramis ran to his side, and the rest of the ship erupted in laughter.

"I'm so sorry!" Crouching near his supine form, she was distressed. Innes tried to smile bravely through his labored wheezing, but couldn't yet speak. "Innes, are you all right? I thought that your display of acrobatics from our meeting meant you had some experience..." She puzzled at the memory of his earlier show. "I had been practicing on that thing with guy ropes for balance each time I had ascended or descended until just before your arrival."

"N... No problem, Seramis," Innes barely managed to squeeze out in a painfully strained voice. "I'll... I'll just rest—here a bit before going on."

. . .

She was a Portuguese ship, *A Agilidade das Nuvens*, and a crewman was repainting the name in English on the stern: *The Agility of Clouds*. The ship was built in the style of the old *caravel redonda*, having four masts total, with the foremast at front the only one to have multiple square sails. The rest of the sails, one giant construct of canvas per mast, were rigged in the lateen, or triangular, manner under great raking spars, or yards (longer even than the masts were tall), but leaned back, or raked, instead of straight like the masts.

The ship was unusual (except perhaps amongst those of pirates or their commissioned brethren, the privateers) for having a fully rigged mizzenmast at the aft, or rear, of the ship, as well as the aforementioned foremast—both topped with crows' nests for observation. The English flag of St. George, the country of her new owner, flew from the foremast even in port, while of course all the sails were furled, wrapped tight until the voyage should begin.

Presiding over her was the Captain Rogero Francisco de Ibarra y Valdez, who shared (mostly) the same name as his great-grandfather, the conquistador and explorer. He also inherited a disdain for authority outside his own, and a thirst for adventure. His experience was only matched by his self-esteem, and both paled in comparison to his joviality.

Seramis had purchased the ship and equipped it for less than five thousand pounds sterling, half the purchase price paying off the debt its previous owner had acquired. Said previous owner had been a Scot—a working owner who sailed with the ship when he purchased cotton in the West Indies, then sold it for tobacco in Virginia—who did not complete the unholy triangle of commerce, as he passed on the purchase of slaves in Africa.

As his ethical considerations of commerce failed to descend to the contemporary standards of trade, only luck could keep him in business. When *Fortuna* failed to smile upon him, he sold the ship and the services of its crew to Seramis, who had in mind a nobler purpose and had paid in bullion from a small part of her treasure.

The *Agility* could be crewed by a minimum of a dozen sailors, and although perhaps ten times that number could work within her, her current complement was only just under forty, including a Cypriot bosun and a Sicilian bosun's mate to round out the command crew. In addition, a French cook kept the crew fed, and a Swedish carpenter kept the ship afloat. The last position wasn't particularly demanding, as the ironbark keel and otherwise nondescript but competent construction rendered the ship solid.

New sailors, about a quarter of the complement, had replaced those who rotated ashore. No new cabin boy was brought aboard to replace the old one, who had been a distant relative of the previous owner, so Innes was asked to sign articles for that capacity. Since the position paid nothing, required no skills, and had no set duties, and as there was no shared profit on this expedition, its existence was a mere formality. But it meant that Innes was a member of the crew, with access to the crew and the ship that a guest of the owner would never have.

Seramis, with advice from the colonel, had made the purchase on expedience and availability. But, all in all she was a fine ship. She would average four or five knots, being able to travel more than a hundred miles per day. (The discreet captain knew she could in fact do twice that, but would never advertise the fact except by example, if the situation called for it.)

To Seramis's sensibilities, the possibilities of experiments and adventure of the life onboard appealed greatly. A previous owner or captain had also taken liberties, apparently, for unlike other ships of her class, there were a number of additional portholes belowdecks, next to the gunports. As a so-called 'ship of the sixth class' she was categorized according to the number of guns: in this case, ten, each with its own port. But someone had equipped the ship with oarholes alongside the guns, so that she could be rowed if becalmed, or against the wind, or even upstream.

Although Seramis was nicknamed 'Commodore' this was more than a title. They had all agreed that she was in charge when in port, or when boarded by an English authority. And in those cases her word was law.

Otherwise, the captain was in charge of the boat while sailing, and her orders had to go through him, as the sailors would only obey the captain; to disobey him was mutiny. If they were to go ashore—and that was the plan if they were to discover what had happened to the Natchez—the colonel would be in charge.

The new members of the crew had been chosen for double duty both as sailors and soldiers when they took to ground. Soldiers ready to fight and die, if need be, and knowing that both were likely.

C.J. Pitchford

Chapter Sixteen: The Departure

In which a party of exploration prepares for war

"We'll be leaving as soon as the tide goes out," Captain de Ibarra announced. "It will be a few days until we reach Port Charleston after we round Pamlico Sound and, of course, Cape Fear." When the quartermaster had returned with the stores Seramis requested, the captain called an improvised council in preparation for departure. Pausing, he turned to the colonel.

"Based on the talk I picked up," the colonel started, his voice echoing the concern he felt regarding the sources he'd found, "the Natchez were moving into the Carolinas to take up new residence on the lands emptied by the Yamasee war and yet to be settled by the English." Shaking his head, he said sadly, "Our guests upriver were the only survivors of the band that I've been able to find any mention of. That would mean only four families survived of thirty or so that came here." He inhaled as if to steel his resolve against such violence. "I think our quarry would have long departed the territory there, but that means that they have the whole continent to get lost in."

Seramis picked up where he left off. "So, our plan is to get to St. Augustine, reconnoiter, and if we find nothing, proceed around the Keys to find out what we can in Spanish Florida before we backtrack if there's no word. Or, if we find a trace of our quarry, proceed to the French territories." She then turned to the captain. "How long until we reach Mobile or New Orleans or any of the French territories?"

"Not including the reconnaissance you mention," the captain said, smiling, "it will be two weeks' sailing in favorable winds." Addressing the colonel as well, he continued, "Speaking of wind, I will remind you that we are not quite finished with the storm season yet. Hurricanes in the areas in which we are sailing have swallowed communities whole along with their inhabitants—never to be seen again."

"I believe you will chart our course wisely, Captain," Seramis lifted her chin as she spoke.

"Ha! I like your spirit!" Captain de Ibarra bellowed. "Mistress, you provide the destination, and I will get you there!"

"I can do better than that, Captain," Seramis replied mysteriously, "as I have more discoveries to share with you both. While I was in Lisbon, I found—stole, really—plans for a warcraft that exceeded even the imagination of Lord De La Warr."

"Oh, he's an imaginative one, he is. Especially when it comes to battle. There is more to you, mistress, than meets the eye!" the captain exclaimed.

"I'll ask you not to repeat this, of course, Captain," the colonel demanded, to everyone's surprise. Looking at Seramis, he made another promise. "While I understand and appreciate your honesty, I will try to protect you as best I can, including a certain... deniability, if charges are ever pressed."

"Thank you, Colonel. Also, although I acquired these plans while in the service of Lord De La Warr, I should note that I did so under duress. But, to the point, this may have a direct bearing on our mission here. Not the specific documents, but the fact that here, in the New World, there are plans to embroil the whole world in war—"

"But aren't there always plans for war? It is the very condition of our so-called civilized age," the captain added sarcastically.

"Of course," Seramis continued. "But the plans I liberated describe a weapon that seeks to make even 'Magdeburg mercy' appear temperate!"

"Miss Seramis," the colonel interrupted, "you lost me there with that reference, although usually I try to keep up..."

Captain de Ibarra answered, "The siege of Magdeburg, Colonel, about a hundred years ago, in the Thirty Years' War. A battle where maybe five thousand of thirty thousand souls survived," he sighed. "From an atrocity perpetrated by my faith against yours... Until now, with the massacres on both sides of the conflict here in the New World, I didn't think such atrocities would ever be repeated."

"Gentlemen." Seramis's features appeared to harden like flint. "We're about to go to war for the one cause I can find acceptable: to stop war itself from happening."

"Miss, I don't see how you can fight a war—" the colonel started.

"You don't have to," the captain interrupted, a cold and calculated smile on his face. "That will be another one of your surprises, eh, mistress?"

"Actually, having already seen the tactical brilliance of Colonel McClure at work," Seramis replied, "I think that he will provide the surprises!"

. . .

Although the commanders were solemn, it was a festive mood for the rest of the ship as the *Agility* left the dock and floated out with the evening tide. A red autumn sunset faded slowly behind them as they let the headwinds push them out to sea. The sky soon filled with stars before the moonrise, as the Milky Way lighted a swath of the sky from horizon to horizon. Even when eight bells sounded the change of the watch, the captain stayed at the wheel. Getting a feel for the tiller and the overall craft, he sailed beneath the stars while the bosun's mate, the third watch chief, stood at his side.

The colonel had retired to the captain's staterooms below, where he, the ship commanders, and Innes as cabin boy would be barracked. Seramis was about to turn in, heading for the actual cabin boy's and quartermaster's cabin, which she had all to herself, when she unexpectedly met up with Innes in the narrow companionway.

"Permission to speak, Commodore?" he asked, in mock seriousness.

"Innes?" She kept her tone neutral, nearly flat.

"Cabin Boy First Class Innes, reporting, Miss!"

"Enough, Innes. You're the last person I expect to stand on ceremony, so teasing me about it only rubs salt in the wound!"

"For that I apologize, dear Seramis." The term he used didn't escape her attention, but she chose not to draw attention to it. Innes, noting that, forged on. "I think it suits you, however. I can picture you commanding a fleet of vessels such as this! Think what you could achieve!"

"Stop." Although she was pleased at his compliments, modesty required that she appear otherwise. "Really, what would I do with a fleet?"

"Think about it. Look around you." Innes was earnest. "See those stars, what are their names?"

"Sirius—"

"Yes, I'm serious."

"No, that's Sirius." Seramis pointed. "And up north, Polaris..."

Innes laughed. "See? That's what I mean! You're brilliant, and this world could use brilliant explorers—"

"No, the world could use brave and upstanding explorers. I'll read about their adventures, thank you very much!"

He moved closer to her as she leaned back against the deck railing.

"Doesn't this remind you of our first voyage together?" she asked, feeling warm despite the chill air. "You were so kind to listen to me go on and on."

"I was, wasn't I?"

"Oh, really?" She laughed, nudging him in his ribs, incidentally allowing her to get closer. "Well, is it your turn? Do I get to hear about you and yours?"

"I was an orphan." While he seemed sad, something about what he said next made the hairs on Seramis's neck stand on end. Whatever the cause, it was not due to the night breeze. "Without any known relatives." Innes continued with neither much thought nor much emotion that Seramis could detect. "To this day, there is no clue to my origin."

Seramis reeled, although she didn't know why, and straightened quickly. "My apologies, Squire Innes, I quite suddenly feel a chill come upon me." She lied as she stepped away from him.

"What is it, my dear?"

Looking into his face, searching for something she couldn't name, Seramis didn't know why she felt as she did. She took several long moments—to her, a pause wide enough to sail a fleet through—to look into Innes's eyes, as if she might find the answer to her discomfort there.

But there was nothing besides Innes, and she shook her head as she left. "I'm sorry. I don't know why, but I'm very tired. Until tomorrow, good sir! Until tomorrow..."

. . .

The next morning, Seramis was up and about early after a long night where she tried to calm her restless nerves through work. Seramis closed the notebook she had been sketching and calculating in as Innes strode across the main deck towards where she stood on the forecastle.

Smells of breakfast wafted up from the galley below, as the morning fog broke and a chill mid-autumnal sun weakly, but steadily, shone from above. The chills of the night had passed, and Seramis had been working on a plan since waking. And since the sea was calm, she had been writing in her notebook on deck while waiting for her morning meal.

Innes called out cheerily, "Will you break your fast with me, my dear?"

"It's almost ready!" came the voice of the cook working the galley within the forecastle, "but you don't have to call me dear."

Choosing not to encourage the cook with a reply, Innes addressed Seramis directly. "Might I wait with you, Miss Seramis?"

"Please!" she replied. She was dressed in a canvas greatcoat and a plain broad-brimmed hat but with light gloves for the chill.

Small talk ensued in which Innes commented she looked lovely, and she admitted she appreciated his appearance as well, as he had long ago given up the frilly fashionable clothes of their first encounter, and today wore the traditional double-buttoned overshirt and long pants of a seaman—the latter of which covered the legs better than hose when swinging through the rigging—and upon his head sat a modest, thin-brimmed sailing hat.

"Aren't we a pair," he effused as he sat next to her. "I would never have imagined this turn of events when I met you! You are a remarkable woman, Seramis Helleborine."

"Thank you, dear Innes, for your enthusiasm and encouragement. I have a feeling I'll need all of both that can be spared!" She seemed to consider for a moment. "There's something I'm working on, and if you've got a moment..."

"Of course, my dear! But I can't imagine what help I could provide—"

"Well, listen," Seramis interrupted. "I doubt that there's a connection to the burning-eyed, self-proclaimed deity we seek, but I learned of actual plans to sail a ship through the air." Innes's eyes went wide as she continued, "And I would try to find out if it's possible or just fantasy."

"It sounds fantastic to me," he said. "How would you solve this riddle with your science?"

"There are many avenues in scientific application, Innes. I could begin with trying to find a precedent, but upon what should we focus? There aren't many precedents amongst animals for floating; flying, rather? Yes. Birds and insects all have wings, and I believe that the gentleman from Vinci had in mind an ornithopter when he designed a machine that could fly."

"But what manner of wing could pull an entire vessel through the air? Like those of the gulls that wheel about above us?"

"No, there's no material I can work with that would be both light enough and strong enough..."

"You can work with? Do you plan on building such a thing?"

"Such a thing may already have been built," Seramis urgently replied. "And we'd better be ready..."

"Mistress," the cook called out, "your meal's ready! Cabin boy, you might as well eat, too."

"Such a warm invitation," Innes smiled wryly. "Who can resist?"

They both went down to the main deck, continuing their conversation as the cook handed them bowls each with a melange of mixed ingredients, such as spiced and chopped potatoes, ham, eggs and cheese, all mixed and cooked together. They sat down on the deck with their backs to the capstan winch and agreed that it was delicious and they'd never tasted anything like it. "That cook can make a stew out of anything!" Innes claimed.

"Aye," the cook said as he brought forth some rolls. "And so will you," he said to Innes, "as I will appreciate your help later."

"Aye aye! I'll work if it keeps you happy, just so you keep making meals like this!"

Seramis nodded her thanks to the cook, then turned to Innes. "Again, I appreciate your help."

"Well, cooking and cleaning are clearly areas where I can help. Science and flying ships? I don't know. But what a sight that would be! A whole fleet floating aloft like the Fire Lantern Festival at Majorca..."

"The what?" Seramis asked, distracted from her designs.

"Ah! You must never have seen it, or you wouldn't ask. And I wish I could shut my mouth and just show you, as it is as unforgettable a sight as I've ever seen." Innes sounded a bit condescending for a change, since it was rare that he knew of something that Seramis didn't. "The fire lantern is a little... paper... box?" He struggled with the description. "It's open at the bottom, but that's where you put the candle. Wait. I'm not telling this right..."

"It's fine. Go on," Seramis encouraged.

"Very well, the candle hangs on string below paper folded into the shape of a box, but where the bottom of the box should be, it's open—that's where the candle is tied! And it's just a little candle, too. Nothing to it, really." He appeared to have gotten a grasp on his description of the festival, and became more animated as he continued. "But you light the candle so that the vapors of the flame are caught by the paper, lifting it up to the sky. And there are hundreds... No, thousands of them! And they're all released at once, so that they float upwards until they're caught by a draft, when they all start to follow the breeze as if they have an instinct to do so!"

"Innes, you're a genius!" Seramis exclaimed.

"I am? I mean, yes. Yes, I am," he replied smugly.

"That is how the original flying ship was supposed to work, according to the plans I sto— ...um, found," she laughed. "But that could never be," she remembered the plans as if she was looking at them presently. "Yet that was the intent. It had to be."

"What intent?"

"The original plans I mentioned had multiple bags acting just like the fire lanterns you mentioned, with the 'vapors' or heated air forced into them from great furnaces and bellows. Can't you just picture it? A ship like this one, and where you and I are sitting—in fact, on every surface deck—furnaces with roaring fires, to replace the candles of the floating lanterns that you mentioned, and huge bellows pumping the heated air into giant bags fixed to the mast of the ship. But the bags... Well, they'd have to be huge! Warm air rises—and caused the Fire Lanterns to rise—but its buoyancy is purely a matter of volume that would have to expand in contrast to the density of the surrounding air..."

Seramis froze, and Innes watched as she proceeded to work through some concepts at a pace which to her was too slow. Pusing away her unfinished breakfast, and opening her notebook, she helped him to follow along.

"Out of tragedy—I'll tell you about that later—there is an answer! Innes! Forget the furnaces! In fact, they'd be a horrible, horrible mix with what I have in mind. Based on the original plans, I estimate that a ship using heated air would need to have lift equivalent to dozens of tons—not the tonnage that the vessel displaces, but the tons which it weighs, and the volume of air needed for that would be like this..." Seramis showed him her drawing of the resulting design.

"But that's a circle with a dot beneath it," Innes stated, simply pointing out the obvious.

"Precisely. That dot is the ship!" She shook her head. "Of course, they could fill multiple bags with hot air..." Her mind was already considering the possibilities.

"And the plans you mention, do they look like that?" he asked.

"Exactly not like that! Which is why the plans would never work." Her voice fell to a conspiratorial whisper. "But if the gas filling the bags was not merely heated air, but instead a compound which I have distilled from plain water and is by far the lightest element I've ever encountered..."

Looking at him, she was almost inaudible as she said in abject wonder, "It. Could. Work."

Chapter Seventeen: The Consequences

In which betrayal is sudden

The work over the few days of sailing down the Carolina coast produced more schematics, calculations, and promising results for Seramis in her studies of flight. Yet, she couldn't erase from her mind the picture of her destroyed study at the old Helleborine Hall, nor could she escape the general feeling of unease that she'd had for the duration of the journey. Due to her focus on her studies, she was unable to pinpoint the source or the inception of that unease.

Waking one morning to the sounds of work going on outside her cabin—the bells of the watch hadn't yet sounded—Seramis noted that her hands shook as she dressed and joined the crew. *Nerves, I'm sure.* She was again surprised to see the captain, as it wasn't his watch. "What is it, Captain? What's going on?"

"I would very much like to know for myself what's going on," the captain shouted. "And as sure as I don't know how it happened, I sure know the results: we're crippled!"

Turning, he shouted at his men. "Get yer oars and get to your stations, but wait for my order." To the bosun, he said, "Take your readings and get our position. I'll confirm and we'll make for shore."

"Oars? Shore? Captain, what is it?" Seramis asked.

"Sabotage!" he said, chewing the word with distaste.

"Of that we can't be certain yet," said the colonel as he joined them. "I heard your voices, so I have suspended my investigation for the moment. Do you both want the report?"

"It was sabotage!" the captain exclaimed once again. "My ship does not simply 'break' in the middle of the night, Colonel!"

McClure kept his voice even. "The facts are these: the tiller broke along a seam, and was neither cut nor sawed through—"

"We'll lash the rudder, and make adjustments such as we can. We can't steer—only point," interrupted the captain, spitting on the word 'point' as he turned to the crew. "Why aren't you men at your stations! Move!"

"...and several sails are torn, as well as rigging winches wrecked," the colonel continued.

"It sounds like the perfect storm. But there was no storm last night, was there?" Seramis asked, knowing the answer.

"'Tis no storm—'tis sabotage!" raged the captain.

"Or simple wear," said McClure, raising a hand to stay the captain from another outburst. "At least, that's what it appears." The colonel looked seriously at Seramis, who was quite certain he was not revealing all, by his choice of words.

"We're equipped with replacements, correct?" Seramis asked.

"Not the tiller arm, mistress! It's several yards if it's an inch!" Ibarra had not calmed even a degree, still blustering like a wind before a storm front. "But I talked to the quartermaster and the carpenter already. We can replace the winches and the fouled rigging and cut a replacement for the tiller once we're ashore."

"And where will that be?"

"Somewhere between hell and heathens," he growled. "We are floating right into a powder keg. The Spanish have been sending troops up from St. Augustine, the English down from Charleston, and the French in the west have tried to conquer the whole region from bases in Mobile and Bilozi."

"Biloxi," corrected the colonel. "He's right. The English plan on settling here, a new 'savannah' for their fields of cotton to compete with the islands of the Cay and West Indies. But that doesn't mean that every tin-horn Maximilian isn't going to try to stake out his share of the land first."

"So while repairing the ship, we mustn't be caught on the beach unprepared," Seramis reasoned, knowing that the stakes had just been raised. "It looks like we get to try our hand at reconnaissance once we reach the shore, gentlemen."

"I still like your spirit," Captain de Ibarra exclaimed, slapping her back affectionately and perhaps a little too enthusiastically. "And I hope it sees us all through!"

. . .

"Will we make for the shore there, Captain?" Seramis asked, pointing to a broad beach towards which the no-longer agile *Agility* rowed. They were on the Atlantic seaboard between English Carolina and Spanish Florida, and the tall forests behind the flat beaches appeared mysterious to her.

"I'm afraid not, mistress," Captain de Ibarra answered, "unless we wish to advertise our presence to passing pirates."

"Pirates?"

"Yes," he continued, making a show of looking both ways before uttering the next word. "Tales are told that Blackbeard himself buried his own treasure on this very island."

"You seem to know a great deal about piracy, Captain." Seramis said.

"I would say that it pays to know such information, mistress." He gave no more explanation than that. "But please know I've never profited from naught but honest ventures!"

Offering her his spyglass, the captain pointed beyond the island. "We'll make for that sound and the swamps beyond, which should lead to a river where we can find the combination of timber and good landing we need to allow us to make repairs."

Seramis took the spyglass and scanned the shore before quickly turning and following the horizon round, scanning the ocean for pirates.

"You've got a feel for it: slow, steady," the captain appraised her study of the waters. "Let the sea come to you."

Returning her gaze through the spyglass to the woods upon the shore, having found no pirates or any other vessels at sea at this time, Seramis asked, "Are we riding in with the tide, Captain?"

"That we are, miss. That we are."

. . .

"Thank you, no, sir! I'm not trained in the use of firearms, so carrying one would only be a waste of vital equipment." Seramis rejected the colonel's request, as a small squad gathered to investigate the forest where the *Agility* had landed and was undergoing repair. "It appears that I will just have to use my wits and make myself a poor target instead," she concluded.

She had just finished putting on her heavier gloves that went went up her arms and covered the sleeves of her riding coat. Her breeches were tucked into her boots, and a flat-brimmed hat covered her head.

"Are you sure that you wish to add Innes to our group?" the colonel asked, then cryptically added, "I understand that he could be very helpful with the repairs here." Seramis had still not determined the truth of the situation: that either Colonel McClure had never really taken to Innes since his arrival, or he was being somewhat overprotective.

Neither she nor Innes had spoken directly of the unease they evidently felt, as Seramis knew she was becoming attracted to him, but she felt anxious and uncomfortable with that attraction whenever she thought about it too much. Her work had kept her busy for this trip, and they had talked little, as opposed to their constant conversation and companionship during the ocean voyage they had shared.

She also knew the colonel suspected Innes of committing the sabotage that had forced the *Agility* to stop, but hadn't said anything—neither did he need to, nor would he until he had proof. *What possible cause could there be for Innes to do that*? wondered Seramis.

Innes's innocent face held no answers to that question, as he arrived, and he, too, rejected the musket offered by the colonel. "I'd only be a danger to you with that thing," Innes said. "Leave it to me to carry the stores!" Foregoing his shipboard attire, Innes wore buckskin, and showed the others the flask and rucksack he carried. "I'll bring supper!"

The colonel nodded, and then called out, "Let's move!" He planned for them to scout the forest due west of their position, and as marshes lay to the north of where they had beached, they would then cut south before returning.

The men he ordered ahead appeared to be mercenaries to Seramis, but without the usual boastful and violent temperament. She thought that the colonel had picked them for their cool demeanor, hoping that coolness in the face of conflict would serve better than heat in all the time before. They fanned out as they left the beach and walked into the high forest, like a small legion of woodsmen.

The colonel and Innes guarded her closely, the three forming a tight unit, unlike the others, who spread out and walked in the sight of just one other ahead and one behind. Dispersed like this, they hoped to avoid being caught all at once in an ambush, yet remain close enough to join and concentrate their fire if they encountered any hostile force. While the mercenaries wore moccasins in the dry, cool autumn air, Seramis and her two companions wore boots; at times it felt to her like the three were just strolling alone through the forest, accompanied by the crunch of fallen leaves and small twigs.

After strolling for several hours and finding nothing of note, the colonel whistled for the attention of the nearest woodsman and waved him into position for a turn to the south, who did the same to the next man, who stopped at the sound and passed the order along the line. The colonel stood waiting as each man passed, until finally, the one who was on point as they walked west was now last and they could resume their search

Although the ground was uneven, it was largely clear of undergrowth, and their progress south continued much as it had previously. The sun shone clear and hung higher in the sky than Seramis was accustomed to, but she focused her attention on observing all that she could through the tall trees. She was no trapper, however, and one tree looked much like the next and the last; neither did the forest floor divulge any secrets to her, she would have had to confess if asked.

"We're going to cut back at an angle now," the colonel said, "until we cross our tracks." Again he whistled, but instead of waving, he held up a fist and stopped, while the next in the group did the same. "We'll rest here for a moment while I get a report from the men. Keep your eyes open and watch around you," he added helpfully but unnecessarily.

Seramis and Innes looked around in silence while the colonel talked to the next woodsman, and then disappeared from Innes's sight as he went to talk to the next.

"What's that?" Innes exclaimed, pointing away from the rest of the men, and touching Seramis lightly on the arm. "Did you see it?"

"What?" she asked, letting herself be tugged slightly by him, as he enthusiastically but gently led her back from where they'd come. *Is he flirting with me? Is this a trap?* She was disappointed that she would believe in a danger that she couldn't sense directly. Yet, she couldn't shake the feeling.

"Didn't you see it? Is it still there?" he asked excitedly. He was stepping quietly, leading her away from the group.

"Should we tell the others?" She hesitated but smiled in good humor and leaned forward with Innes. She felt that denying her natural caution might help her to learn either more about herself or at least more about Innes if she went along with him.

"About this? No!" He was good-natured in his denial. "Shh! I didn't think we should see any this time of year!"

"What is it?" It was hard to resist the enthusiasm he displayed. She felt herself swept up in the events as they unfolded, instead of perpetually waiting and held back by the slowness of time or by her own caution. "What did you see?"

"Quickly! Come look!" Innes took her by his left hand as he swiftly but quietly led her past a clump of brush where he stopped, effectively cut off from the sight of the rest. "No. You didn't see it."

"What was it?" She was enjoying herself and wondered why she had ever held herself back from being fully in the moment, as it were.

"Nothing," Innes replied, grinning broadly and smoothly. "Here," he said, casually handing her his sack. "Hold this." He reached inside, once it was in her hands.

"Innes..." was all she could say before the smile froze on her face at the sight of him pulling a flintlock pistol from the bag. He brought it down fast—even compared to her reflexes, which normally would have been more than fast enough—and hard on her head.

Had it come from anyone else, she could have easily avoided the blow. However, in this situation she simply froze, caught between her feelings of affection and Innes's violent betrayal. Stunned as she was, her vision slowly swam from side to side as she fell back into the brush like a giant conifer swaying in the moment it was cut down. Unable to focus, she could barely see Innes reverse the weapon by lightly tossing the pistol into the air and catching it with both of his hands, one on the handle and the other pulling back the flint hammer into position just as Colonel McClure bounded into Seramis's hazy sight. Innes coolly reacted by stretching out his arm straight at the colonel's chest and pulling the trigger.

Seramis wondered at the silence—the complete lack of any sound from the pistol's shot—as the colonel disappeared within a cloud of smoke that engulfed him. Still falling, Seramis didn't reach out to catch herself, but instead reached out to her protector—Innes's latest victim—as she pitched to the ground, her vision mercifully dimming out the tragedy before her just as she fell into oblivion.

Chapter Eighteen: The Loss

In which betrayal leads to captivity

As Seramis sank into unconsciousness, the woods seemingly erupted with native warriors. The Creek (or so they seemed by their language and dress) launched a violent attack with the purpose of hunting down and killing the rest of the woodsmen. They left Colonel McClure for dead and unmolested as they had been ordered to travel light. In fact, the colonel was not dead, but the bloody mess on his jacket revealed a terrible although not life-threatening wound. He would have died, except for the planning and contingencies that experience had taught him time and time again; once more, they served him well.

Just as the colonel had secretly ordered one of the workers to act independently and observe the situation from a distance when the Natchez unexpectedly appeared at New Helleborine Hall, he had ordered one of his soldiers to prepare separately from the others and stay behind just a while when they left the landing site that morning, to trail silently after the group as they went through the forest. The scout had almost stumbled upon them when they stopped walking west earlier, so he hung back a bit farther when they turned south. This meant that he was too far back to help during the attack, as of course he had heard the gunshot and shouts from too great a distance.

When he did arrive, it was to find Colonel McClure gravely wounded but alive. Miss Seramis and Innes were gone, but before he found the colonel he had noted with surprise and disgust that Innes's tracks went off with those of the attacking natives, and sank deeper into the soft ground, suggesting that he had carried Miss Seramis away from the skirmish. As soon as he traced the tracks back to the colonel, he only had time to surmise that Innes had been the one to shoot the colonel before he started dressing the horrible wound.

. . .

Innes carried Seramis through the forest, accompanied by the Creek warriors, striding throughout the day and into the setting sun with apparent invincibility and divine purpose. They made their way into a clearing where Chickasaw sided with Cherokee, Creek with Susquehanna, Choctaw with Mohawk, and more. Without exception, Innes could see clearly as he arrived that the melange of people acted and treated each other as kin, despite their diverse languages, customs, and manners.

Graceful, strong, and intelligent, the assembled groups represented the finest of their kind, or of any kind, as they regularly and mercilessly culled the weakest from their ranks. And while elsewhere Appalachee fought Shawnee and Congaree fought Catawba at one time or shifted allegiances at another, here they lived and worked as one. As Innes walked past, one group paused in their preparing of meals, another halted their fashioning of hides and skins into clothes, while the vast majority remaining set aside their preparing of armaments for the battles to come, in order to witness his arrival.

Drawing together this mix and ruling over them all was one man dressed entirely in black, standing in front of a tent larger than the others, and set upon an improvised platform, taller than the rest as well. All eyes turned to him and all faces were set towards him, in silent expectation, as Innes hefted the unconscious Seramis up crude steps to deposit her at the feet of the man whose eyes shone with dominant intensity.

"Father Time, your appearances in my dreams have brought me to you!" Innes intoned loudly. A human echo sounded in all directions as Innes spoke, his words repeated first by those who knew English and could translate each statement into the various languages spoken by the assembled community, and then repeated by every speaker of that language until the woods shook with hundreds of voices in dozens of languages.

Patrick Tempus appreciated the ritual, and also appreciated the instructions sent by Innes via courier from Newport letting him know when and where he should appear in order to claim the Helleborine girl.

Innes continued, pausing after each phrasing. "Commanded by your will! Hundreds of leagues were no impediment to your command!" Each statement was transformed into a repeated version of itself and amplified a hundredfold. "No enemy could thwart your plans! I sabotaged and brought to a halt your enemies, just as you commanded!"

Innes knelt as he spoke, casting his arms wide. Every member of the assembled tribes followed his lead, dropping to one knee. "I was alone! Surrounded by foes and beset by fear and doubt! But your voice sustained me! Your vision propelled me! You filled the emptiness and gave me purpose!"

Wave after wave of similar statements filled the forest with a Babel of conformity. But the words of devotion and supplication were filled with anger and ire. "When I submitted to you, everything became clear! You are my first thought, my last act, and your will is my only command!"

Innes threw his hands upwards and arched his head back, and again, as if all were one, so did every witness. Inconceivably twisted, each statement professed love and offering, but was voiced through gritted teeth within snarling mouths. "Take from me this gift, as it is yours. Take from me all that I can ever say or do, as it only reflects what you would have from me." The sustained chorus lifted Innes's own words above all, as he bellowed, "Take from me my life, as it came from you, is yours to do with as you will, and will always and forever be yours!"

Seramis, at this moment, stirred from her concussion. Her mind just barely lifted from the bottom of a deep well, and the braying and bilious tumult from the hundreds of voices in dozens of languages that surrounded her only slightly registered upon her hearing as the most distant of whispers. And as the very last of the repetitions came to a close, Patrick Tempus, here addressed by Innes as 'Father Time,' only said a single word.

"*Peh,*" he said quietly.

And with Innes first falling prostrate before him, followed by all of the rest, there was a muffled, but powerfully plosive echo from the group: "*Peh.*"

"*Mach,*" Patrick said, calmly and meditatively.

"*Mach,*" the group echoed. Like a mallet, each repetition pounded into Seramis, alone and without solace or comfort as she lay upon the platform in a heap.

"*De zim,*" Patrick announced beatifically.

"*De zim,*" shouted everyone else. Seramis wasn't yet fully aware of her surroundings, and was unable to move or even form a coherent thought as her body struggled and slowly recovered from unconsciousness.

The rhythm evoked the hammering of a smith, with Patrick Tempus providing the guiding tap that the smith uses in order to rhythmically and precisely aim the mighty slam of the hammer that immediately follows. "*A be,*" the gentle tap from Patrick, "*A be,*" hammered the group in response.

"*Je bong,*" tap. "*Je bong,*" hammer.

Words formed in Seramis's struggling mind from sources she couldn't comprehend. She heard "Life from the dead is in that word," as spoken in a susurrus of distant and impossible whispers.

"*Peh mach de zim a be je bong,*" spoke Patrick Tempus and his followers in a sing-song round of imitation; "*Kah ge nig pe mahd' zim,*" they repeated, forming patterns of anguish and confusion in her tortured mind.

"It is immortality," spake the harsh voices inside Seramis's head.

In a torment of pain, her body sprang upwards to a sitting position, as if a coiled spring had suddenly snapped. Dizzy and reeling and only partially aware of any other physical condition, she cried out, "NO!"

Afterwards, she held her injured head with her hands, while her eyes squeezed out tears. In pain and sorrow, she cried as the crowd erupted in ululations and shouts.

Confused and greatly distressed, Seramis could make no sense of anything that was happening around her or even within herself. But her stirring had enraged the ensemble, who vocally poured their insensate hatred upon her.

The war cries rang out until Father Time lifted his hands, and all were stilled. His stern features and fierce countenance were belied by beatific eyes that shone so they nearly burned. "Awake, my soul, and with the sun, thy daily stage of duty run." This time the crowd answered in a translated repetition, "*Um ba koosh koo zin nin je chaug, kee zis a zhe meen wa we zid.*"

Seramis shook with pain and confusion, finally seeing through squinted and tear-blurred eyes that Innes was face-down in front of her, and that they were both on a platform with Lord De La Warr's Irish spy, Father Patrick, who was standing and speaking next to her.

The questions in her mind regarding the nature of the connection between Innes, Father Patrick, and Lord De La Warr would have to wait, however, as the image of Innes clubbing her with the butt of a pistol surged to the front of her memory. The image provided an explanation for the pain she felt but also added doleful misery and heartbreak at the betrayal. At this she sobbed deeply, causing the pain in her head to explode, constricting her vision further still. The image of Innes's first attack was replaced by the memory of Colonel McClure's body disappearing behind a cloud of exploding powder as Innes shot and killed him.

Father Time continued: "Shake off dull sloth, and early rise, to pay thy morning sacrifice." And as the assembled warriors cried out, "*Nah saub e zhe meen wa we zin, ke ke zhab dush ah nuh me aun,*" Seramis knew as the voices rang in her ears that when the ritual concluded she would join the colonel in death—before the night was through.

Chapter Nineteen: The Sacrifice

In which rituals are planned

The sacrifice of Seramis Helleborine was not intended to be a public spectacle, as that purpose had already been served by the ritual just completed. Patrick Tempus and Innes half-carried, half-dragged the unresisting young woman into the tent where the private killing would occur. Seramis was terrified as her sorrow drained from her.

She had no response to Innes's taunts. "Where is your 'science' now?" he said. "What? No comeback? No retort?"

Patrick and Innes fastened leather thongs to pegs placed at the points of a pentagram, painted in animal blood upon the floor. Fluttering candles lit the interior of the hide-bound tent as, outside, the life of the community returned to its routine.

Seramis's thoughts flew outside of the tent, not in escape, but first in sorrow to Mrs. McClure, who she imagined would be distraught but stoic at that future time when she would learn of her husband's death. Even as Seramis was forced to the floor and tied to the pegs, she sobbed in a whisper, "I'm so sorry," as she wept for Mrs. McClure's loss.

This angered Innes. "No. Oh, no. Not as sorry as you're going to be!" In response he raised his hand to strike her, aiming for the innocent face he had once desired, just below the purpling bruise now rising upon her bare forehead.

In that moment Seramis asked, "Why?" Patrick touched Innes, who froze in conditioned response, becoming completely inert.

"There is no why," Patrick whispered as he knelt beside her, "except for my will. My 'why'—if you will—is the only thing that matters." He finished securing her, although she was still and didn't struggle, as he continued. "There is no 'why' for you. You will have no other answer from me, but 'me'—I am the answer."

Seramis attempted to turn her head away, but he cruelly grabbed her by the jaw, pulling her face towards his. "I know there is something inside you that understands this." Patrick's words sinuously slid through her hearing of them.

"You are alone. You are mortal." The false priest's gaze seemed to pierce her vision. "You yearn for a touch you cannot feel, for a connection that cannot be shared." He had apparently charmed countless others in this manner, with his voice echoing in his victims' ears, his eyes locked upon theirs. But she felt only the loss and sadness, until that, too, drained from her.

His words failed to have their desired effect. "You are deranged by hate," Seramis whispered through her pain, "but you can't diminish me like you have the others."

"What? But I already have!" Patrick said. "You were nothing but the main attraction in a show to my followers, and soon you will be nothing but a shell to be discarded after I have picked from you your secrets and your knowledge."

"You could do that and more, but you will still have nothing but your anger," Seramis became stronger and more focused as she realized the truth of it.

"I will have the world!" He stood, towering above her. "I will have all of time itself!" he shouted. "I will have everything I want, and I will take it at my whim. Do you see how I control this?" He pointed to Innes, who blankly stared at nothing while he stood at the ready. "Did you see how I control whole populations, who—before my coming—fought and killed at the mere sight of each other, but cast that aside at my bidding? And know you how I will achieve my conquest, untouched by any adversary?"

Patrick scanned Seramis's features, looking for acknowledgment. "I shall control the skies from horizon to horizon! My volition merely needed the right spark to inflame the world! I will start here, with those who are most beset: the slaves and the heathens who will be my cannon fodder as I march forth! Every city and every nation will fall!"

"From what? From this? This isolated collection of natives?"

He smiled and leaned towards Innes but never allowed his gaze to waver from her own, and asked, "Did you bring it?"

Innes then resumed moving under his own will, and answered as if he had never paused. "Yes, Father," he said, producing Seramis's notes from his coat's inner pocket. "It is all here."

Nodding slowly to Seramis, Patrick smirked as he answered her question. "No." Pointing to the notebook containing her studies of the lighter-than-air elements and plans for airships he concluded, "From this."

. . .

A sound of scratching at the platform just outside the tent attracted Patrick's attention. "Innes! Go see what that is."

"Yes, Father."

Turning back to her, he continued, "What brought you to this, little lady Seramis? Don't you see how I have you? I'm your master, and you will acknowledge me!"

Seramis turned away as the pain throbbed and pulsed through her head, constricting her vision and clouding her thoughts as once more they turned to Mrs. McClure. Although the pain of seeing the bitter end of her friend at Innes's treacherous hand stung, she burned in agony at what the loss would mean to Mrs. McClure.

Seramis vowed at that moment, if she should live, she would always support and be there for her, and try to provide the same comfort she had received from Princess Sophie Dorothea. Her vision cleared somewhat at the thoughts of those two women, only to be interrupted by Patrick once again cruelly turning her face towards his.

"You keep looking away, my dear! But you can't leave, can you?"

"You are alone as well," Seramis said as a retort that came to her as an intuition. But her pain grew unbearable, leaving her to sink into silence, and also leaving unspoken her fervent wish: my friends will come for me.

"You think? I am many places, even now! I can see for leagues, and into your future of pain, as well..." At that moment, Innes returned to the tent, looking concerned, but not directly interrupting. "Well?" Patrick stood upright as he looked at his lackey, "what is it?"

"Father, it is a band of men from Seramis's ship. They've circled around and are quickly coming from the west to rescue the girl and avenge their losses. They'll be here very soon."

"So? Take a sufficient number and destroy them, take their weapons when you've finished, but leave the dead."

"Father, they aren't alone. Redcoats, with field artillery—brass cannons—are marching from where they've landed in the east. And from the north, a remnant of the Natchez that survived an earlier attack are making their way here through the marshlands. Overall, the scouts estimate that there are at least one hundred about to attack us."

"What? Like Edward the Confessor, I can defeat one or two enemies only to turn and be annihilated by a present-day William the Conqueror."

Father Patrick appeared momentarily stunned. Seramis guessed that while his forces were roughly equal to their opponents in number, Patrick had yet to equip his minions with armaments to match those of the British regular forces.

"We cannot face such a threat, now, Father!" Innes said.

"I have foreseen such an occurrence, but thought it unlikely," Patrick claimed, while Seramis thought it a lie. "Do you trust me, Innes?"

"With all that I am, Father."

"Then come with me. We go to the south, sooner than our plans would have set for us, but soon enough and well enough."

"All are assembled without, Father, ready for your divine will. What of the Helleborine girl?" Innes asked, as if she was not listening at that very moment. "Shall we take her with us?" He paused. "Shall I kill her, Father?" The Irishman nearly begged the last, to Seramis's visible chills at the desire with which he sought to please his master.

"No, we shall leave De La Warr's broken plaything right here to slow down the pursuers as they wait for her to be fixed," Patrick replied cruelly, looking at Seramis, who met him with sorrow. "If she was dead, they would quickly join forces to pursue us in

vengeance." Turning back to their captive, he smiled malevolently. "As the bard says,
'Our haste from hence is of so quick condition
That it prefers itself, and leaves unquestion'd
Matters of needful value.'

"And so I take my leave of you again, Simple Seramis. Don't bother saying fare thee well, as we are not to be finished here, rather,
'...to the hopeful execution do I leave you
Of your commissions.'"

. . .

Thirst and pain were Seramis's most pressing sensations, but other sights and sounds came to her as she drifted in and out of consciousness. After Patrick and Innes left the tent, Seramis could hear Patrick preaching to his followers and weaving stories of bloody conquest and rich plunder, as driven by a plot of divine guidance and vengeful retribution.

After he had finished and the roars and shouts had died out, natives swarmed the tent where she lay, ignoring her as they packed Patrick's items in his absence. As far as Seramis could surmise, he had apparently already left towards the south where he claimed their greater glory awaited.

Alone now as the birds called out the coming morn, Seramis lay bound upon the exposed platform and a fever started to burn within her. In her state, she dreamt of her father and of De La Warr. They argued over her as she lay scattered about in painful pieces, just out of her reach. She was unable to put herself together in the same way as she was unable to speak, let alone stop the men from fighting.

Why are they fighting?

The colonel and the captain appeared in her dream, imploring Seramis's father and Lord De La Warr to do something, but unable to assist of their own volition. Then, Patrick and Innes sneaked past all the others, so that they might steal little bits and pieces of her. She couldn't even voice her anguish or ask for help.

Why is this happening?

As the arguments and pleading and pestering reached a peak, Princess Sophia Dorothea appeared as a spectral phantasm. At first, she was hazy and ill-defined, but grew larger and more detailed and solid over time. And as she grew, the princess became more forceful, much to the dismay of the Duke of Cambridge and Baron West, who noisily voiced their displeasure. Soon, the princess was ten feet tall, towering over the others, and casually brushed aside the diminutive forms of the arguing pair. Seramis would have cried out in relief, but she still had no voice, as parts of her were yet scattered across the dark and vaguely defined dreamscape.

What will become of me?

Then, in a sight that terrified the despondent dreamer, Mrs. McClure appeared before her, wearing a homespun apron covered in blood. Seramis tried to give her voiceless solace and sympathy for her dead husband, but Mrs. McClure ignored her and went about assembling the myriad pieces that were what remained of her. The colonel and the captain began to shout for joy, cheering that something indeed was being done, and ran about farther and farther afield. They ignored Seramis, as well as ignoring the increasingly violent attacks of Patrick and Innes.

How much longer can this go on?

In fact, their violence became more insistent, and on occasion, they would knock about and unhelpfully scatter the remaining still-to-be-assembled pieces of her body. Princess Sophie Dorothea had grown too large to do anything to stop them, and Mrs. McClure was too busy fixing her. And Seramis still had no voice of her own to plead with the women to help, nor to command the men to stop. Mrs. McClure was soon finished, but still Seramis couldn't speak until another figure appeared, made entirely of light that was too painful to look at, but radiating warmth and kindness as it got closer. Seramis felt her voice returning, while Patrick snarled at the sight of this new figure and Innes sank to his knees in hopeful supplication. As the shape became more distinct, it appeared feminine to Seramis, as she fought to understand. Her newly assembled body shook as she struggled. As a result of these efforts, her reconnected limbs could now move as if they had been cut free from bonds, and she felt she could speak as she was bodily lifted, both physically as well as in her dream, now nearly able to see who the new figure was. Opening her eyes, she beheld the mustachioed and concerned face of Captain de Ibarra in the morning light whispering words of comfort and succor, but all Seramis could say in response was...

"You're not my mother."

PART THREE: The End of the World

The Agility of Clouds takes flight.

Chapter Twenty: The Recovery

In which restitution makes for a new start

"And then I knew you to be on the right road to recovery, mistress," the captain was saying to Seramis, who lay in a bed made in his own stateroom where she had been recovering. "But if you would have actually mistaken me for your mother, then I'd be worried!" Smiling and patting her arms, he chuckled. "As it was, I was relieved!"

"Still," Seramis said, "please forgive me, as I lay fevered and from what little I can remember I was having the most unusual dreams."

"It's been three days, mistress, so you needn't ask forgiveness like it was just this morning!"

"Three? Oh, but to me, it has been only since this morning, except for brief moments of half-awareness, when we arrived on board, and as my maids ministered to me." Seramis's eyes teared with the memories. "I am so grateful at your kindness, and so sad at what has happened..."

"Oh, I'll have none of that, mistress!" the captain said as he stood. "Now that you are up a bit, there is someone who made me promise that instantly upon your waking I should immediately send for him, and I know you'll be pleased to see..."

"Who?" Seramis asked.

Smiling, he opened the stateroom door, and in walked Lord De La Warr.

Seramis blanched, and sank slightly into her bedding, as Captain de Ibarra hissed to the new arrival, "Out! Get out now, man!"

Lord De La Warr's eyes widened. "You dare address me thus?" He, too whispered in deference to Seramis's condition, but he took a menacing step towards the captain who, measure for measure, stepped up to him until their broad chests were touching.

"I would dare have you flogged for disobeying me on my ship," Ibarra said in a voice like a sword being drawn from a sheath.

De La Warr did indeed step back, replying in a voice cold as that drawn steel, "You wouldn't live to see your order carried out, I assure you." He turned to address Seramis but uttered not so much as a syllable.

"Don't," said the captain. "Out. Now." And De La Warr turned on his heel to leave.

Seramis had turned away from the stateroom door, but heard the captain say, "I'm so sorry, mistress, here he is." Seramis heard uneven steps and the captain encouraging someone, "Come on, you're almost here!"

"Welcome back." The words were spoken by a ragged and entirely unexpected voice. Seramis snapped around to see Colonel McClure resting an arm upon the captain's shoulder, bandages around his chest.

"Colonel!" Seramis exclaimed. "How? But Innes?"

"He did say he would be a danger to me," the colonel answered, with a slight smile, though it hurt to speak. "He didn't say how bad he was at aiming, however."

. . .

After briefly visiting with the colonel, who left after checking on her and assuring her that he was on the mend, Seramis rested a bit before accepting Lord De La Warr's request to meet. She fervently wished that she wouldn't have to meet him alone but knew he would never agree otherwise. So she hoped for the best, and that she could brave it out, but prepared for the worst. Fortunately, she was able to speak with Captain de Ibarra in the meantime; she told him nearly all of her story as quickly as she could before he stopped her when she got to the part of her arriving in Jamestown.

"Oh, you needn't tell me any more. Your brave maids—they insisted on traveling with Lord De La Warr, wouldn't you know—told me a great deal regarding your time in the Virginia colony. They seemed especially appreciative of hearing stories of adventure while you slept, and in turn, told me all that they knew," Captain de Ibarra said, while taking in the changes to his stateroom. "This place suits you better, although I imagine you might wish to add some more books and instruments to make it more like home."

"Captain, you are too kind," Seramis said. "As soon as I'm better, I would very much like to return the living arrangements to their previous state."

"I don't know, as I think at least one of your maids should stay here with you."

"Perhaps we'll discuss this later, as I see that you're never short of persuasion when you wish! But tell me—before De La Warr arrives—what is he doing here? How did he even get here?"

"He runs a tight ship filled with sailors having the tightest, most closed teeth of any I know! Not even my cleverest crewmates could wheedle the slightest bit of information from the lowest of sailors on that bucket..." It was clear to Seramis that the captain partly admired, and partly suspected, De La Warr's discipline.

"But I do know that he went all the way up the James River to your home in Henrico. I heard from the maids that he tried to convince Mrs. McClure to travel, suggesting that she could help her husband, but she refused out of loyalty to you. He didn't waste much time, and as you see he was close behind us the whole way. The ship might have actually passed us by, but if it arrived in St. Augustine, the baron would have realized we were not yet there. That vessel—the *Royal Sovereign*, it's called—must have put the fear into the Spanish. They might have imagined a new war was at hand, and they hadn't heard the declarations yet. The colonel had just been returned to us safely when we saw their colors. Of course, we wasted no time in assembling a detail and were off to recover you."

"And I was right behind," said Lord De La Warr as he entered. He doffed his feathered cap, and Seramis noticed for the first time the gray in his hair and beard, and the wrinkles upon his face. He was showing his age, Seramis thought, and looking more haggard than either the captain or the colonel.

"I want to thank you both for a rescue that saved me from a fate truly worse than death, as much as that cliché is overused." Seramis shuddered at the thought of her tormentor. "I think that Patrick Tempus would have done everything he could have imagined to make death a sweet release from his tortures."

"Oh, mistress, I was only doing my duty as a faithful servant," the captain said as he was leaving, but couldn't resist one last gibe as he left. "But I don't know about this one," he said, indicating De La Warr. "He may have mistaken you for an inestimable prize to be won, if he chased long enough."

"Good day, Captain," Lord De La Warr replied with forced cheerfulness. "By the way, I see your carpenter has fashioned a new tiller. Perhaps you can chase down the rest of your crew and see to your fine ship's needed repairs?" Turning, he exclaimed to Seramis as he bowed in greeting, "My dear Lady Seramis!"

"My lord, permit me some confusion in addition to my gratitude." To the captain, Seramis called out a farewell, as the baron sat in a deck chair next to the bed that had been fashioned for her. Then to the baron, she spoke to her point straightaway. "Forgive my directness, but why do you address me by my former honorific?"

"My lady, there is much to discuss, but first, I want to apologize for my ignorance and my blindness to the twisted malevolence that is that creature, Patrick Tempus, who caused you such pain."

"My lord, I could not hold you accountable for actions meant to injure you as well," Seramis replied, noting the concern in De La Warr's voice. "Even his minion, Innes, was held under much closer control than you had over him." Seramis felt a cool fury at the memory of Innes's betrayal. "But I will hold him to account for his betrayal, and not anyone else. Looking back, it's clear that 'Father Patrick' is more dangerous, more powerful, and more fiendishly mad than either you or anyone else could have possibly known."

"And it was foolhardy of me to send you into the unknown, unprepared and unassisted in this venture," he confessed. "Further, my lady, my own betrayal of your trust and belief in my word is a stain that I may only remove by my life, which I devote to your service."

"Please don't think me churlish, my lord. Although your appearance here is without doubt the reason for my continued existence, I'm not presently inclined to accept your service. Especially as I have no idea why or how you are even here! I left you hundreds of leagues away, yet here you have appeared in what would seem to be the most extreme of coincidences to stagger the mind in comprehension—"

"My lady, there is much to tell, but I'll be brief so you may rest. And I hope my story proves to be restorative! Except for my regrettable involvement, there is only good news to share.

"I shall start, if I may, with my return to England, where you were fêted as a hero. It seems that the unfortunate accident of the fire at Helleborine Hall was a story shared by all. Your neighbors and peers told and retold the tale of how you saved the lives of your guests, risking your own life in the process. And how poor Elizabeth of Shrewsbury was in such a state of shock that she naturally had the wildest tale to tell of her unlikely survival. Her accusations were dismissed as nonsense, although her reputation suffers not in the telling, due to the extreme conditions to which you were all subject in that tragic accident."

De La Warr paused, and then seemed to slump a little in his chair. "I confess I took advantage of the situation, and deeply regret what I have done. I am very sorry and I know what I did was wrong. You have every right to never speak to me again. But I would have you hear the rest of what I have to say, if I may, my lady. And then I will leave."

Lady Seramis was silent, but nodded. She was overwhelmed by what she had heard, but she was determined to hear him out. What more could be said, she wondered. Could she accept his apology?

"There is someone from the admiralty who would like to express his good wishes. It was he who casually asked for an audience with the king, in which I was called to account. Without discussing the... um... diplomacy involved in Lisbon, I explained that you were on a mission for me. The admiral, being a peer of course, knew about the transfer of your title and lands and, to be honest, his inquiries and ties to certain ministers of Parliament made His Majesty very nervous.

"The king feared an actual mutiny of the navy would be on his hands, so he rescinded the transfer..." As an aside, he added, "The arrest warrant never existed, of course." Returning to his conversational tone, he continued, "And lastly I was commanded to retrieve and restore you, the heroine of Helleborine Hall." Standing, he bowed again as he prepared to leave.

"Now that is something I never expected to hear," Lady Seramis said. "And I was referring to that ridiculous nickname, not your apology." Truthfully, she would not have believed the existence of the latter, had she not heard it with her own ears. "But tell me before you go, who was this admiral?"

"I believe you know him. He's the Duke of Gloucester, Lord Albion, and currently in command of His Majesty's squadrons in the western Atlantic. I am told he would be glad of a visit when you are well enough."

. . .

In due time, Lady Seramis returned to good health, and accepted the invitation from the Duke of Gloucester aboard *HMS Royal Sovereign.* A gig from the flagship was sent over to the shore where the *Agility* was undergoing the last of her repairs, and Lady Seramis was taken out beyond the shoals and little islands where the great man-o-war lay anchored.

Even from shore the *Royal Sovereign* appeared huge, its coppered hull gleaming solidly in the wintry midday sun. Upon arrival, Lady Seramis marveled as she was assisted onto a plank hanging from a winch—upon which she sat as upon a swing—that served as a means to lift her high enough to attain the main deck merely by stepping upon it.

When Lady Seramis set foot on board, she felt very small indeed at the huge expanse of the ship that was twice—thrice?—perhaps many times more the size of the *Agility*. Looking up from under her hooded cape, she was shocked and made to feel smaller still as the hundreds and hundreds of sailors that were the entire ship's complement were 'standing to' in formation upon the deck, leaving but a single cleared path that ran to the aftcastle.

A swain's whistle pierced the air from across the deck, and a voice bellowed "Attend all!" causing the entire assembled crew to snap to attention. Dressed in an officer's uniform, the second-in-command of the vessel announced "Her Ladyship, the Marchioness of Cambridgeshire!" Doffing his naval bicorn, he gestured for Lady Seramis to follow two marines in traditional red coats who preceded her down the clearing on the deck, while he himself followed at a discreet distance.

Unable as she was to see past her marine escort, Lady Seramis could neither see who awaited her at the end of the path, but she steeled herself and continued between the rows of saluting sailors. Finally, they turned and stepped aside, revealing the same gentleman who had once read her a poem, standing next to their host from that same event, which now seemed as if it had occurred a lifetime ago.

His Majesty's Admiral, the Duke of Gloucester, Lord Henry Albion, stood rather imposingly in all his martial finery upon one of the steps leading to the aftcastle. He held a ribbon in his white gloved hands. Behind him was the proud visage of Baron Thomas West next to the other officers of the *Royal Sovereign*.

From behind Lady Seramis, the officer whispered, "Might I humbly ask your ladyship to do us all the honor of stepping forward and curtseying to His Grace?" Lady Seramis, wondering at the spectacle, her heart racing at the unexpected turn, bravely pulled the hood of her cloak back and did as she was requested.

When she had curtseyed, Lord De La Warr boomed, "Lady Seramis Helleborine, upon this proclamation decreed by His Majesty, King George the Second, Sovereign of the Most Honourable Military Order of the Bath, and confirmed by the Great Master of the Order, Sir John Montagu, you shall henceforth be a Commander Dame of the Order!" The duke stepped forth, and let the medallion drape down from the ribbon he carried. The sun flashed and sparkled on the ornamented gilt of the star cross medallion as he then lifted and placed the ribbon around Lady Seramis's neck, lastly adjusting it upon her shoulders.

Before stepping back again, His Grace mentioned in a conversational tone, "My grandmother, the dowager duchess, thinks you should be awarded this for your musical skills alone." Stepping back, he smiled and bid Lady Seramis—now also Dame Seramis—rise.

Lord De La Warr continued, "For bravery and sacrifice in the face of danger, for exceptional dedication in service to the kingdom and for inspired leadership throughout the realm and beyond!" Pausing, he looked straight at Dame Seramis. "We salute you!" With that, the duke and De La Warr bowed low. And following them as one, the assembled crew knelt.

"Brace yourself," whispered the officer behind her in time for her to ready herself as the thirty-two-pounders roared, sending their padding and packing flying—but no shot of course—as no cannonballs were loaded for this ceremonial salute. The explosion of the cannons reverberated around them as the smoke billowed upwards from the gun deck, followed close by the entire company cheering a rousing "Hurrah!"

Chapter Twenty-One: The Pact

In which a transition is marked by departures

Dispersed in sections by the watch commanders, the crew returned to stations or left for their quarters. The Duke of Gloucester, for his part, invited Dame Seramis and Lord De La Warr to the captain's staterooms. "Shall we take some refreshment? Ceremonies like these should be celebrated. At the very least, we should rest for a moment before discussing the implications of recent events."

As they entered the stateroom, Seramis said, "Once again, Your Grace, I am grateful but feel unworthy, and most certainly confused by all this—"

"I have a bad habit of interrupting, but please indulge me as I recite—in prose, not verse—what I know to be true," said the duke. "You risked life and limb rescuing your guests from a horrible fire; you apparently risked life and limb on a mission about which I officially know nothing except that it occurred in Lisbon, where my grandmother was delighted by your musical performance; and, you risked more than your life unhesitatingly leading an expedition against the most peculiar threat I've ever heard!" Albion smiled as he finished, "But let's not go into the details, shall we?"

"Your Grace, I don't know what to say—" Seramis faltered.

"Then don't! But please, do take some tea." Pouring it himself, he offered her a cup and saucer which she politely declined. Nodding, he turned to the baron, who took it while Gloucester instead offered her some cake. "My baker doesn't often get the opportunity to practice his more indulgent side, but I've always loved his cakes on my grandmother's birthdays. Please, try some. And I hope you will forgive my indulgence in celebrating your accomplishments. We are all so grateful that you were rescued safely and expect to rapidly recover from your terrible ordeal."

"For that, I am at your service, Your Grace," she said.

"I would not, for my own sake, ever ask for you to enter said service," Albion said sadly. "But now that you are a Commander of the Order, I may have to press upon you to serve in another cause."

"And I will be direct with you, Dame Seramis," Lord De La Warr joined in. "I need your help once again."

"All this?" Seramis asked incredulously, indicating the cake she held with one hand, and the ceremony just concluded on the other side of the stateroom door with the other. "Was it a mere show? Did you hope to persuade me with pomp and circumstance? And cake?"

"No. Oh no, dear lady," pleaded Albion. "You are a Commander of the Order, and can determine whatever course of action you deem best. If you wish to offer advice from your rebuilt home in Cambridgeshire, or from your new home which I have heard you have constructed in the Virginia colony, your wish will be respected." Looking at De La Warr, he pressed, "Isn't that correct, Thomas?"

"You were ever right to suspect me," Lord De La Warr said. "And you may wish never to hear from me again. But the need is dire, and the enigma apparently insoluble! I fear that the business with Patrick Tempus is unfinished, and there is another wrinkle to this that I would share."

"Shall we join in a compact, then?" Lady Seramis put her cake back upon her plate. "I wish to conclude this business with Patrick Tempus and his ally, Innes—to stop him from waging war upon all the world. And I need your help, gentlemen, to counter his threat of spreading death from the skies."

"Then we are at your service, my lady. And we need your help, too, in finding out why we've lost all contact with our colony in Bermuda." Gloucester unfurled some maps he had close at hand. "That's the 'other wrinkle' that Thomas mentioned. No ship returns from any of the squadrons that have been sent, with no clue ever found as to why."

"And your quarry may be on his way there now," De La Warr added, pointing to Bermuda on the charts. "After we inadvertently spooked the garrison at St. Augustine, they recalled their fleet to defend their territorial waters, but left their inland fort largely undefended and unable to withstand Patrick's assault." Lord De La

Warr snarled as he continued. "He threatened to slaughter every man, woman, and child in the entire town unless the Spanish surrendered their ships, which—of course—they did.

"He took their fleet and disappeared. The only place where we are blind is Bermuda, so we think he is there."

"We must get to work right away, then. For what I have in mind, winter's chill makes working even here unsuitable," Lady Seramis said. "And there are special provisions and equipment from Williamsburg that I need in order to refit the *Agility* so I can follow Patrick's flight. Would it be presumptuous of me to request His Majesty's flagship to taxi about some cargo for me, and bring it about to, say, the West End of the Bahamas?"

"My lady," the Duke of Gloucester smiled as he answered, "you may ask His Majesty's entire royal navy to follow you to the end of the world, if you wish!"

. . .

Dame Seramis looked forward to one more happy reunion and steeled herself to face sharing one more heavy decision as she arrived back at the shore where the *Agility* was now completed in its repairs. Asking the sailors from the *Royal Sovereign* to wait a moment before returning, she turned towards the crew loading raw material aboard the *Agility*.

The group that greeted her upon her arrival praised her for the golden star cross medallion she wore, and the news spread quickly amongst the rest of the crew and passengers. It appeared, however, that the happy reunion would have to wait, as the recipient of her heavy decision strode down the gangplank to shore.

"Did they give you some shiny bauble and then recruit you for another dangerous mission, to clean up their dirty work for them?" the colonel asked. His healing was far from complete, but his concern for Seramis lent him energy he might not otherwise have had.

"No," she said indignantly. "Well, yes. But it matters not to you, good Colonel"—Seramis wished she might get her decision out of the way as quickly as possible—"as you will be going home to your missus after procuring some materials I need in Williamsburg. I've had a list of items drawn up on the *Royal Sovereign* for you to send back with them."

"What, mistress? Are you dismissing me?"

"Oh, no, Colonel! I'm fulfilling a promise that stands paramount to any other consideration!" Dame Seramis took Colonel McClure's hand. "The vision I have of you leaping to my rescue and sacrificing yourself to Innes's mindless violence will stay with me forever. I know your dedication and bravery will never flag nor fail me—"

"But I did fail!"

"Never! Your plan worked exactly as it should." Seramis was steadfast in voice and bearing. "And we should all acknowledge that we can sometimes stand to use a little help, whether our plans work out or not." Less strident now, more beseeching, she gazed up at his face imploringly. "I need your help, now, as a leader."

While she spoke, her first thought was that she needed to send him home to Mrs. McClure, as she had promised herself when captured. "Please, go to New Helleborine Hall and lead Sunday sermons. Lead our young community in peaceful relations with our neighbors. But all the while make your contingency plans for when hostilities are fomented by belligerents who will rue the day they face the leadership that only you can provide!"

The fight drained from the colonel, but his expression stayed firm, and his voice rasped. "But I promised my Sarah I would bring you home again."

Dame Seramis's eyes filled with tears and her throat tightened as she listened to the slowly spoken words of devotion from her good friend. "But you will. You will bring me home again! I know it! But I have to finish this." She paused, intent on convincing him she spoke truth. "Somehow... And if I lose my way, I will send for you to join me before I return to Virginia. We'll go home together, you'll see!"

Sniffing, she straightened, and attempted to recover. "But first, you will need to heal yourself, and do all those things at New Helleborine Hall that I'm counting upon you to establish!"

"I would refuse if I could," he said. He paused, looking into her eyes. "If I could, but no. I will work towards that day when you send for me." Breathing in slowly, he added, "Of course, I had a feeling, so, naturally, I made a plan for this contingency and I'm already packed."

"Oh, Colonel," Seramis cried, "you are always ready for anything!" She bounded forwards to hug him.

"Ow!" he exclaimed after as they quickly parted, especially separating the star cross medallion from where it had poked his wound. "Except for that, mistress."

"I'm sorry! And you can call me Dame Seramis now, apparently." Referring to the medal of the order, she said, "At least in the king's eyes, I've grown up!"

The colonel asked for his bags to be retrieved, and it was actually Captain de Ibarra who brought them personally. "Farewell, my friend," the captain said to him. "I look forward to acquitting myself as well in your domain, as you have in mine! Until then!" The colonel made his farewells and boarded the longboat with the assistance of the sailors.

Captain de Ibarra nodded towards Dame Seramis's medallion. "You are still full of surprises!"

"I have a rather large surprise to unveil to you," she replied, "and I hope to persuade you of the necessity of it and then, of course, work with you to achieve it!"

"I hope you will surprise me with a course that sets us racing against that overgrown bucket of a ship, so that I might show the English the true meaning of speed! We set sail at your command, my lady."

He saluted and left the newly-minted Commander of the Order of the Bath staring after him in amused confusion. She wondered whether the new show of respect was mere coincidence, or if Captain de Ibarra somehow overheard her talking to the colonel earlier. Or was there was something else that he recognized as fundamentally changed in her, and she had, in a sense, grown up? Turning around she found herself facing the person she had been hoping to talk to since her vivid dream during her capture.

"Hanaawa," she said, "child of the Great Sun! I am grateful for your presence."

"Seramis, Great Woman!" Hanaawa of the Natchez nodded towards the preparations to get underway. "Before you leave, I must confer with you."

"You have my devotion, Hanaawa. And I have a great favor to ask of you."

"You've done me a great favor already, so I'm honored to extend one in return—but even before I can do so, I have another favor to ask as well! This is my niece, White Apple, who arrived today." Hanaawa presented a proud, young native girl in a homespun dress, cloak, bonnet, and shoes typical of any young lady in the colonies, the effect of which was to make her dark features and long black hair all the more pronounced.

"The passing of her honored brother, whose spirit you helped to achieve the next realm, makes her the last of her family. I wish to seek out an opportunity for her to learn with you, if you will take her in, as—" he faltered, apparently searching for the right words.

"The term is 'lady-in-waiting' and rather archaic. But if she wishes to join us in whatever capacity she would choose, I would be honored." Dame Seramis looked to White Apple, smiling and speaking just a bit condescendingly, "I am Lady Seramis Helleborine—"

"The Marchioness of Cambridgeshire," White Apple finished Lady Seramis's sentence with a straight face. She continued matter-of-factly, "a shire on the coast of England between East Anglia and the Midlands with its county seat in Cambridge. Marchioness is the feminine form of a hereditary title of the English nobility, similar to Baroness but with the added distinction of protecting the kingdom's borders, known as the March."

Raising an eyebrow, Seramis listened while White Apple continued in even tones. "Fens, or marshes, are a distinct part of the landscape in Cambridgeshire, so the title reflects its geographical as well as historical roots."

The dame stood astounded into silence, so White Apple continued proudly, "I can read, recite, recount history, do sums, geometry and... and anything else you wish to teach, my lady." Upon finishing her self-introduction, White Apple's solemn expression at once transformed into a big, toothy smile that sent Seramis into a fit of bright laughter.

"...And I will be delighted to have such a promising pupil!" Shaking her head, Seramis turned to the Natchez chief. "Hanaawa, I am honored at your request."

Her features turned solemn as she continued. "I desperately need a guide to help me understand what I've already been through but clearly don't comprehend. And as we could easily journey into realms where what maps we have are useless, I feel that only you can provide that guidance. The favor that I want to ask of you is: can you help me, please?"

"I am honored to serve you," Hanaawa answered. "And I have followed you this far because it is clear that you will need all of the help you have available in the struggle to come."

Seramis noted that he gave no indication of whether his help would be enough, and resigned herself to being able to do little other than hope.

Chapter Twenty-Two: The Aspiration

In which our company attempts the impossible

When crew and passengers had boarded the *Agility*, Captain de Ibarra put to sea immediately. Although the winds were light and pushing into the shore as the winter's day drew to a close, the captain had put the sails into a bad tack against the rigging and made straight for the *Royal Sovereign*, cutting across the wind and turning at the last possible moment to avoid the man-o-war as it weighed anchor and slowly made its way up the coast to the Virginia colony.

The captain cut across Lady Seramis's protestations as well, directing the maids and the newly arrived Natchez maiden, White Apple, to stay in the more spacious stateroom that had belonged to him.

He then revealed bunks built into the stateroom walls where the new inhabitants would be sleeping, much to the delight of the maids (who had tired of the hammocks they had been using). Hanaawa would bunk with the captain, taking the place of the colonel, and so it was settled.

The next morning, as the *Agility* sailed down along Florida's coast, Captain de Ibarra and Dame Commander Seramis spoke on the quarterdeck. "What's our course and heading, Captain?"

"Fair enough," he replied, "we're heading due south until we reach 26°40' North, and then we turn left. We should be at West End, Gran Bajamar, or what you English call the Bahamas, in three days." Smiling broadly, he asked in return, "What's your surprise to be this time, my lady?"

Seramis folded her arms across her chest, her eyes sparkling. "I want to teach you to fly!"

"Oh, I knew about that! Unless you mean to tar and feather me and slap a beak across my face, I thought that would be what you had that in mind for me…" His smile faded, the merriment left his eyes and voice, and he said quietly, "But what exactly are you proposing to do to my ship, my lady?"

"That would be the more difficult task to explain, Captain." She proceeded to outline the changes to the *Agility* that she had in mind, keeping her voice low. The discussion didn't stay quiet for long, however.

"No cannons?" he roared, when the topic came up.

"There's simply no need for that much weight!" Lady Seramis replied. "Surely, you've hunted birds? Flight is the ultimate escape. And who wants to be around gunpowder and—"

"True enough, my lady. I merely attempt to point out to you the flaws in your plan, not to say yea or nay. Please, continue."

However, Captain de Ibarra couldn't see past two outstanding issues. "My lady, proposing that we sail upon the air is fine, but we'll always be at the mercy of the wind! My ship can sail against the wind as it has a keel and a rudder deep in the water to fight inch by bloody inch as we tack into the weather, as we did last night when passing the *Royal Sovereign*, first in one direction, then stepping off to sail in the other! But what are we going to hold onto and dig our keel into while up in the air? The clouds? How would that work?"

"What do you do when there is no wind? How did we make it to shore after we were sabotaged?" Lady Seramis asked rhetorically. "I have in mind a mechanism that would transform the oars into rippling fans, where just a small crew can row our way through the sky and add greatly to our maneuverability!"

"I see. Actually, I don't. But you do, and that isn't surprising!" he said, smiling. "I believe that if anyone can make this happen, it will be you, my lady. You are going to make this work."

"But I'm not the only one! Remember, Captain. Innes stole my notes that now feed Patrick's ambitions to make the aerial warships he desires." Lady Seramis paused as she considered the additional information Lord Albion had provided. "He also now has a fleet."

"But you said that the plans would never work, right?"

"Correct." She began to pace. "The original plans are flawed—"

"Well, then, how can they make their ships fly?"

“They also have the information about the hydrogolic element I isolated, and despite its extreme flammability, they could use it to make the plans work.”

“But you aren’t thinking of using those same elements, are you?” This was the second of the outstanding issues he wished to address. It was most important, as all others paled in significance. “My lady, I have fought pirates and bloodthirsty islanders. I have risked life and limb upon the high seas. I am not a man easily frightened, but the tale of how your experimentation left your manor house a smoking ruin gives me pause. Thinking on it overmuch nearly leads me to turn to a less life-threatening line of work. I prefer to keep my ship's hull and sails free of fire.”

“I won’t be using the hydrogolic gas if the pitchblende experiments are successful, no.” Lady Seramis stopped pacing, and met his gaze evenly. “Not if I can help it.”

“Heaven help us all if you can’t!”

. . .

The weather in the West End of the Grand Bahamas was perfect, and Lady Seramis would have never imagined early November to be so favorable and so warm. The sabotage of the tiller by Innes, the first of the treacherous deeds that she could recount, had had an unexpected benefit in preparing her to consider how to control a ship.

But no one—least of all, the traitor Innes—could have imagined that it would lead to what Lady Seramis and her crew hastily constructed: a model ship’s deck, only a few yards in width and breadth, with an open structure covering the wheel with canvas that can be lowered to enclose the wheel entirely. But this model also had a series of wheels and cranks underneath it, tied to pulleys that were wound by crewmates at each side of the model deck. One crewmember could turn a crank that altered the deck’s attitude, or the angle it faced up or down to the front, while another altered the deck's banking angle, or the degrees it leaned to the right or left. A third altered the position of the model deck on a rack that allowed for movement front and back, while the last of the 'motion simulators' could rotate the entire deck. But these last two were more constrained than the others.

Of course, Captain de Ibarra insisted he be the first to experience the trial, so Lady Seramis began her experiments. Naturally, he was able to stand, turn, walk to and fro, even hop (he declined to skip) at any angle, or any motion no matter how quickly or unevenly the crew cranked the motion simulators. Lady Seramis wasn't surprised, unlike White Apple, who stopped in her drafting and drawing (she was quite good at the task, and had picked up the style needed for the carpenter to make equipment), and simply stared at the captain's cavorting about the model deck.

"Is this all you've got?" called Ibarra, fairly dancing on the moving boards. The crewmen working the simulators glanced to one another. The canvas shrouding the structure dropped.

"What d'you mean? I can't see!" But the protests were ignored. The leader of the work crew nodded, and within moments the captain regretted having issued the challenge. The leader grinned as he offered his captain a hand up.

As the good-natured laughter died away, Lady Seramis asked the captain to examine the modified ship's wheel. It was smaller, he noted, and in addition to spinning, it moved right to left in addition to forward and back. Watching him test the movements, she offered brief explanation. "I'm sure you understand that the wheel will control the banking or yaw of your flight, and you can further deduce that pushing and pulling the wheel forward and back will control your attitude."

"My attitude is just fine, thank you, my lady! What's the objective?"

"Simply to keep level! The wheel is geared so that you can counter the motions with your controls. Please note that the gears are variable, and will change to simulate shifts in balance, air currents, et cetera."

Lady Seramis wondered if this was the first time she had ever called out 'et cetera' but that thought was quickly set aside as Ibarra shouted "Arriba!" As the crew immediately started to crank the motion simulators, he responded by spinning the wheel. The model deck pitched steeply and promptly flung him to the ground, where he fell sputtering onto the soft sand.

"Let me try that again!" he said as he remounted the model deck. Again he shouted "Arriba!" and again he was pitched to the ground—albeit on the other side.

"Again! I nearly had it that time!" With another "Arriba!" he mounted his third attack; his feet slid out from under him while the deck tilted first one way, then another, sending him sliding off the boards and onto the ground, headfirst.

"Auugggh!" he shouted, holding his head. "Unless you've created a mechanism merely to vex me, I will conquer this!"

"Captain, that was never my intent! You will feel acceleration as a change in pitch, but your senses are lying to you. Might I suggest that you lash your boot to the plank with the cords for that purpose next to the wheel," Lady Seramis explained. "The plank is held in place by a spring that will detach, so you can use it for leverage, but don't expect it to carry your full weight." The captain laughed at this, which allowed the crew to release their pent-up amusement.

"That I will!" He had every intention of doing so. Unfortunately, the feedback and the gearing proved to be too much for the captain, until Lady Seramis added to the wheel a spirit level—glass tubes, marked and etched at their centers and filled with oil, save for a single bubble.

"You will need to learn to navigate using these instruments, good captain!"

"What?"

"It's no different than using a compass, sir. You know how to use a compass, correct?"

"Oh, we'll see about that..." With the aid of said spirit levels, Captain de Ibarra was able to almost match the motions and (mostly) keep the deck from bouncing too much. Lady Seramis had found a toy spinning top, and added some magnets to it so she could induce the spin. The carpenter provided a copper filigreed globe to house the toy, with a watch underneath set to rotate the magnets every few minutes. The captain and White Apple gazed at it in admiration as the spinning toy registered the speed of its motion and any changes in its orientation. It was added last, and soon the bosun and bosun's mate were able to keep the deck steady nearly as well as the captain, regardless of how it twisted and slipped.

Now, Seramis needed only to match the control mechanism to a ship that could actually take to the air.

. . .

Work had already begun on the *Agility*, despite the *Royal Sovereign* being several days out at best, possibly still a week away. The gearing and linkages designed for the model deck and motion simulators were being adapted and replicated in the replacement of the oars, the new 'air fan' which would replace the oars on the gun deck. Everyone had a turn at the 'rowing machine' as the captain had named it, and the crew got used to the unfamiliar task of facing in the direction of their travel from the rowing benches while pulling on the rowing arms. The arms themselves were attached to gears that turned still more gears on casters that would allow them to continue spinning even when the rowing arms stopped.

Whether going forwards or back, the gears were turned continuously in the same direction, all of which served to keep the hundreds of moving fans (one hundred and ninety-two on each side, actually), rippling or waving from front to back or vice versa, depending on the position and rotation of the new control wheel. The new 'aerialwave' devices that would be the heart and soul of the *Agility's* mobility were tested and made ready.

For about a week, members of the crew joined in the design roundtable, rotating in and out as their duties permitted as Lady Seramis and White Apple drew up plans, built models, and otherwise transformed the maritime vessel into one worthy of the air. Until Seramis could begin her experiments on the pitchblende, she had to make several assumptions regarding the buoyancy of the gas; she also factored the flammable gas into her calculations and modeling, as it was at least a known factor, if not what they would actually have to use.

The models and plans took on startling and remarkable forms, as no ideas were rejected if they could be described and quantified. Sometimes, the less practical ideas would still be made into models, even if only to examine what the model could describe in other plans, or to be used as negative examples if the concepts didn't work out as expected. The day of the earliest possible arrival of the *Royal Sovereign* came and went without more than a passing comment, as everyone was occupied with making changes to the *Agility*. Still, the next couple of days were a blur of activity, and even a *bon voyage* of sorts as a final plan was argued over and decided upon.

But on the third day of waiting for His Majesty's flagship to appear on the horizon, conversation turned to the expected arrival more frequently and more reservedly as the tension grew. Lady Seramis, least of all, displayed little unease at the delay, and used this time as a pretext for distilling the flammable hydrogolic element for testing purposes. Of course, she warned everyone that flames, even sparks of any kind, would be disastrous, and the cautionary tale of what had happened at Helleborine Hall was repeated. Seramis thought this task too dangerous for White Apple, who expressed an extreme disappointment in being excluded—the first time she had ever shown displeasure, according to Hanaawa.

When a full week had passed after the day of their expected arrival, Lady Seramis privately discussed the absence of the *Royal Sovereign* with Captain de Ibarra. "I wouldn't be anxious if a commercial vessel, save one captained by you, of course, were this late. But as you remarked on the efficiency of the command and crew, what do you think?"

"I would be glad to be rid of her," the captain said, shocking Seramis at first, "but for the esteem in which you show its commander!"

"Seriously, Captain!" She reprimanded with her tone, although she knew that he joked to relieve the tension.

"You are quite right, my lady. And right as well in that that De La Warr fellow owes you a debt that I don't think even the English monarch could absolve him from." That was something spoken aloud that Seramis didn't fully agree with, but she said nothing as he continued. "He has broken with convention in the past, so I think he would find a way to return to us, without the *Royal Sovereign* if need be."

"Yes, and that delay might be considerable," Seramis agreed. "But I think that unlikely, as it may just be possible that the commander of the *Royal Sovereign* holds me in some small esteem as well!" They both laughed at her affected haughtiness, serving to quell the anxiety they shared.

"As I see it, then," the captain said, "we will have to change this from an exploratory mission to a mission of mercy. We will have to come to the aid of that tub—but what will you do about lifting our airship without the pitchblende?"

"There's simply nothing to do but to use the hydrogolic gas," Lady Seramis said, but was caught short when Captain de Ibarra interrupted quietly.

"That will get us all killed!" he exclaimed, and Seramis knew he was serious. "Have you ever heard of St. Elmo's fire, my lady?"

"Sir? Yes, I have heard the term, but—"

"Have you ever heard of the lightning that dances along the rigging and lashes of the tall ships? I have seen storms that produced bolt after bolt of terrible charges that burned at the touch! But that is not all, not by half! I've also seen the scirocco blow past the Wadl Al'Harra! Wind so dry it will pull the moisture from your body. Did you ever see two canvas sails flap and strain and actually spark when the sheets were pulled apart? If you are going to transform my ship into a bomb, you had best not aim straight for a fire!"

"But Captain, what can I do?"

"That is where you will surprise me once again." Having regained his breath, the captain smiled as he returned his tricorn to his head. "I know that you will find a solution, as you know we are all counting on you to do so..."

Chapter Twenty-Three: The Plan

In which the impossible becomes possible

The next morning Seramis announced to the assembled crew, "We are heading into a storm!"

Storms were not new to the sailors, but this situation was like none other they had ever experienced. The solution and its presentation had occurred to her the previous night after talking with Captain de Ibarra. Alone with her thoughts as her bunkmates slept, Lady Seramis faced a dilemma. His words echoed in her ears, but the thought of simply abandoning those who had come to her rescue—even Lord De La Warr—would not be allowed.

The solution to the spark problem occurred to her in a flash, as she thought she could re-create the ground of a copper 'pile' simply by tightly spiraling a copper wire around a conductive iron rod, all of which would be held in a nonconductive ceramic pot. The copper would be traced throughout the outer rigging and would attract a charge, leading it to 'ground.'

But material solutions were only part of what was needed. The captain's concern must be reflected in a change of attitude, and that was up to Lady Seramis, who called everyone together.

"The storm will show no mercy," she told them all. "The storm will be constant. The storm will never be afraid, never hesitate, and never give up." The repetition had gotten their attention.

"The storm will also be invisible. It may look like this perfect morning here and now. But it is deadly, and a misstep will be your last, and it may even be the last of everyone here. This storm forces us to hold one another's lives in our hands, all the time, with every action we take."

Emphasizing each word of that last statement, she looked out over the crew, and even the most stern among them was still, listening in rapt enthrallment as they had never been spoken to by anyone—let alone a woman like Dame Seramis—this way before. She could easily remember the way in which the colonel would exhort his workers and soldiers, so she took on his mannerisms, and in this way became a leader in the crew's estimation.

"The storm will know exactly what to do to kill us. We will need to know exactly what to do to stay alive. We will train." She had frightened them; now she gave them something solid to hang their hopes upon. "We will prepare our every move so that no matter what the storm throws at us, we will know what to do without even thinking about it."

Now she had to point them and their attention in the right direction. "The center of that storm is fire. Our enemy is flame. Heat. A spark. From now on, there will be no dealing with the enemy in any shape or form except through me. There will be no fire of any sort, not even match flame, as fire is our deadliest foe."

She paused, having just taken away the crew's—indeed, mankind's—first weapon against their perpetual enemies. "But to meet that foe—once our ally, our tool—we have to take to the air. To the skies! By extending our reach into the skies, we have become the aggressor and will take our fight to the enemy. To the skies! The storm will fight us, but we will be strong. We will not yield."

And then, in what was likely to be the least popular but most necessary decision she would make, Commander Dame Seramis announced: "We will lash ourselves to the guy lines on deck at all times. No matter where you are or what you are doing, you will do so. Starting now, when you are on the deck of the *Agility*, you have a single goal. To the skies! You are in a storm, and in order to survive, you have to remember where you are going. To the skies!" Looking at each of them, she could see hope, determination, and pride in their faces. "Where are we going?"

The crew answered as one. "To the skies!"

. . .

After another picture-perfect day of waiting for the *Royal Sovereign* and completing the refit, *The Agility of Clouds* was about to demonstrate whether it could live up to its name. Gone were the raking spars that had leant casually from the main-, quarter- and mizzenmasts. The only sails were a small spinnaker flying from the aft, a new lateen from the foremast to the bowsprit, and the mainsail, the single square sail that retained its place on the foremast.

Of course, this was enough to get the ship off the beach with the tide, but the great spars were now in two different places. One was loosely connected to each of the masts lengthwise to the ship almost at the very top, and had canvas furled to both sides of it.

The other two spars actually protruded at right angles to the direction of the ship, and instead of sails furled along their lengths, had canvas rolled the length of the sides of the ship. It still looked like a caravel, only one that had been taken apart and then put back together by someone who had little to no idea how caravels, or sailings ships in general, actually worked.

"Steady as she goes!" shouted the captain.

Then, conversationally to Lady Seramis, he said, "I know you explained the process, but shouldn't we be flying? What, with all that hydradollelol—hibragigol... hydro-go-whatsit, ah, devil gas! Whatever ye call it—on board?"

"When it's compressed, Captain, it's no more buoyant than you or I. But that changes now!" She then shouted to the crew, "Ready the main envelopes!" The canvas stretched along the upper spar was no longer rigged to pull the ship, as now its purpose was to lift the ship up out of the water.

Two of the crew were stationed at the top of each mast to help unfurl the protective canvas, which shielded the sealed silk that actually held the gas (and thus, the term 'envelope' was used, as the whole system was composed of layers without and baffles within). However, instead of the canvas below draping into sails, when Lady Seramis shouted "To the skies!" and turned the handles of the valves next to her, the envelope started to billow and bloom upwards, while the crew chanted "To the skies! To the skies!"

As the main envelopes blossomed, filling with gas, the ship's presentation shifted. Turbulence buffeted at the mainsail and bowsprit. As her draft was pulled upwards out of the water, the keel and rudder lost their purchase. As a swift little vessel, the *Agility* almost never sailed stiff and straight, and in a gale, could be seen almost on its nose, so to speak. But now, it was actually turning at an angle to which it was being pushed by the wind without tilting in the same direction—something the captain had never experienced before.

"My lady?" he asked casually. Only his eyebrows revealed the surprise he surely felt.

"What was that saying, Captain? Steady as she..." but the words fell away for a moment as the buoyant main envelopes filled and lifted *The Agility of Clouds* right out of the water. The rigging snapped taut, the masts groaned, and the ship slipped free of the sea and took to the sky.

"...goes!" Lady Seramis shouted, and the crew cheered as one. The long, cylindrical main envelopes were now straining at the hydrogolic elements, so she closed the valves on the copper pipes that led to them. To the captain, the ship felt as if it slipped out from under him at times, but he kept a steady hand at the wheel despite knowing that he could only minimally affect the ship's direction at present. Spars attached to the rudder that floated while the ship sailed fanned downward now that they were airborne, extending the rudder outward and down as if it had a sail of its own.

"Deploy the lead kite!" Lady Seramis shouted, to be echoed by White Apple, whose task it was to keep an eye out for the air currents ahead, as indicated by the immense box kite launched from the bow. With a steady tailwind, Seramis had planned to use the kite as a hint at what she was racing towards, although she had yet to surpass three knots, according to her gyro-accelerometers.

"Ready the secondary envelopes!" There were two on each side of the main envelopes, and when they were deployed, they were rigged to affect the attitude of the ship. "Prepare for ten degrees rise!" she called hoarsely, as her voice was becoming a bit strained from the excitement, and, of course, the shouting. They were perhaps a hundred feet above the sea when the secondary envelopes started to noticeably add to the lift. Two hundred feet, and they were still climbing into the sky.

Looking up at the envelopes, the captain exclaimed, "It's like my ship has grown a puffy parasol!" Smiling at Lady Seramis, he praised her. "You did it, my lady! You did it!"

"Ship ahoy!" announced the lookout, but even without a spyglass, Seramis could see that it wasn't the *Royal Sovereign*.

"I wonder if they see us?" asked White Apple, who was answered by puffs of smoke appearing on the deck of the galleon. Pops from it were heard as the airship passed overhead, far out of range of the futile fusillade.

"How rude!" White Apple remarked, worried. Lady Seramis worried too, aware not for the first time that being visibly different was something she'd spent most of her life trying to avoid. However, as one floats hundreds of feet above the sea in a caravel buoyed by lighter-than-air gas, one grows used to appearing different rather quickly, she thought, not without a measure of pride.

"Let's put on a show for those sea-crawlers below, and then find a more appreciative yet still envious audience in the *Royal Sovereign*." She exhorted her crew. "Ready the aerialwave! Deploy same!"

Unfolding like a bird's would, the hundreds of 'wings' of the aerialwave moved into position perpendicular to the sides of the airship and caught the air. With only a moderate push to get started, the cyclic gears began the rippling motion that waved through the wings from front to back and gave the device its name. The captain and Seramis looked at each other as the the pulsing of the wings and gears vibrated under them, throbbing throughout the deck.

"Ready for a turn?" Lady Seramis asked.

"Thought you'd never ask!" Ibarra laughed. "All hands! Prepare to come about to starboard on my mark! Mark!" The bowsprit and the mainsail drooped while the spinnaker tacked to port, forcing the aft of the *Agility* around while the captain turned the wheel. "Zero degree rise!"

"Zero degree rise," Seramis quietly echoed, as she adjusted the valves to stop the flow of the gas to the forward envelopes.

"Wind abeam!" the captain announced as he had turned the ship ninety degrees to their desired direction. The port aerialwave had been in full flight, rhythmically pulsing as each individual wing ascended and descended, while that motion flowed through the rest.

White Apple called out, "The kite! It's no longer stalled! We're pulling into the wind!"

"Steady! Ready to tack!" Ibarra called out, "On my mark! Mark!"

“The aerialwave is acting like the keel,” Lady Seramis observed, feeling the rhythmic pulse of the beating wings. We’re actually tacking into the wind, she thought.

White Apple confirmed, “We’re pulling into the wind about a half-knot, Captain!

“And we’re not even trying!” he shouted. “We’ll give her a good workout one of these days! But for now, let’s find that bucket! Eh, my lady? Shall we go and look for that ship? She’s big enough—surely you can’t miss her!”

. . .

Hanaawa came out of his cabin, staring in wonder at the sight of the twin cylindrical, gas-filled envelopes overhead. The realization was slow to come upon him, but apparent, as he was clinging from guy-rope to guy-rope, placing his clip upon a new one as he tried to ascend to the wheel deck but couldn’t as he was momentarily stuck, having forgotten to unclip the old one. When he finally managed to get to the railing near Captain de Ibarra and Commander Dame Seramis, his mouth was agape as he realized he was looking down upon clouds. However, after a moment, his face darkened and his expression grew serious.

“What is it, Hanaawa?” Seramis asked. “For a moment, you looked as if all this was a momentous achievement for the ages, then it all changed.”

“Something has changed,” Hanaawa said cryptically.

“Well, of course!” she agreed.

“Did I miss anything?” Hanaawa asked.

Without even taking a breath, Ibarra interrupted. “Only the most incredible achievement by a group of people since that time when someone looked out upon a desert in Egypt and said, ‘Do you know, this could be a great spot for some pyramids?’ Or, when someone was merely relaxing in Rhodes and said, ‘What this place really needs is a colossus.' This is simply amazing! We are flying! Do you know what this means?"

"No," answered Hanaawa.

"Neither do I, really," Seramis admitted. "But think of it, gentlemen! We can go anywhere! We can fly to the end of the world!"

"And we'll get there much quicker than you think, Great Woman!" Hanaawa spoke softly, his gaze turning away slowly.

Captain de Ibarra interrupted again. "There's a cloud wall up ahead, my lady. We're only half-way from the top, but I recommend we go around it."

"That's too far out of the way, Captain. Why not go through it?"

"Well, I don't like the looks of it, for one. It looks wrong to me, but I don't know why." Pulling out his spyglass and shaking it to its extended length with one hand—he never let go of the wheel with his other—he looked at it more closely. "It looks ordinary enough: no lightning, no tops... But something's just not right," he added, puzzled.

"Something is very wrong," Hanaawa said. "Get us up and over it or around, but do not go in or near it!" Turning to the fore of the ship, he shouted, "White Apple! Are you there?"

"I'm here, Uncle!" came the cry from the forward crow's nest.

"Look at the clouds ahead. Look carefully. Tell me what you see." The entire crew had stopped to listen by that time.

"Careful, people! Mind your stations!" The captain called out to Hanaawa with a concern. "Could you provide an insight, good sir, as to just why you're spooking the crew, please?"

"You said the clouds looked wrong, Captain," Hanaawa protested innocently.

"The clouds are wrong, uncle!" White Apple shouted.

"See?" Hanaawa said.

"Bah!" Ibarra grumbled, shouting then to White Apple, "White Apple, dear? What is it? What do you see?"

"Can't you see it, Captain?" White Apple's voice was uncharacteristically level. "The clouds aren't moving."

Chapter Twenty-Four: The Rescue

In which our company find their lost companions

The trade winds were blowing strong and cold at a mile above the sea, and hampered the *Agility's* progress. That is, until she crossed the edge of the clouds well below her, where she was becalmed. Or would have been, if not for the aerial wave. She had been traveling briefly at a simply unheard-of twenty knots, according to the instruments. But now, for the dozens of miles she would travel above the clouds, she had to provide her own power.

Another crew rotated onto the oar deck, and Commander Dame Seramis made the decision to head for the eye of the cyclone. The captain took less than kindly to this choice, urging her to reconsider the facts: there were no winds around the clouds—and even the clouds themselves didn't move!

"My lady, what if this should prove the utter antithesis of a cyclone? What if, at the eye, it is not calm and silent, but rather a deafening howl and raging gales? An anti-cyclone, if you will? What then?" Ibarra made no attempt to hide his fear from her, allowing it to infiltrate his voice, yet managed to outwardly maintain the demeanor his crew expected.

"There is no normal to this," Hanaawa said flatly. "Whether or not it is an 'anti-cyclone' as you call it, I do not think anyone has ever encountered anything like this before."

"Certainly not," Lady Seramis agreed, looking through her spyglass at the storm's center. "Look! There's smoke drifting up from the eye."

"Indeed there is," the captain said. "Finally! Something moving. That answers the question about the winds in the eye, or the lack of same—"

“Let’s get in closer!” Seramis said, forgetting for a moment who was in charge.

When they arrived at the center, they peered down and espied what looked like nothing so much as a toy sitting at the bottom of a well. It was a ship, possibly the *Royal Sovereign*. At least it looked like His Majesty’s ship, although its sails were furled and mighty flags hung limp from *Agility’s* vantage point, far above the vessel.

Before anyone from that ship could start shooting, Lady Seramis asked the bosun’s mate to drop a message attached to a parachute, an example of which White Apple had drawn for him in the manner of da Vinci. The message said simply: “To the Captain: Please extinguish all fires and every manner of flame or combustion, and we shall be down shortly. Signed, the Marchioness of Cambridgeshire.”

Enabling the venting of the dangerous gas in a controlled manner had proven to be a design challenge, but for Lady Seramis, the end result was simply operating a lever. She hoped she never confused the two in flight, that is, the two valves: one for filling the envelopes, one for venting them.

The *Agility* descended slowly, but soon they were close enough to see signal flags and various sailors waving their caps. Soon, they were close enough to hear the cheering of the *Royal Sovereign’s* crew.

“Steady! Mind your stations!” Captain de Ibarra warned his own crew. “There’ll be time enough for celebrating later! But we’re not done yet, not by a long shot!”

“Any sign of smoke?”

“No,” the bosun’s mate replied. Acting as signal officer, he had been in contact with the ship, which was indeed the *Royal Sovereign*. “They sent first their compliance; then, a warning: do not contact the clouds or the rain.”

“Rain?” Captain de Ibarra arched an eyebrow and once again pulled out his spyglass, peering through it. “It doesn’t sound like it’s raining. It doesn’t *look* like it’s raining.”

“That’s the third message, sir. ‘The rain is not normal,’ it said, and also, ‘The rain is stuck.’”

“Stuck?” Ibarra shook his head in amazement.

“Aye, sir! That’s what it said, sir,” the bosun’s mate repeated.

"I see it!" White Apple announced from the bow. "The rain is all around, but it's just raindrops hovering in the air; they don't fall. They are stuck!"

"They don't move?" Seramis asked, trying to piece together what she thought she saw and what she was actually seeing.

But the captain had other pressing concerns. "Let's worry about that after we get my ship safely down out of the sky!"

"Why, Captain, you sound as if you have some doubts!" Lady Seramis chided.

"Let's just say that I have always thought it unlikely, once we got up into the sky, that we'd get back down again as smoothly!" Calling to his crew he shouted, "Furl those sails, they won't do us any good here. Rowers! Keep us in place. Maintain present position."

"Captain, it looks like we're going to return to the sea just aside the *Royal Sovereign!* Congratulations on finding her, and on your first aerial rescue!"

"Thank you, my lady! Now, if you could only discern why the *Royal Sovereign* is trapped out here, and maybe find a way out at the same time, I'm sure they'll be grateful as well!"

. . .

As the *Agility* successfully landed and the crew started to vent and furl the mighty gas envelopes, the *Royal Sovereign* launched its gig, bearing Admiral Duke of Gloucester Lord Henry Albion and Lord De La Warr and being rowed by several sailors. Arriving at the *Agility*, they announced themselves. "Permission to come aboard?"

"Granted!" shouted Captain de Ibarra and Lady Seramis in unison.

"So, now I'm merely a pilot aboard my own ship?" the captain asked of her, leaning away slightly and arching a bushy brow.

"I apologize. I forgot my place in my excitement, Captain!"

"No, no. Please! Go greet our guests!" He folded his arms, but his smile was casual and good-natured.

Lady Seramis left the aftcastle and arrived amidships as Admiral Albion climbed over the railings. "My lords, welcome to *The Agility of Clouds*!" Lady Seramis announced. The admiral smiled weakly as Lord De La Warr also climbed aboard.

"This is an incredible achievement, my lady!" the admiral proclaimed. "We were on our way from Newport with your supplies when the storm came upon us and then somehow transformed into this hellish trap. We were lucky to make it this far with as many survivors as we did. Sadly, there's no way out for us."

Lord De La Warr agreed. "At least we know that you and your ship will be able to continue on without us."

"My lords, what kind of talk is this?" Seramis was incredulous. "What have you suffered, that you are so convinced of failure you'd so readily admit defeat?"

Lord De La Warr answered first. "To sail through this storm is to invite certain death, my lady."

"Commander Dame Seramis," Admiral Albion continued, "I must report I have lost nearly a quarter of my complement to the storm—good men who perished in this unearthly trap—and as I warned, whatever you do, do not come in contact with the rain."

The crew of the *Agility* looked about nervously, noting that they were surrounded on all sides by the unmoving raindrops, seemingly stuck in time, a shimmering, deadly wall.

"Although the raindrops are just ordinary water, they are fixed in place," he continued. "If you touch one, it will pass right into you, at first drowning that small location with its water, and then—through a process I don't fully understand—if you move, wherever the water has touched you all moisture will be removed. Blood or bile—it's all gone when you move in any direction once your skin has come into contact with the immobile raindrop."

"It is like being burned without the fire—the result is the same!" Lord De La Warr adds. "The suffering of our victims has been horrible, and the losses catastrophic!"

"My lords, we are prepared for storms," Lady Seramis turned to rally her crew. "Our enemy is flame, and this, by twist of fate, is the same!"

Turning back to Gloucester, she spoke calmly, matter-of-factly. "I suspect that the binding properties of water, which create its surface tension, are what cause the loss of water from tissues that are touched by the immobile drops." She paused, thinking, then asked, "But do you recall how this came about? What happened, my lords?"

Lord De La Warr shook his head. "I wouldn't have believed it, had I not seen it myself. Fantastic storms! Hail! Ice! Rushing in at incredible speeds, only to stop and beat against us—"

Admiral Albion picked up the narrative. "We lost fully half of our sails to the hail and ice alone, piling up upon the deck faster than we could clear it away, before we encountered this storm! We were already in its midst when the storm stopped frozen in time just as you see it before you!"

"Welcome to my world," Seramis Helleborine said cryptically, thinking of Cambridgeshire and the life she had left behind long ago. She had left that world behind, but it followed her still.

"My lady?" De La Warr asked, then added after a moment of silence, "We've put the ice to good use, at least, since we had so much of it. Ministering to the wounded for now, anyway."

"I just had a thought, my lords!" Lady Seramis turned towards the unmoving wall of rain, studying it as closely as she dared. "Have you seen how the raindrops are affected by heat or cold?"

"We tried to burn our way through," Lord Albion answered, "but each boiling raindrop simply transformed into a roiling immobile vapor, which was just as deadly."

"Ice, my lords! Did you try the ice?" Seramis was thinking rapidly, and she forced herself to speak slowly and clearly.

"No, my lady, what effect would it have?"

"Let's find out!" She turned to Captain de Ibarra and called, "We forgot to bring ice, Captain! Please tell the quartermaster to include that in our stores next time! In the meantime, have the bosun's mate signal the *Royal Sovereign*, gather all of the ice that can be spared, and have them prepare for their admiral's return!"

. . .

Lady Seramis shipped out with the admiral and Lord De La Warr to the *Royal Sovereign*, rowed hastily by the sailors who, for their part, reacted as if possible salvation was near at hand. For her part, Seramis reasoned that if the physical properties of the rain were mutable, as evidenced by its turning to vapor when heated, then binding the molecules into crystals, or ice, would remove the threat of its binding to a body's own water.

The overall effect was staggering: a hurricane stopped in place. Seramis wondered at it, but wouldn't let the impossibility of it hamper her attempts. Whatever had caused it mattered not at the moment, it was here; what had happened had happened. The first concern was saving the lives of the remaining crew.

For his part, Lord De La Warr appeared fatalistic concerning his chances, but said aloud that he hoped for some small chance to redeem himself before his destined end. "My lady?" he asked as they finished climbing the ladders to the main deck of the *Royal Sovereign*. "How do you plan to proceed?"

"Lord De La Warr, you have that look about you." Lady Seramis looked at him suspiciously. "You are making plans again, unless I miss my mark. I appreciate your concern, but I am the only one capable of performing this experiment."

"How can that be? Why must you put yourself at risk?" De La Warr asked.

"We are all at risk, my lord." Seramis lowered her voice. "But I have the experiences of a lifetime of maneuvering around seemingly immobile objects—experiences that I don't think anyone else shares."

That wasn't so hard, thought Seramis. *Being honest about one's differences seems so much easier than hiding the truth.* But she knew that it wasn't always easy, and dismissed her thoughts for the moment. Lord De La Warr seemed to accept her reasoning, so there was that.

"We'll know very soon whether this plan is feasible," Seramis said. "If not? Then, we will regroup and try another approach! Ah! Here's the ice! Load a small amount into the captain's gig, please." To the sailors within earshot she called out, "You will have to break your old habits of knocking the ice out of the sails, good sirs!"

She shouted to the assembled sailors. "Your ice-bound sails should be draped ahead of you from the bowsprit and foremast! Protect your rowers as they pull you free of this trap; they will be your salvation!" Cheering, the men moved to obey.

"Admiral? Permission to launch the gig?" Seramis called out to Gloucester.

"Godspeed, my lady!" he said.

"Please signal the *Agility* to follow—"

"Commander," a signal officer interrupted. "The Captain of the *Agility* has signaled a request for a tow behind us."

De La Warr said, "If that captain consents to be towed by this ship, you have commanded his loyalty well!"

"I'm sure he'll be looking forward to telling the tale of how he came to the rescue of His Majesty's flagship, so there might be more at work here than loyalty!" Lady Seramis said as she climbed down to the gig.

Two marines joined her, carrying a canvas stretcher filled with ice. As she boarded the smaller boat, Seramis was filled with doubt. Although she radiated outward confidence, she couldn't be certain that any special abilities she possessed would, in fact, help her in this situation. However, it was clear that the marines and the sailors aboard the gig were as disciplined as they were buoyed by her presence. They had seen first hand what had happened to the victims, and yet still they pressed on without so much as a sideways glance.

Standing in the bow of the gig, Lady Seramis hoisted the stretcher as they encountered their first static and unmoving raindrop. How can something so small and as insignificant as a drop of water, thought Seramis, become a deadly trap when manipulated by time?

"Hold!" she called out, and the rowers pressed forward neatly, bringing them to a complete stop. There was a raindrop just in front of her, but as Lady Seramis first hauled upwards and then slowly released the rigging tethered to the canvas carrying the ice, it disappeared. "Three-count pulls, rowers, slow and steady!" And at the next raindrop, and the next, the result was the same. As each drop froze and crystallized, it bound itself with the ice in the canvas.

"It's working!" shouted one of the marines. The gig was pressing ahead into the unmoving rain, and wherever the drops came into contact with the ice, a path was cleared.

"Signal the *Royal Sovereign* to proceed at minimum." Commander Dame Seramis Helleborine was in charge, and the inflection of her voice matched her instructions. "Have them get their wounded up on deck behind the ice. We're escaping this trap."

Chapter Twenty-Five: The Enemy

In which action dispels dark shadows

By the time the vessels had cleared the deadly storm, the bows of the ships were entirely encrusted with ice. The cheers of the crew of the *Royal Sovereign* were steady, but muted, as the wounded were a visible reminder of what they had recently suffered.

Commander Dame Seramis ordered the gig around while the marines knocked the canvas and the rest of the ship free of the rapidly melting ice. Once the gig was lifted directly into place and stowed, she joined Admiral Albion and Lord De La Warr on the quarterdeck amidships, where she was thanked profusely.

"Once again, you've proven your mettle and earned my admiration, Commander," the admiral said. "The elegance of your solution is worthy of poetry—which I'll commission from an actual poet, never fear—and for my part, merely bask in the glow of your achievements."

"Thank you, Your Grace," she replied, practically chirping with relief. "I'd welcome the chance to hear your take on what you've experienced in the storm, provided that you leave my part out—I think I'll be too embarrassed to brave such a display!"

"Lady Seramis, your bravery and intelligence outshine those of the rest of us," admitted Lord De La Warr as he bowed deeply. "And I'm again indebted to you."

Nearly speaking into the gloved hand with which he stroked his beard, he continued. "Speaking of debts, you'll find that I settled all the accounts in Virginia while we acquired the supplies you requested. It was the very least I could do."

"Lord De La Warr, I'm grateful!" Seramis said.

"And so are the members of your household, as they've been provided for as well," he added. "Saving His Majesty's flagship was worth every shilling."

"We're not safe yet," Admiral Albion admonished the baron, "but I don't want to get ahead of myself and spoil the mood after such an incredible achievement—"

"No, no, my lord! You are quite right!" Seramis said. "I should get the supplies you brought to the *Agility* as quickly as possible so we can be underway."

Gloucester's eyes shone with admiration. "And the only compensation I can imagine sufficient to your absence would see you take to the skies once again!"

"The appearance of the *Agility* over the eye of the storm was a sight worthy of a lifetime. I imagine you understand better than most, the immense risk you took and are about to take again. I want you to know that every moment that you're in the air, I pray for your safe return." De La Warr's face clouded at the distressing worry he expressed.

"My lord, I would not question your feelings or motivations at present, but please note that I do have questions—a great many of them—that I shall ask when I return." The marchioness coolly regarded the man she knew had, at the very least, previously plotted her downfall. "But know that it's not atonement I seek, only answers. And right now there are simply too many more pressing matters that require my attention, or I would have them from you."

"My lady, I am at your disposal for anything that you seek." The baron's voice shook. "You may think the less of me when you hear the answers, if it is possible for you to do so."

Admiral Albion had discreetly removed himself from this exchange, but took this moment to interject. "Noble peers, might I be so indelicate as to suggest that such sentiments must needs wait? If we are to determine what has happened to His Majesty's naval squadrons, or even whether the island of Bermuda still exists, we had best renew our mission!"

"Admiral, you are quite right!" Lady Seramis said. "And I wish your crew a speedy recovery and your ship a speedier repair! Might I ask your ship to send a signal..."

"Commander?" Once again, a signal officer interrupted. "The captain of the *Agility* has signaled a request to come alongside us and take on cargo."

The admiral laughed. "Truly, you and your crew are of a like mind! Further, I bow to your future judgment—I hereby order a field commission to Commander Dame Seramis Helleborine as Fleet Captain, effective immediately. We've already had one ceremony, so I hope you don't mind if we skip having another!" Although he was smiling, Admiral Albion was serious. "With your leave, I'll see to the repairs of this ship. Then, we're at your command!"

"To Bermuda is my first command," the newly commissioned fleet captain replied, "and let us hope it shall not be my last!"

. . .

The supplies were quickly brought on board, and Fleet Captain Dame Seramis Helleborine rallied her crew and passengers. "You are the bravest collection of humanity that I have ever witnessed! Thanks to you, we flew!" She walked among them, shaking their hands, and pressing their shoulders.

"But we are about to transform this airship, and our journey ahead will still be dangerous! However, just because we can cross one threat off our list does not mean we are safe. Our enemy is still fire, but it will be the fire of our foes in the form of cannon shot or bullets."

She paused, thinking also of that flesh-and-blood enemy, Patrick Tempus, and how he, too, threatened her with harm worse than death. "But we have proved ourselves, quicker, smarter—and at the very least, luckier—and if we work together, we can give fortune an opportunity to provide for us a victory!"

Hanaawa stepped forward, asking, "But what is our victory, Great Woman?"

"Survival is victory, friend and mentor! And if what we've witnessed so far is any indication, we are sure to invite hostility if we continue on this course. Once again, we will fly to the heart of the storm. Our foes will clearly seek our destruction. Let us work together to solve the mysteries we've seen and those we've yet to see!"

"Survival is victory," said White Apple, standing and addressing Lady Seramis.

"Survival is victory!" added Captain de Ibarra, who was joined by the crew. Voices rang in the rigging.

"Survival is victory!"

. . .

Using the equipment she had fabricated in the Bahamas, Lady Seramis successfully replaced the compressed hydrogolic element with the liquified gas extracted from the pitchblende. Demonstrating its safety, she inhaled a small amount, which transformed her voice into a high-pitched version of its normal timbre. The crew responded with peals of mirth.

Pretending not to have heard her, Captain de Ibarra arrived and demanded, "What's going on here?"

The only suitable answer was for him to be given a similar treatment, to which he responded as if nothing had changed, affecting a deadpan expression as he squeaked: "What?"

This caused everyone within earshot to roll with spasms of laughter. In mock confusion, the captain chirped repeated commands for the crew to stop, lecturing them on their apparent disloyalty and further admonishing his helpless crew in his tinny, tiny voice until the effects dissipated.

"Ahem," he finished with a droll smile. "Carry on."

. . .

The Agility of Clouds was ready to undertake its second aerial mission, and signaled the newly repaired *Royal Sovereign* its intentions. Once again, Captain de Ibarra took the wheel while Fleet Captain Helleborine and the crew readied themselves for flight. This time, however, they had an audience: the six hundred surviving crew (out of over eight hundred commissioned) of the *Royal Sovereign* assembled to watch them lift off.

A slight breeze pushed the airship out slowly from its audience, who shouted cheers as the main envelopes were deployed and filled. The bulk of the gas envelopes was aerodynamically tempered by a cylindrical shape that was slowly revealed as they filled with gas. The cheers grew even louder as the *Agility* lifted free from the sea. The airship's secondary envelopes were deployed, and as they inflated, they appeared to rake from fore to aft, as if they provided not only buoyancy but a suggestion of speed, and the *Royal Sovereign* cheered to that as well while the *Agility* climbed into the sky.

But the loudest cheer came at the deploying of the aerialwave, at which the astonished sailors cried out that the airship appeared to swim through the very air. The *Agility* responded to the cheers and put on a show, lifting its nose and performing a neat tack back towards the water-bound vessel. It then executed a complete three-hundred- and-sixty degree turn as it rose still higher and higher into the air. The watch commanders of the *Royal Sovereign* signaled the crew to stations, and the warship followed the *Agility* to Bermuda.

Now free of the immobile cyclone, the airship and the warship faced brief but violent storms. While the *Agility* could outmaneuver and even rise above the local disturbances, each storm thrashed at the mightier and sturdier *Royal Sovereign*, which soaked up the storms as it would swallow broadsides in battle while unceasingly billowing ahead. But this meant that progress was slow, and Lady Seramis chafed at the delay. Still they encountered no vessels, and the *Agility* could easily cover three or more times the distance that the slower vessel could.

Fleet Captain Dame Seramis Helleborine and her crew used the time to practice aerial maneuvers. Each attempt, while spectacular in terms of precision and mobility, could be very tiring, so after each one they would settle to sea and float while they discussed what worked and what didn't after each attempt.

Seramis had rigged a bellows to pump ordinary air into sealed inner bags so that the gas from the pitchblende wouldn't have to be vented but could instead be liquified and recompressed when the envelopes needed to maintain their full size. However, the *Agility* most certainly failed to live up to its name when it sat upon the ocean with its envelopes nearly full of ordinary air. Lady Seramis quickly learned to leave most of the buoyant gas in the envelopes in order to keep the ship upright.

Just before a new maneuver was about to begin, White Apple saw it first. A thin vertical line appeared on the horizon just at the point where Bermuda should be, and ascended straight into the sky and out of sight, like an impossibly tall mast of a ship the bulk of which lay just past the horizon.

The *Agility* flew swiftly through the air to meet this unlikely phenomenon. At one thousand feet above the ocean, the crew could see more than twenty leagues to the horizon, and when the shores of Bermuda first appeared in the misty haze at that distance, they realized that the thin line was actually a very broad strip, as wide as a boulevard but most certainly not made by any known method of manufacture. It was impossibly taller than any known mountain, stretching into the farthest, unseen heights of the atmosphere.

But they weren't able to linger on the implications of this newly found puzzle, as instead it appeared that all of the missing and captured vessels were anchored or otherwise stationed on Bermuda's shore. And when the commanders of those vessels spied the *Agility*, the ships began to take to the air, each lifted aloft by dozens of round bags attached to their capstans, masts, and rigging, firing their cannons as they flew.

Chapter Twenty-Six: The Battle

In which ability proves no defense against casualty

Captain de Ibarra shouted, "To stations!" But he wasn't overly concerned, as the *Agility* was still well above and far out of range of the cannons, and was using its aerialwave to push directly into the wind, meaning that they could turn and have the wind at their backs if they needed to make a quick exit.

Calling out to the watch, the captain shouted again. "What are their numbers, White Apple?"

"Three English frigates on the water, eight Dutch *fluyts*—appropriately named, I think—taking to the air, and eleven of what appear to be smaller Spanish carracks also readying for flight, Captain!"

Fleet Captain Dame Seramis Helleborine looked at the aerial armada with an analytical eye as well. "Well said, White Apple!" The Natchez maiden's gifts of intelligence had been proven time and again, her position as lookout having become semi-official, or at the very least, nearly permanent. "Captain? Do you have your spyglass ready?"

"Of course!" He was looking through it already. "What should I be looking for?"

"We've already seen the cannons fire from the *fluyts*, so we know how they're armed. What do you see on the carracks? Are those crenellations?"

"Aye! They've gone back a hundred years or two and built actual castles on the forecastles and sterncastles! That makes no sense unless they are using bows and arrows, eh?"

"No, it doesn't make sense. But yes, they are," Seramis said. "Let us stay clear of them, as those are the ships where they must have used the hydrogolic element for buoyancy. Surely, they must know how flammable it truly is?" She had out her own spyglass and confirmed. "And they've put bonfire furnaces aboard the *fluyts*. They're using heated air for lift... Do you see the bellows? Those *fluyts* had best stay away from the carracks as well!"

"Shall I put us above the *fluyts*, Fleet Captain?"

"Yes, Captain, let's put an end to this. Full speed ahead!" That was all she needed to say, as the *Agility* lived up to its name and shot forward and down slightly in the direction of the *fluyts* while the crew readied their own munitions. In addition, the wind gently pushed the *fluyts* towards the *Agility*, but their furnaces and bellows couldn't provide the lift needed for them to ascend except at an achingly slow rate.

Slowing and pulling up over the first of the *fluyts* in a maneuver they had repeatedly practiced, the crew dropped a half dozen javelins that spiraled through their terminal velocity before they plunged through the canvas gasbags, sending the *fluyt* slowly back to earth. The *Agility* tacked and turned to deliver another round upon the next vessel, and the next.

By the time Lady Seramis and her crew had disabled half of the *fluyts*, the first of the carracks had lifted as well. This proved disastrously unfortunate for them, as the *fluyts* were still wildly firing cannons and muskets in nearly all directions—but only generally in the direction of the *Agility*, for reasons that were not entirely clear. In nearly every case, the smaller carracks fell from but a single errant shot from their own squadron that resulted in a catastrophic explosion and a sickening, fiery dive to the shore below.

The one exception proved to be when the captain of the second-to-last of all the carracks pitched its entire stores, its ballast, and anything else that wasn't bolted down. This caused the vessel to jerk and spasm upwards in fits and starts until it collided with a *fluyt* that had yet to stop its firing, only to burn in a blaze of leaking hydrogolic gases that had escaped from the ill-fitting gas bags of the carrack beneath. Tragically, both vessels burst into flame and plummeted downwards onto a hellish shore littered with burning vessels and blackened by fire and charred remains.

Lady Seramis was distraught at the carnage. *What nightmare is this? What have I done?* She was torn twixt the desire to stop her attack and retreat from the carnage below and the wish to put an end to the *fluyts*' ability to wage any kind of war themselves.

"Oh, Captain!" Lady Seramis cried. "This is mayhem and madness!"

"Steel yourself to the task, Fleet Captain, and my advice is to make swift your mercy," he called out.

The captain then called her attention to the squadron of English frigates. "Yet, we could warn the *Royal Sovereign* she may have company soon. By my reckoning, that slow tub could even now be just over the horizon. She may have her hands full with three of the enemy, and I'm not one to run away from a fight..."

"Hanaawa!" Seramis shouted, "Are you seeing this?"

From the crow's nest he shared with his niece on the foremast, Hanaawa called out, "I'm seeing more than I can say. It's a terrible reckoning, but I think my lost kin have been accounted for among the dead, who died by their by their own misdeeds. Yet, I would still bring justice to the one who is truly guilty of all this!"

"Should we press on, then, and finish this? Look to the frigates! Should we go back to warn the admiral, instead?"

"Take a look around you, Great Woman!" Hanaawa demanded of Seramis. "What do you see?"

Fleet Captain Dame Seramis Helleborine called out to the crew: "Hold, everyone."

Then to Ibarra she said, "Hold us in place; I'm moving us up!" Adjusting the levers as the airship climbed rapidly into the sky, Seramis looked around her, slowly.

The first thing that drew her attention was not the horrifying results of the battle, but rather the impossible oddity that had become figuratively overshadowed when the battle had commenced: a jutting spar of land she could now see, spotted with rock and vertical streaks of minerals as if it were no more than an ordinary parcel of earth, regardless of its impossible position and existence. Furthermore, she could see now that the spar was shaped cylindrically and stretched upwards like a column at least a hundred yards in width, but countless miles high.

But as impossible and unlikely as its upward stretching straightness, the root or anchor point where the column met the earth defied any attempt at rational explanation. All around the column, which appeared to continue down towards the center of the earth without ceasing, the land itself was being folded into the dark void where column pierced shaft, but never touched upon the sides. Bursting forth in unnamed colors, streaming far too fast for the rest of the crew to see, shimmering jets of light shot from the gap between column and shaft, convincing Lady Seramis that this transformation of the world was malignant as far as she and the rest of humanity—indeed, all life—were concerned.

"White Apple, is that column of rock growing?" Lady Seramis called out.

"Yes, my lady, although I can't see the top I can see that the features of the great column are slowly moving upwards. Not only that, but it also appears that the void around the column is swallowing the earth, dragging the land—this island—down into the bedrock!"

Lady Seramis trusted in the young girl's vision. "To answer your question, Hanaawa, I think we're seeing the end of the world!"

. . .

Fleet Captain Dame Seramis Helleborine decided that warning the *Royal Sovereign* was clearly warranted, as Patrick Tempus's aerial fleet had been a suicidal and pointless disaster in actual practice as opposed to the awe-inspiring terror it had been in theory. She thought herself fortunate that Patrick had not seemingly given the slightest thought to maneuverability. It might not have even occurred to him that another airship would oppose him—certainly not one like the *Agility*—as evidenced by the tactics he attempted.

Seramis could imagine Patrick's warlike intent of sailing up to ports from New Orleans and Biloxi on the Gulf to Boston on the eastern seaboard. Perhaps even up the St. Lawrence to Montreal, and with a fleet of airships at his back, he would have haughtily demanded their surrender. Or, mercilessly destroyed any who opposed him.

Just as the *Agility* was free to rain down destruction upon the slower airships, those same vessels would have reigned unchallenged above the ordinary defenses of any city Seramis could name. She realized that the advent of the airship meant a new destructive era of warfare, as nation will race against nation in a competition full of menace and threat, and she imagined the results of the destruction she had just perpetrated upon the shore spread across the globe.

With the wind behind them, the captain ordered full sail, including the new inverted triangular sails rigged from the secondary envelopes to the horizontal spars amidships (there wasn't time to rig even more sails upon those, as Captain de Ibarra would have liked), and the *Agility* soon overtook the frigates. As fast as she was, the frigates were likely faster and more maneuverable than the warship, and three of them would just about even the odds if they could cross the *Royal Sovereign's* path in a line formation and pour their broadsides into her before she could turn.

The captain spent the time racing to the *Royal Sovereign* sharing with Lady Seramis the tactics he would use if he were in charge of either the frigates or the warship, and how he would counter either. She listened distractedly to the endless stalemates described by the captain, until he mentioned, half in jest, "If ye'd let me put a cannon back on board, milady—"

"Captain. For all of the meaningless destruction we've witnessed, you would add to our armament?" Seramis sobbed quietly, and turning, buried her face in her sleeves.

"I wish you never had to see any of this," Ibarra said in an attempt at consolation. "You are a brilliant and sensitive woman, and anyone with half your gifts should be sheltered from what we've done and seen."

He gestured to the crew, saying, "You've given us all so much, and ask of us to uphold the highest of standards; do you hear any complaints? Any? Well, from anyone except White Apple..."

"I heard that, sailor-man!" White Apple said, as everyone knew she would, yet laughed at it anyway.

"See? We're ready to follow you wherever you lead, no matter how grim the situation!" The rest of the crew looked on, following the conversation intently. "You could ask us to stop here and now, and we would."

Captain de Ibarra raised himself to his full height. At this, Lady Seramis looked up, and also noticed the whole crew gazing at her, in consolation and kindred empathy. But, there was also a steely resolve that had not been present before they had been in battle.

Captain de Ibarra continued, "We know that you hold yourself to the highest standards. And we don't think you can just leave the end of the world without at least trying to set it right, can you?"

. . .

Once again, cheers arose from the decks of the *Royal Sovereign* as the *Agility* floated to meet it, coming alongside and hovering above the crow's nest just to port. The frigates were just over the horizon, still at least an hour out, likely intending to force a battle just before nightfall. The warship was tacking into the wind, yielding the advantage to the frigates who would have been able to rush at the warship with the wind at their backs.

The signals from the *Agility* slowly shared the news, with word of the destruction of the enemy fleet causing another cheer among the British tars. The oncoming frigates of the fifth rate were eventually described, and the reply from the *Royal Sovereign's* bullhorn could be clearly heard by all: "Leave us an enemy or three!"

The inexplicable column was just coming into view for those aboard the warship, and as fleet captain, Seramis Helleborine asked the messenger to describe it as a "towering pillar of earth" and "the end of the world" which she hoped would convey more than just a poetic idea. She further requested to meet up in the morning on Bermuda's leeward side, opposite the trade winds. After acknowledging the messages, the *Agility* resumed its lift and the *Royal Sovereign* tacked farther to starboard.

The frigates responded as soon as they noticed the new course, and turned hard out of the wind to keep in front of the warship. The maneuver also slowed them down in the process. The *Agility* was soon leveling out at one thousand feet, and running directly towards the frigates under the propulsion of the aerialwave.

The captain turned to Seramis with a wry smile. "'Tis a good thing frigates don't carry mortars, as we might find ourselves wanting a bit more room between us and the guns below!" She privately thought that the prospect would happen in some not-so-distant future, should aerial fleets become commonplace as she had feared earlier. Both the captain and the marchioness agreed that their luck was eventually going to run out, and it appeared unlikely that they would come through this unscathed.

"Despite our current unsporting advantages, let's just even the odds for our comrades-in-arms, shall we?" Lady Seramis said evenly, wearying of battle even before it began, and wishing it would be over.

She quickly received confirmation that the battle would indeed be over soon, as the *Agility* swooped down to drop two dozen cannonballs with crippling accuracy on the largest of the three frigates. Not that the missiles did much actual damage to the ship proper, but in a single pass, the *Agility* had destroyed most of the sails and fouled the rigging, putting the ship out of the fight before it had a chance to fire its guns. In fact, the ship actually struck its ensign and unfurled a white flag of surrender.

Despite this, upon their nearest approach at only seven or eight hundred feet above the ocean's surface, Lady Seramis thought she could hear bullets and ammunition pass ineffectively under the *Agility*, although with the continuous roar of the cannons, she couldn't be sure. Apparently 'surrender' wasn't quite the cessation of hostilities she imagined it to be.

The remaining two vessels apparently still thought well of their chances, and tried to cross the path of the *Royal Sovereign*. Naturally, the *Agility* was the quickest of all of them, and came around for another pass. This time, Lady Seramis flinched when she heard the shots thunder below her. Another crippling blow and the second frigate was struck. Even as the *Royal Sovereign* turned to arrange their guns in a broadside, the damaged ship couldn't turn away at the last minute so it fired a volley at the *Royal Sovereign*. But it was alone in its attack as the last remaining maneuverable frigate turned away, abandoning its crippled partner.

The cannonade of the *Royal Sovereign* as it returned fire against the lone attacking frigate was merciless. The resulting onslaught tore massive holes in the frigate's hull, between wind and water as it listed. Of course, that caused the frigate to list even further, and soon it started to sink just as it briefly righted itself after the barrage.

Lady Seramis turned away from the devastation and looked towards the retreating frigate. She couldn't judge the captain for his apparent cowardice. She had fought under duress, and knew how that might affect different people. However, she quickly decided that letting him escape—the frigate would soon be out of range of the *Royal Sovereign*—would only give Patrick Tempus more ammunition to continue his war.

"Let's put this last frigate out of commission, shall we? Then, we can let our compatriots mop up after our victory!" She shouted to her crew, who readied their cannonshot as Captain de Ibarra shouted the orders and maneuvered the *Agility* around for their swooping pass, bringing them within five hundred feet of the enemy.

Again, Seramis could hear the missiles pass by—but this time, the enemy had arranged sharpshooters in their rigging and on their masts. All but one bullet in the fusillade, apparently, slipped by the *Agility*. Fortune, or their opponent's changing tactics, had dealt them their first casualty: the starboard aerialwave directly in front of where Seramis stood was struck by a single ball and the ship shuddered as its intricate rhythm (not to mention its forward momentum) was interrupted by the splintering of wood and the grinding of gears. As she had before, Lady Seramis flinched at the shot, and she even felt a sting on her forehead after the bullet did its damage to the ship, although she was too focused on her station to notice anything further.

"Steady!" shouted the captain. "Prepare for spiral aim!" he called out. As part of the maneuver they had practiced and readied should one of the aerialwave 'wings' become damaged, Seramis focused on increasing the lift on the side opposite the damage and dramatically raising the foredeck another ten degrees. "On my mark!" he called out.

"We have five seconds," the captain shouted to Seramis without looking at her. "If the musketeers aboard that frigate know their training, they will be ready for another round." Despite none of the muskets being accurate at this range, if enough fired at once, at least one would surely get lucky again. Seramis worried that they might puncture an envelope, or worse, injure one of the crew.

"Mark!" The captain's signal to reverse the flow of the working aerialwave wing at full speed, in combination with the drag of the damaged but still deployed opposing wing, caused the *Agility* to pivot in place. Seramis did her part to push the airship through the clouds as she flooded the envelopes with buoyant gas from the storage cylinders. The airship launched itself upwards just prior to the next incoming volley, which ineffectively passed by without touching the *Agility* or its crew. Seramis felt as if she and the clouds were one, and despite the damage to the airship, she sensed a nimbleness in her passage through the sky she had never thought possible.

"Make this shot count!" Lady Seramis called out to the weapons crew, as the rowers took to the rigging to unfurl sails that caught the wind, putting the *Agility* over their target. Dropping their ammunition with a vengeance, the crew readied yet another battery before their first attack dealt its deadly effect. The bombardment wreaked havoc upon the men in the rigging and on the masts where the cannonballs smashed into them or into the spars or ropes where they fought, and in many cases, died.

Fleet Captain Seramis Helleborine thought she tasted blood. She had ordered the taking of the lives of others in combat, and she was instantly reminded of this by the cool, coppery and unpleasant sensation in her mouth and a wet stinging in her eyes which she couldn't just blink away. She felt a little confused and unfocused...

"My lady! You're wounded," Captain de Ibarra cried out. "Surgeon! Get ye aft, man." Turning to his fleet captain and friend, he said soothingly, "Try to set yourself down. Gently, now." Of course, he didn't move from the wheel, and he claimed he would never endanger the ship for the single life of any of the crew. But the surgeon and the bosun—who hadn't any need to be called as he had leaped from his station when he heard the cry of distress from the captain—arrived quickly. Still, they were too late to prevent a stunned Seramis from slipping down to her knees just as she was caught in the arms of her rescuer.

Chapter Twenty-Seven: The Confrontation

In which tragedy is followed by an escape

Lady Seramis awoke in her bed, surrounded by her friends and peers. At first, she didn't recall anything out of the ordinary. It made no sense that she should wake up being the object of such scrutiny, so she thought at first that she was dreaming. She looked around, concerned, as this was not a pleasant dream, especially as she had spent her life avoiding observation whenever she could.

Within moments, as she grew more awake and more alert, she remembered the battles of the previous day, and was glad to see Hanaawa and Captain de Ibarra, and knew this not to be a dream as details of her friends took on their familiar look and feel. Seeing the Duke of Gloucester and Baron West, the latter fitfully snoring in a chair, brought forth a mixture of feelings and memories, not the least of which were the confusing sensations and visions of herself on the wheel deck, the last thing she remembered. When the memories returned, she reached up to feel a bandage upon her forehead.

"Ah, good! You're awake and thinking about your battle scars!" Lord Albion announced. The rest of the men present started at his voice, including Lord De La Warr, who jumped up into a defensive stance, but sheepishly relaxed before bowing deeply towards Lady Seramis.

"Gentlemen! My lord! Your Grace! I feel fine!" Seramis protested as she sat up in bed. One of her maids came over to offer her some water. "Thank you," she said, "thank you all! But I would be even more grateful for an explanation, if possible..."

Hanaawa offered, "I'll leave that to others, except to say that I'll pass along the news of your waking to White Apple, who hasn't left her duty station except to ask of you!"

"You keep surprising me, of course, my lady!" Captain de Ibarra said. "The chances of a piece of shrapnel glancing off your brow are remarkable! But that's all it was." Glancing to Lord Albion, he opined, "I think we all know your scars will not show. I, too, will leave, to go check on the status of the repairs. We've been working all night, anchored to the east of Bermuda's Castle Harbour. We should be ready for your orders in an hour, but I'll personally confirm that."

He left, and Lord Albion picked up where he had left off. "Fleet Captain, allow me to report that we scuttled one of the surrendering frigates—the one that got a lucky shot upon you—after we transferred the prisoners to the ship you first disabled. We've towed it behind us." He chuckled, mostly at himself. "Speaking of towing, I wonder why the captain didn't mention that we towed the airship as well? What a sight! The first aerial tow, with the longest tow rope I've ever seen. That need not be in the official report, of course. And, also unofficially, you have single-handedly destroyed or grounded Patrick's aerial fleet, albeit most of the damage was self-inflicted."

"You can be assured that I've already interrogated the prisoners, my lady," Lord De La Warr said matter-of-factly. "It appears that Patrick Tempus had installed hand-picked natives as commanders of the frigates, but they were only knowledgeable enough to give general orders." He stroked his beard with his gloved hand in his usual affectation, his expression firm. "And I'm told that the surrendering vessels mutinied in order to capitulate. It's likely that the ship that attacked the *Royal Sovereign* only to be destroyed sailed under duress, as well."

Fleet Captain Dame Seramis Helleborine thought about this for a moment, realizing her responsibility extended beyond this ship and this situation. "We have to stop Patrick before he can do any more damage. Whole navies and cities have suffered at his hands. And I know only too well from personal experience what he is capable of. Leaving him wounded only leaves him smarter and more capable the next time. I fear he will..." Feeling light-headed, she paused in her speaking and patted her bandage lightly.

"You should rest, my lady," the baron said, furrowing his brow in concern.

"No. I mean—yes. Yes, I will." Taking a deep breath, she continued, "But first, has anything changed regarding that pillar of earth?"

Lord Albion straightened as he spoke. "It has Patrick's attention as well. I sent a contingent of marines ashore when we arrived. They report that he and that Innes fellow are aboard the last of their aerial ships—one that appears to be unarmed. The marines won't engage them; only observe." He broke off reporting as he saw Seramis's eyes close briefly. "We should leave, but we'll be right outside if you need us."

She thanked them as they departed and started to sink back into the bed, but not before White Apple rushed into the room. "My lady!" she cried out, running directly to the bedside and failing to stop before falling atop Seramis in a very undignified manner.

Seramis hugged White Apple as the girl crashed into her. "Now, now. I'm fine!" She stroked the girl's raven hair gently, smiling as a mother might. "It's nothing more than a little loss of blood, something I've dealt with monthly since... My dear? Have you reached the age of *menarche*?" she asked as she took in White Apple's puzzled look.

"I? Oh, no, my lady," White Apple answered, having considered the question for a moment.

"Then we should talk soon. But until then, know that I'm fine. I'll just have a light meal and drink some more water. But you should get some rest!"

"Oh, I'm fine, my lady! Like a bird, I slept in the nest!" White Apple said with a smile so disarming Seramis laughed until her throbbing head forced her to stop.

. . .

"This is just wrong!" Captain de Ibarra complained, once Lady Seramis recovered and the *Agility* returned to pursue Patrick Tempus. "It looks wrong. It feels wrong. We should turn back now!"

Despite his objections, the captain was steering the *Agility* towards the pillar of earth, flying a few hundred feet above the beaches, trees, and plantations that comprised the island of Bermuda. It was warm and clear as the sun climbed higher into the sky, in contrast to the captain's dark foreboding. "But I've got the impression, my lady, that you will continue despite my misgivings and the plain and simple truth that a sailing ship should at least be over water, if not actually in it."

"I recall hearing a fine captain once tell me that I need only name the destination, and that said captain would get me there!" Fleet Captain Dame Seramis Helleborine replied, smiling. She was still bandaged, but her flat-brimmed hat covered most of the dressing. She had rested, and while her head still ached, she was determined to press on.

Lord De La Warr was aboard the *Agility*, accompanying Lady Seramis and silently seething as he prepared to meet his former spy. The rest of the crew and passengers gave him a wide berth, as he only replied in low ominous tones when spoken to, and otherwise stood quietly by and waited.

But he was not the only one who was reserved. Even the naturally gregarious among the crew of the *Agility* were stunned into a disbelieving silence at the sight of the massive and impossibly tall column growing out of the island to an unknown height. Its rate of growth was now noticeable to all, and not merely to White Apple. The once broad center of the island appeared visibly pinched as it was consumed by the pillar's continuous formation process, while the ground trembled and shook; ripples radiated from the pillar, as if a giant hand were gathering the fabric of the earth.

Under this towering impossibility, and near the chasm from which the pillar grew, floated the last of the stolen and repurposed *fluyts*, one of the Dutch ships captured by Patrick Tempus and turned into a floating warship. As the marines had reported, there were no guns to be seen on the weather deck. From each gunport sprouted a great fan, about a dozen in all, in simple imitation of the aerialwave of the *Agility*, but they all moved slowly and erratically side to side as opposed to the swift, smooth up-and-down motion of the original design. The fans, however, served their purpose in keeping the floating vessel in place and confirmed Lady Seramis's fears regarding how quickly Patrick adapted and learned from their encounters.

As the *Agility* drew close, its own aerialwave bringing the vessel to a stop in front of the *fluyt*, Patrick waved a white shirt in a signal of parley from amidships. Hanaawa called out from the crow's nest, "I see the would-be master, but where is its pawn?"

"Keep a lookout," the captain answered, but Hanaawa was on the move, down the rigging to the deck. Ibarra's gaze firmly trained on the enemy, he spoke in level tones to Seramis. "I've steered you to your destination, but what is your plan?"

"We're here to stop Patrick Tempus," the fleet captain replied evenly, "although I admit that it's not the most concrete of plans. It's more of a goal than an actual plan at this point..."

Patrick shouted across the distance, barely audible above the rush of the wind and the constant rumble erupting from the ground hundreds of feet below, "Will you parley?"

In answer, Lord De La Warr shouted, "There will be no parley, Traitor Patrick! As the representative of the king in this, his territory, I am here to arrest you! And if you resist..."

"Thomas!" Fleet Captain Helleborine admonished. "While you're on this vessel, you will be subject to my authority—"

"She's right, Baron." Gloucester frowned at De La Warr, then added, "But my lady, surely you don't mean to—" He never got to finish his question as several voices shouted warnings simultaneously.

Launching himself from the topmost of the gas bags keeping the *fluyt* airborne, Innes jumped towards the *Agility* while tossing overhand a trawler's hook tied to a long rope fastened around his waist. The vertical stacking of the large number of bags used for buoyancy on the *fluyt* had given Innes the height needed to cross the space between the two ships, but he would have plummeted to his death had the hook not ripped into the nearest secondary envelope, shredding its outer layer (but not the gas-filled inner compartment) before snagging upon the rigging that held the canvas shrouds in place. Mirroring the first acrobatic display Seramis had witnessed him perform, except for the expression of hatred now masking his face, Innes swung at the end of the improvised ratline wound about him and pulled himself into the rigging of the *Agility*.

Shouts and consternation broke out amongst the crew as Innes drew an immense knife and cut himself free in order to throw himself downwards, straight at the marchioness. Today she was not stunned into immobility as she had been the last time Innes attacked her. Then, she had been completely frozen in shock at his attack, but this time she calmly and swiftly dove and rolled to the side, protecting her throbbing head and quickly escaping danger.

Into her place, however, leapt Lord De La Warr, who couldn't have known that Innes's deadly knife should have found no point of cruel entry had he stayed safely where he had been as Lady Seramis easily escaped. He had instead jumped to a point just in front of where she had been standing less than a heartbeat earlier, and Innes's knife cut deep into him.

Lady Seramis screamed in defiance as she saw what happened. Gloucester had drawn his sword and swiftly crossed the distance where Innes had murderously tumbled into the baron, the latter crumpling with a groan.

The combatants rolled apart, recoiling from the force of Innes's attack. Each lay still where he fell. Innes's knife was buried in its final resting place within the baron's chest. Shocking all who had witnessed the attack was the hilt of Lord De La Warr's court dagger jutting out from under Innes's jaw, where the blade had pierced his throat and stabbed upwards into his brain, killing him instantly.

Lady Seramis's eyes filled with tears for a loss which she could not, at present, name. Her orders to attack were a scream of anguished retribution. The crew on the *Agility* launched its hooked nets like fishermen casting off, and Hanaawa led the scramble across the gap between the ships when the hooks bit into the rigging of the *fluyt*. To those enemies now tethered to the *Agility*, the attacking crew looked not unlike angered spiders flowing over their webs as they crossed the nets that separated them from the empty air and distant ground below.

Patrick was swiftly overwhelmed, and was soon bound and tied before being swung like mere cargo from the *fluyt* to the *Agility*. Dumped unceremoniously upon the deck, Patrick couldn't move and merely sneered haughtily while Hanaawa stood over him, pitying him. Javelins were launched to pierce the gasbags of the *fluyt* while the *Agility* pulled away swiftly. The last remaining craft of Patrick's aerial battle fleet sank ignominiously towards the chasm at the base of the pillar.

As the *fluyt* touched the stone, not far from the chasm where the column emerged from the earth, it shifted curiously, as if twisted and pulled sideways towards the column by an unknown gravity. The failing buoyancy of the deflating gasbags caused them to bob and shift as they approached the column as well, until the rigging failed under the strain and the upper structures broke free of the hull. Most of the remaining bulk came to rest against the pillar, while other parts fell down to earth. That which fell into the chasm at the base of the growing column twisted and exploded, and solid objects appeared to stretch and distort as they disappeared in showering sparks of colors and light.

"Imagine the most massive object your pitiful minds can conceive," Patrick Tempus shouted haughtily at no one particular. "And know that there are objects that exist that will dwarf even that." He continued with his peculiar pedantry, struggling to breathe even as either the ropes or his prone position constricted his chest.

"What would happen if you compressed not one, but two of those massive objects that were once millions upon millions of times the size of this earth into a sphere you could fit in your puny hand!" Patrick's voice became strained as he spoke. "But you could never hold it, not if you had the strength of every man that ever lived, for even in its diminished size it retains every particle and every bit of its original massive shape. The two singular points of unbelievable density would spiral at a fantastic rate, cutting through solid ground and reshaping all that came in contact with them. And it did! Right here! And you are too ignorant to even guess at what I am describing!"

"What are you babbling about, you madman?" snarled Lord Albion. "Fleet Captain? I beg your leave to gag and remove this stain from your presence."

Hanaawa peered at Patrick Tempus closely and could see that he was undergoing a transformation even as he watched. White

Apple called out in the distance, "Something's wrong!" just as Hanaawa warned everyone back.

"I have come in contact with immense power, as well, you insects! And I have found that the opposite of that compression can happen, too! And I can control it! I can control it all! Father Time rules you all!" Patrick's voice diminished to a spectral whisper as he floated bodily up off of the deck and simultaneously started growing in size, while he, his clothes, and the ropes that bound him appeared to fade.

Appearing to finally notice the fallen Lord De La Warr, Patrick said, "*The evil that men do lives after them.*" Turning to Lady Seramis, he continued his quotation, "*The good is oft interred with their bones!*" He spat the final word at her, who realized she was looking straight through the rapidly disappearing body of Patrick Tempus into the face of a stunned Hanaawa. Lord Albion rushed forth, slicing his sword through the air, but only ineffectively cutting through the apparition that dissipated like a wisp of expanding steam.

"What sorcery is this?" Captain de Ibarra exclaimed as the last traces of 'Father Time' vanished.

In the lull that followed, as all had become still, Hanaawa answered, "What you would call sorcery is just the application of will by as yet indescribable means."

Seramis still focused on the fallen men, and had but time to voice a single thought—"Goodbye, cruel and gentle men both"—before pandemonium broke forth upon all points of the sky from the pillar of earth.

The noise was beyond deafening in its intensity, a wave of pressure that pushed inwards and shut out all other senses, including sight and touch. As one, all present put their hands to their ears and offered up a silent cry of supplication. The religious among them prayed silently as they fell, wracked by unfathomable pain. Not one was left standing as the blast passed through and beyond them.

At first, sensing only by touch, Lady Seramis could but guess that the shivers and thuds upon the deck were the result of Lord Albion crawling and rolling towards her. Finally, she could laboriously force her eyes open through her tears. She could dimly see him approach through her tight-closed eyelids as well as sense his painful progress through vibrations of the wooden deck as she lay upon her side. Throbbing was all she could feel, and a high-pitched ringing was all she could hear as she struggled to her knees, shouting—at least she thought she was shouting, but couldn't hear her own voice—"The tiller! The wheel!"

Lord Albion reached her just as she gained some measure of stability upon her hands and knees, where they both pushed and pulled and supported each other as they staggered upright. Once standing, they rushed to Captain de Ibarra, who was writhing upon the deck in pain and disorientation but waved the two towards the wheel. Lady Seramis slipped off the tie that lashed it into place and spun it to port. She then pointed to the mizzen rig behind her where Lord Albion could swing the sail out of a bad tack.

The shockwave from the explosion had pushed the *Agility* away from where the pillar of earth had once stood, but now that they were pointed back towards the east and the *Royal Sovereign*, they could ride the winds towards water. Gloucester took the wheel as Lady Seramis staggered to the controls, venting the pitchblende gas and initiating a gentle descent towards the flagship.

What was once an inexplicable and inconceivably tall column of dirt, gravel, and rock had exploded—vaporized—and instead of falling to earth, the tiny fragments were spreading in all directions, blocking out the sun. Soon, Bermuda was enshrouded in a sickening, blood-red darkness.

From her altitude upon the airship, Seramis Helleborine could watch the swelling shadows engulf the bright blue waters in every direction, as if the realm of Hades itself were invading the earth, unstoppable and implacable in its spread. Wordlessly, Lady Seramis and Lord Albion looked at the resulting two worlds, one of light and one of shadow, and briefly at each other as well. In desperation, each slipped a hand into the clasp of the other, the simple act of kindness the only defense against the growing horror they witnessed.

To Be Continued in Volume Two of the Helleborine Chronicles: The Fury of Storms

(the First Chapter of Which Follows)

PART FOUR: The World, Split Into Two

Chapter The Last: The Parting

In which our players depart in decidedly different directions

The results of the devastating blast were seen from all stations aboard the English flagship, HMS *Royal Sovereign*. Immediately, all eyes turned upon the first to feel the effects, the improbable airship, *The Agility of Clouds*. At first, the enhanced and re-purposed caravel was buffeted in all directions, out of control while floating—sinking, really—towards the much larger British Man-o-War of the First Rate. The ropes binding the envelopes of lighter-than-air gas to the airship appeared to stretch nearly to the breaking point, while the dozens of mechanical wings on each side tore at the air in futile gestures.

Hundreds of sailors on the *Royal Sovereign* who owed their lives to the previous heroic actions of the daring airship stood in silence, fearing that the *Agility* would soon crash.

When the initial blast subsided, however, both crews had recovered and had resumed control of their vessels. All around them, as the former clear blue skies and seas vanished, it appeared that the world would never be the same again. Bermuda was now enshrouded in darkness as the fragmented dust and detritus drifted away from the column that formerly sprouted from the island and had consumed much of the land in its inexplicable growth.

For her part, when she could pause in her struggle at the wheel of the airship, Seramis Helleborine looked at the growing clouds and, in shock at the hellish transformation, wondered which direction she herself would take next.

Captain de Ibarra recovered and, thanking Lady Seramis, once again took the wheel. He called out for assistance, rousing the crew to their stations. His rough voice sounded thin to Seramis, although it could be the ringing in her ears that casued that effect.

The Natchez chief Hanaawa and his niece White Apple also recovered quickly, and returned to the crow's nest to guide the Captain to ground. Indeed, the rest of the crew of the *Agility* were soon at their stations, and each were looking to their leader, the Dame Commander Seramis Helleborine, for direction and leadership but as yet finding none.

Wordlessly, each of her friends approached Lady Seramis in turn, but left in silence, as she would neither speak nor meet their imploring expressions. They quietly undertook tasks of their own, leaving Seramis silent in her sorrow. Upon the airship's gentle landing on the darkened waters, Lord Admiral Albion sadly took his leave and resumed command of the *Royal Sovereign*.

But Seramis followed Lord Albion, and had taken upon herself the role of surgeon's assistant in preparing the last rites and disposition of the bodies of the two men who had harmed her most in life, the murderous Innes and the scheming Lord De La Warr. In her shock at the deaths of these two men, she retreated into routine, and had taken charge of the transfer of their bodies to the *Royal Sovereign* from the *Agility* where they had briefly clashed and died.

The surgeon of the *Royal Sovereign*, for his part, largely ignored the silent Marchioness with a studious air he had cultivated ignoring those screaming in pain and groaning in supplication. Both of the deceased had already bled out, but the surgeon carefully removed and discarded the clothes of the men while Lady Seramis modestly and passively watched the spreading gloom, despite it being mid-day.

Orderlies brought fresh clothes for Lord De La Warr and canvas to wrap the body of Innes, a shroud for his impending burial at sea. The assistants poured lead shot into Innes's abdominal cavity before wrapping him, to ensure his sinking to the depths of the ocean. But before they could complete the wrapping of his head, Lady Seramis returned her attention to the man who had violently betrayed her.

Innes's face, passive and unreadable in death but reflecting the emptiness that had once been within him, felt cold to the touch. Just as he had once been an empty vessel—a mere tool of Patrick Tempus to be filled with whatever ambition the master desired of its slave—his face revealed nothing to the searching gaze of Seramis. Silently, she said good-bye to the first man she had opened herself up to, and thus, said good-bye to her innocence. Briefly, visions of their time together flooded her sight, filling her eyes with a picture of laughter. But that had been pretense. The last vision, the one that she would carry always, was the mental image of Innes raising his flintlock pistol in violent fury and betrayal.

While the orderlies completed roughly wrapping Innes for his burial at sea, the surgeon had finished the first stages of embalming Lord De La Warr using camphor and myrrh. Just before the surgeon was to set the deceased's features for the journey back to England, Seramis interrupted the process.

She expressionlessly looked at the stern features of her former patron and Nuncle, that even in death appeared strong yet pained. She had once feared him as a patriarch and a patron, and not long ago despised him for his own betrayal of promises made. But for all that, she couldn't bring herself to condemn the man who so evidently cared for her and had even died in her defense.

Lady Seramis's head started to throb, almost as a physical manifestation of the warring feelings within her. Her head was indeed filled with unresolved issues, the questions she still carried about her patron and how now none of that would ever be resolved directly. A gasp of pain and frustration escaped from Lady Seramis's lips, quickly summoning Lord Albion, who had hovered just out of sight while performing his duties.

"Milady, if you wish to return to your craft, I will have the gig readied—" he began.

"Your Grace—" she started, her hand lifting to her brow.

"Please, call me Henry," he interrupted, obviously concerned for her well-being.

Her answering smile was brief, and her eyes shone with tears. "This disaster was my doing, but I'm afraid that I haven't the resources to try to set things right..."

"I will be so bold as to disagree with both assessments, milady."

Formally, as if being Dame Commander was as natural as any other role she had been asked to perform, she said, "Can you send a summons for the Captain and Officers of *The Agility of Clouds* for a conference?"

Turning to a communications officer to his left, but still looking askance at Lady Seramis as if locked by her gaze, Lord Albion said quietly, "Comm? Just as ordered by the Fleet Captain."

"Aye, sir," said the officer, who then departed as if a very model of efficiency.

"A garrison officer has taken charge in Bermuda, Milady," Lord Albion said, turning back to Seramis. "But we have no further intelligence as to the plans of Patrick Tempus or how he could have just vanished into thin air! There is so much more at play here than I can hope to understand. It seems that just as one mystery is solved, two more are just as quickly revealed—"

"I'm so sorry that I ever involved you in this. My vendetta against Innes and my clashing with Lord De La Warr has wrought this disaster upon us all—"

"Oh, no, dear Seramis! How can you shoulder the responsibility for such a plot beyond reckoning?" Lord Albion's voice softened in gratitude and appreciation. "I'll remind you that you've once come to my rescue and saved me. A hurricane—frozen in time—would have been my undoing, if not for you."

Continuing more loudly, he continued, "Patrick Tempus styled himself Father Time, but the frozen hurricane, the pillar of earth and now this perpetual gloom are clearly beyond any one man's doing. There's more at work here than can be accounted for."

White Apple innocently asked, "Even by someone who can disappear at will, your Grace?" She had just arrived with Captain de Ibarra and Hanaawa, who gently shushed her.

Captain de Ibarra, commander of the airship Seramis had herself designed, bowed to Lady Seramis. "We were ready for your request, Fleet Captain." His gaze then became defiant. "I assume that because you haven't returned to the *Agility*, that you're staying here on this bucket—"

"Your intelligence and pride are revealed in equal measure, Captain," Lord Albion interrupted.

"Gentlemen," Seramis chided gently. "First, what is the status of the *Agility*, Captain?"

"Ready to depart for any destination on the globe you may wish, Fleet Captain," de Ibarra answered proudly.

Lady Seramis's voice caught, as she struggled with what to say next, "I have to go to England, and to warn the King and ask for his assistance in dealing with this disaster. But, Captain de Ibarra, you and the others must go to Virginia Colony and find out what you can about that so-called Father Time. He may have vanished, but I fear we will see him again."

Turning to the Natchez war chief, Seramis looked at her friend imploringly. "I admit I'm at a loss to explain what has happened here. What can you tell me?"

"I can only point out what your eyes already tell you," Hanaawa said. "Daylight is gone from this part of the world. Eventually it will return, as that is the way of things. But, in the meantime, there will be famine, death, and bloody conflict over diminishing supplies and resources. That, too, is the way of things."

"We must warn them," White Apple spoke up, not needing to explain who she meant by 'them'—the families and the colonists who joined together at New Helleborine Hall—before reaching out to Seramis. "But I don't want to go! I... I wish we could have had that conversation you mentioned earlier, milady." She said quietly, referring to the promised but now delayed discussion of life's many changes.

"I'm so sorry," Seramis said as emotion filled her voice, "but we will have that conversation, someday, I promise."

She paused, wondering whether she would be able to keep that promise. "You're correct about raising the alarm, White Apple. In the meantime, I want to ask you to use your keen eyesight to watch over your uncle and your captain."

White Apple nodded, evidently not trusting herself to speak.

"Milady, I've had your maids gather your things, and they're here aboard this bucket as well," Captain de Ibarra said sadly.

"Please ask one to stay, and the others should return with you to assist Mrs. McClure, who will need the help, if Hanaawa is correct in his assessment of humanity's follies and shortcomings," Lady Seramis said.

Hanaawa interjected, "I wish I could be faulted for overestimating the follies of humanity, but, first, I have two questions. What do we do should we actually uncover the truth behind Father Time?"

He paused, knowing that there wasn't yet an answer. Looking at Seramis, he asked a question that had no answer as well, "And does anyone have any idea what we can possibly say to Colonel McClure when he realizes we've returned to New Helleborine Hall without you?"

. . .

Father Time, once known as Patrick Tempus in a mundane existence ill-suited to his current situation, stared through incorporeal eyes in disbelief. He never imagined a daytime sky so black, nor a sun so bright, nor a globe so round and yet in a sense much smaller than he imagined.

He had become much larger than he would have ever thought possible. On two ghostly legs he stood astride the Eastern Seaboard of the North American continent. He had seen maps of the great Atlantic Ocean, but now he could stretch his arms to point to the limits of the real thing.

A hurricane, frozen in time by one of his early experiments, its clouds arranged in neat concentric circles, attracted his attention. Father Time was aware of his hands—although he could not see them as such—and he leaned over and brushed through the hurricane, setting it back into motion. He spun it faster and faster until it dissipated before his sight, becoming as intangible as he, himself, had become.

But, what, exactly had he become? He could sense the planet's rotation... He was surprised that the sunset occurred so quickly (there was no dusk to speak of—just a wink, and the sun was gone), a multitude of stars exploded unblinking into existence upon the night sky.

He could feel his body, that is, the proprioception of where its various parts were located, but he could feel neither warmth nor cold, texture nor any other kind of touch. And, as with the hurricane he had once stopped in its tracks, he had no idea how this had come to be.

Laughter at the realization of his ascension and the magnitude of his being poured forth from Father Time, unheard by any, but felt as an unease in the nightmares of all who slept and dreamt that night. Father Time's vision twisted in his mirth, and a rumbling under his feet suggested a delicateness to his predicament, that he was as he was only by his will alone.

"I have done it!" he shouted in an exulted voice that he could only sense, but not hear.

"No, we have done it," answered a cold, spectral wind. "We have journeyed across the millennia in order to change conditions on this planet to our betterment, and you are our tool."

There was no one source to the voice; seemingly, it came from everywhere. "We become impatient with our tool," the voice continued. "Time, in this scale, moves quickly, as you can see."

"I had hoped! Yes, truly, had I hoped I would attract the higher beings from my dreams—"

"It was not you who attracted us, but instead, we who have been manipulating you..." Haughty and insouciant, the voice was terrifying and yet appealing to Father Time. "For a task of our own design; one which you cannot accomplish by standing here while time flies before your eyes."

Indeed as the voice described, the sun burst forth above the Eastern horizon in a dazzling magnificence that burned away the stars from sight and transformed the cold globe into a lighted sphere. But the sphere was no longer shiny blue and green and white as it might have appeared, as there was a dark stain growing from Bermuda, lessening somewhat as it spread, but still black and plunging the world beneath it into shadow. Even the menacing cloud at this height was settling and dissipating, as if being poured into the lower atmosphere.

"Yes, you notice our handiwork," the voice continued. "We have traveled from what you would call the Five Hundred and Tenth Century in order to remake this world into something more to our suiting. But you are not simply witness to the chaos and destruction that is to follow. You must eliminate any potential challenger to our supremacy."

A pause, and a rage within Father Time erupted as he thought of another who had replaced him in his former employ as a spy for Lord De La Warr. The thought occurred to him, burning through his brain, that she might have been manipulated, too; and further, she would supplant him if possible. "I know of whom you speak! And I shall tear her apart as she burns!"

"You cannot—confront her directly," The voice chided, but somehow, not sounding as sure of itself as previously.

"Why?" Father Time screamed in a voice without sound, attuned to the suggestion of possibility he heard in the voice. "I am not to be caged. I stand at the pinnacle of volition. The very substance of existence bends to my will."

"While it is possible for primitives like you to aspire and even—in some rare cases, attempt—manipulations such as we dispense, for those we have manipulated, we decree that there can be no conflict. You will not be allowed to directly challenge any who we have uplifted, just as they cannot directly diminish you in any capacity."

"I don't understand," Father Time shouted. "You've made me a god! Who can stand before me?"

"We will unmake you if you do not pursue our will." And when the voice had finished, fires of ethereal poison erupted behind Father Time's eyes, melting his thoughts and willpower, leaving naught but pleas of supplication. In an instant, the fires had burned out, and Father Time was left wordless, stunned and humbled before his gods.

When Father Time's voice returned, the question, "What will you have me do?" was almost all that was left. Almost—except for one tiny fire that didn't go out. One spark within Father Time, hidden and controlled, but burning and containing the potential for conflagration, for supremacy...

For revenge.

www.ingramcontent.com/pod-product-compliance
Lightning Source LLC
Chambersburg PA
CBHW071145260626
47162CB00003B/922

* 9 7 8 0 9 8 5 0 8 8 2 3 1 *